W9-ABQ-759

ST. BARTS BREAKDOWN

Also by Don Bruns

Stuff to Die For

South Beach Shakedown

Barbados Heat

Jamaica Blue

A Merry Band of Murderers
(editor & contributor)

Death Dines In
(contributor)

ST. BARTS BREAKDOWN

A NOVEL

DON BRUNS

IPSWICH, MASSACHUSETTS

FIRST EDITION

ISBN 978-1-933515-12-0

Published in the United States by Oceanview Publishing,
Ipswich, Massachusetts
www.oceanviewpub.com

2 4 6 8 10 9 7 5 3 1

PRINTED IN THE UNITED STATES OF AMERICA

To Mr. B., a good friend and the best bartender in the Caribbean.

The world is all the richer for having the devil in it,
so long as we keep our foot upon his neck.

— William James

ACKNOWLEDGMENTS

I could never tell my South Florida/Caribbean tales if it hadn't been for Sue Grafton. Thanks to Dave and Nancy Steiner, Scott and Jennifer Koenig, Frank Simonetti, Bill and Susan Timmermeister, and Michelle Kirkendall. They graciously allowed me to use names and fabricate their personalities. They're really wonderful people. To Don and Dianne Wright for their insight into fabulous St. Barts, to Chris Seddlemeyer who got me home again, and Matt and Andy Thompson from Lucky Bucks who wrote one of my favorite musical lyrics in the book. I acknowledge Linda Bruns who keeps me straight, Medeira James who keeps the Web site up to date (and does a great job), to Mary Stanton who is my good friend and mentor, and Sandy Ingledue who does so much of the graphics, George Foster for the great covers, Nancy Olds who helps in so many ways, and to Mr. B. who introduced me to the nightlife on St. Barts.

MR. B.'S STRAWBERRY DAIQUIRI

½ ounce strawberry schnapps
1 ounce light rum
1 ounce freshly squeezed lime juice
1 teaspoon powdered sugar
1 ounce fresh strawberries

Add ingredients with a bit of ice in a blender. Blend and then strain into a cocktail glass. Garnish with a strawberry.

ST. BARTS BREAKDOWN

CHAPTER ONE

"Not again." Danny Murtz closed his eyes, as if the act would magically erase the vision of what he saw sprawled on the floor. Through tightly closed eyelids he still saw the figure. Opening his eyes he gazed upward to the top of the curved staircase then down to the marble-floored entranceway under the magnificent cut-glass chandelier. Her body lay crumpled, limbs askew. Blood flowed freely from the massive head wound, and her right arm looked to be separated from the rest of her body. Only the curve of her naked buttocks and the small of her back seemed untouched by the fall. Her blond hair fanned out, soaking up the blood and her eyes were open, wide open, with fear frozen in the dilated pupils.

Half an hour ago she'd been in the throes of passion, her legs locked around his waist, screaming at the top of her lungs. Now — he couldn't remember. Like the last time, it was a blur.

He shook, as if the temperature were thirteen degrees and he'd worn only a T-shirt. His dry mouth wanted for a drink, but drink had been partially responsible for the naked corpse. Drink and cocaine. And the handful of pills, and possibly a couple of joints he'd smoked an hour ago. He'd gotten a little out of balance.

He had to call Harvey. Who else could he talk to? Focus. Focus. Wait a minute, a lucid thought. Harvey had said the next time he was on his own. As if Harvey knew there would be a next time. But, of course, he did. The smug attorney knew everything. And that was the problem. Harvey knew too much.

Murtz took his cell phone from the pocket of his thick, terrycloth robe and punched in Harvey's number on speed dial. For the money Murtz paid him, the son of a bitch had better not give him attitude.

"Harvey Schwartz." The voice was cold and distant.

"Harvey? It's Danny." He tried not to slur the words.

"Yeah, Danny. What is it?"

Murtz paid him close to a million a year. The man could sound a little more interested in talking to his number one client. Murtz's secretary said he was only looking out for himself. She didn't trust the son of a bitch, but he had no one else to turn to.

"Harvey," he started shaking again. He needed a drink.

"What is it Danny?"

Murtz walked to the bar and with unsteady hands poured himself a tumbler of Grey Goose vodka.

"Danny? I'm waiting."

Murtz took a long swallow. "You remember four years ago . . . well, of course you do. I —"

"Jesus Christ, Danny," he interrupted. "Tell me it didn't happen again."

"I can't tell you that, Harvey."

Silence, then a long sigh of exasperation. "How many times, Danny? How many times have I cleaned it up?"

He had to show a little backbone here. Can't have Harvey treating him like a spoiled child. "You're going to clean up the mess, Harvey. You work for me, you arrogant prick. I don't care what it costs. Clean it up whatever it takes."

"Who is she?"

"It's not important."

"You don't know, do you?"

"Some wannabe actress. Singer. I didn't ask for a résumé. Just take care of it." He took another gulp of the clear beverage and stared at the shaking tumbler in his hand. Harvey was quiet. Murtz could hear him breathing on the other end. Slow, measured breaths.

"Half a million, Danny. At least that much, maybe more."

"Jesus!"

"Then call the cops. Or do you want me to?"

"Fuck you. You turn on me and the money stops." He could hear the attorney on the other end, breathing slowly, perfectly calm. "You son of a bitch." Nancy, his secretary, was right. He shouldn't trust the guy. "Fix it."

"Half a million."

Murtz drained the glass. "Put it on my tab."

"Don't touch anything, don't move anything, just go to your room, lock the door, and I'll have someone there in ten minutes. And, Danny, lock the front door too. My man will have the key."

He nodded. It was going to be all right. A disappearance, a couple of articles in the second section of some big city newspapers and it would all go away. It always did.

"Are you listening?"

Of course he was listening. "Yeah."

"Pack a bag. We'll have a plane ready in a couple of hours."

He should be relieved. But he wasn't. Harvey knew too much. Threatening him about going to the cops. Murtz's mind tried to wrap itself around the situation, but there was just too much fog. His father had moved the family in the middle of the night, one night when he'd come home drunk. Murtz had been about eight. There was talk that the old man had killed someone in a drunken stupor. The apple didn't fall too far —

"Danny?" Harvey sounded more engaged, like the wheels were turning. "Is her car there?"

"Yeah. Little Toyota something."

"Okay. We'll move that. Far, far away."

"Yeah. The car. And she has a cell phone. She was making a call."

"When? When was she making the call, Danny?"

"Maybe just before. I can't remember."

"Before what?"

"Before she went over the railing."

"The railing?"

"Jesus, Harvey, are you paying attention?"

Silence on the other end of the phone. Finally, "Who was she calling on the cell phone?"

"I don't know." His head ached, and he was slurring his words. God, it was a miserable drunk.

"Shit. Think. Did she mention any name?"

He couldn't think. It was Harvey's job to think. That's why he demanded so damned much money.

"The cell phone is there, right?"

In her bag, on the bed, somewhere. "Yeah." He was so tired, just needed another stiff drink and then a good night's sleep.

"All right. We're going to need that phone. We need to know who she called. Do you understand that? Don't touch anything."

"Like I would."

"Half a million, Danny. Minimum."

"Goddamnit, Harvey, I heard you."

"Danny, was it an accident?"

"She went over the banister."

"Was it an accident?"

"She was coming from the bathroom. We'd just, you know, done it, and maybe she was disoriented."

"Was it an accident? Try to remember." That steady, measured tone that he used — talking to him as if he were a child.

Murtz stared at the empty glass. Then he stared at the naked body on his shiny marble floor. He dropped the glass, the shattering lead crystal echoing in the large entranceway.

"What was that?" Harvey was now fully engaged. "Danny?"

Murtz remained silent.

"I'm going to ask you one more time." Very deliberate words. "Was this an accident?"

"I think I might have pushed her, Harvey. So no, it may not have been an accident. You know, I really don't remember. She's dead. So do your job. Fix it. Do you hear me you arrogant ass? Fix it!"

CHAPTER TWO

"Orchestral Rock, Mick. That big, full sound." Jeff Bloomfield held his hands up, spreading them to emphasize the image. "Surely you remember?" He grinned at Sever, obviously excited about his subject.

Sever remembered. Danny Murtz had been the producer who had invented the heavy orchestral sound for popular music acts in the sixties and seventies. Dubbed *Orchestral Rock*, Murtz had hit it big with the sound of Jeremy and Storm, two white guys who sounded like the Isley Brothers. But their orchestration was magnified about 500 percent, and you were sucked into the depth of the music from the very first note.

"This was before multitracking was so easy," Bloomfield continued. "As you know, today they can play on three hundred tracks if they want to. When Murtz came on the scene, it was very limited, maybe four tracks, so he'd have, like, seven guitars play the same notes at the same time. Maybe five horns, five bass drums, playing the same exact line."

Sever nodded. And Danny Murtz would build an echo chamber that would resonate with every beat. Strings would swell, and the bass would boom, and the percussion would overwhelm the production. He'd heard that Murtz had used ten French horns on the song he'd written, *Living Without You*, and the entire session had been recorded at the bottom of an elevator shaft, just to get the proper echo effect. Even with all the computer effects available today, no one had ever duplicated Danny Murtz's Orchestral Rock.

"A&E is filming a special on Murtz this month, and we'd like you to do a story on him for the *Tribune*." Jeff Bloomfield had been giving him assignments for twenty years.

Sever had been writing entertainment articles for the *Chicago Tribune* for longer than he cared to admit. He'd started as a stringer in high school, covering Chicago-area rock and roll concerts, and even though he'd moved on, working as a freelancer for *Rolling Stone*, *Spin*, and a number of other high-profile publications, he still appreciated assignments from Bloomfield. Whenever his career had stalled, Jeff had always been there, offering him interviews, insight articles, and personality profiles. In his career, Sever had written four books, produced two movie documentaries, and had himself been the subject of numerous media profiles. The books were inside looks at the entertainment industry, and the movies were intriguing insights into the musical British Invasion, and the history of Barry Gordy's Motown. The profiles on Sever's life made him a legend in journalistic circles.

And now, Bloomfield was offering him a chance to interview another legend. Danny Murtz. And even though Murtz had a reputation as a rather nasty character, Sever couldn't help but be intrigued.

Murtz had written and produced *Living Without You,* a classic beyond almost any other classic in the rock and roll genre. Sever and anyone else who grew up in the sixties could immediately identify the first two measures of the song, the rich, full sound, the chord structure, and the magnificent vocals from Jeremy and Storm that hammered the message home.

I've got a sad, sad tale, and only one of us can feel the pain.
Of love and all it takes, of parting and the heartache's sad refrain
There's just one little thing, I'd like you to think of
The passion that we shared for all those
Times that we spent making love.

It was a perfect song for teenage angst. And as a teenager, Sever had bought the message. He remembered the girl's name, Jane. Jane Powers and she'd dumped him, telling him at the tender age of thirteen or fourteen that he was too immature. Well, duh.

I've got a sad, sad tale, and only one of us can feel the pain.

"Jeff, I know the background. Hell, I grew up on his music. I think he's produced hit albums in five different decades."

"He has." The editor took a swig from the bottle of water sitting on his desk. "And, he's been accused of stealing other people's material, taking unfair credit for other people's work."

"And on and on. Producers get that rap."

"And it's usually true. Danny Murtz has had his share of lawsuits, and he's won them all."

"What can I say, Jeff. It's a dirty business. But Murtz has been successful."

"Wildly successful. So, you'll do it?"

Sever surveyed the piles of paper on Bloomfield's desk. God deliver him from a desk job. Being an editor, a publisher, a pencil-pushing clerk was the last thing he could think of doing. He lived for the road. He lusted for the long-distance story, where he could get to the heart of the matter. Especially now. "Where is he?"

"He lives here. In Chicago."

"That keeps it simple."

"But I got a call from his attorney yesterday. He says A&E will be doing an interview on St. Barts."

"St. Barts?"

"Yeah. He was going to do the shoot here, but he's got a place on the island and had to go there at the last minute."

St. Barts. He'd taken his honeymoon on St. Martin, just a fifteen minute plane ride from the French Island of St. Barts. He and Ginny, the ex.

"I don't know, Jeff. I've got some things back here —" He

thought about the tall, leggy, blond singer, Randi Parks, who was working her way up the ladder on *American Idol*, and the interview he was scheduled to do with her for MTV. She'd been so excited about the interview that she'd flooded his answering machine with phone calls, but when he finally called her yesterday to confirm a date, nothing. She never returned the call. So maybe the interview with Murtz was meant to be.

Bloomfield smiled, the deep wrinkles in his pale face showing ten years on Sever. "Come on, Mick. We're paying you to take a great vacation. April on St. Barthélémy. We want to tie into the TV special."

St. Barts. There would be some painful memories.

I've got a sad, sad tale, and only one of us can feel the pain.

"What's he doing on St. Barts?"

"As I said, he's got a villa up in the hills, and I think there's a band over there he's working with. The Indoorfins? Maybe you've heard of them. Anyway, it all came up rather suddenly. Harvey Schwartz, this attorney, called me this morning and said they're in St. Barts. Last week they decided to take his show on the road. Of course, you were our first choice to do the interview."

"His attorney?"

"Yeah, the guy apparently is an attorney, handler, organizer — I don't know. Jack of all trades. You know better than I. Danny Murtz is a star, a legend, and he's got *people*!"

Sever nodded. "An entourage. A star's got to have his people." It sounded like this Schwartz was the buffer who handled Murtz's life for him.

"Anyway, I guess A&E had to scramble to accommodate the move. They were all set to film it here."

"What's the budget?"

"We'll pay you your going rate plus a nice bonus, put you up at a four-star hotel on the beach, and you retain the rights to the story once it's run."

The Caribbean in April. It sounded right. A warm beach, bright sunshine, and escape from the Chicago winter. "I've never met Murtz."

"I thought you'd met and interviewed just about everyone in the business."

He had. The music business, recording business, the business of rock and roll. A fantasy world, where money was everything and trust and honesty meant nothing. That had pretty much shaped his life. He'd met most of them, partied with a majority, and had a small fortune to show for it. That, and little else.

"I'm surprised he's doing the A&E piece. He's like the Howard Hughes of the music industry."

"Yeah, I've been reading up on him. Mansion in Hollywood, townhouse here in Chicago, and a villa in St. Barts, but he doesn't do much with the press. Somewhat of a recluse. The last media interview I could find was about fifteen years ago." Bloomfield handed Sever two pieces of paper stapled together.

Sever glanced down at the two pages. "*Playboy*?"

"They interviewed him for this article titled "Men Behind the Music." He didn't give them much. He rates about two paragraphs in the entire story."

Sever nodded. "But he still gets publicity. The kind he doesn't want."

"Oh yeah. *The National Enquirer* loves him. We've got a file on him that you'll probably want to review. Firearm charges, abuse, resisting arrest, DWI, drunk and disorderly, and assorted other pleasantries."

"Still," Sever heard the song in his head, "he makes some damned fine music."

"Not my style, but he's certainly maintained his popularity. So, I ask you again, will you do it?"

"Sure. He's an interesting guy. If he'll talk, it should be a good interview."

"You're saying yes has nothing to do with the rum drinks and the topless French babes on the beaches?"

Sever ignored him. "When do I leave?"

"Day after tomorrow. Eight a.m. You fly to St. Martin."

Sever cringed. An involuntary cringe. St. Martin, the scene of the honeymoon.

"Then you'll layover for one hour, or two or three if the shuttle decides to be late." Island time. In the Caribbean that meant whenever the hell they felt like it. "Then you take a fifteen-minute ride on the puddle jumper onto St. Barts."

"Okay. Three days should do it. If I can't get a story out of him in three days, I'm not going to get a story at all."

"Oh, and Mick, about twelve years ago, there were charges that Murtz pistol-whipped a guy."

"You told me. With all the charges against him, it's obvious he has a nasty streak."

"Yeah, but I thought you ought to know. This guy he beat up was a reporter doing a story on him."

"I can usually take care of myself." Six feet tall, a little boxing at the Lake Shore Gym, some light workouts with free weights when in town, Sever worked at staying in shape. Sort of.

"Jeff, you said there's a bonus."

The editor brushed back what hair there was left on his balding head. "I've always been straight with you, Mick. There's another angle to this interview."

"How much is the bonus?"

"Sizable. Okay? It depends on whether you want to go the direction we're heading."

Bloomfield had always been fair. But once or twice Sever had turned down an assignment because it just didn't feel right and he had a feeling one of those moments was about to rear its ugly head. Travel to St. Barts may not be in the future plans.

"The A&E piece is going to be a puff piece. They'll do a video on the villa, show him working with this new band, the Indoorfins, interview some associates, but for the most part it's going to be fluff."

"And you don't want fluff."

"Mick, you've never given me fluff. And a couple of times you've stumbled on some very serious stories. Jesus, the Gideon Pike story?"

Sever *had* literally stumbled onto the story of the fabled piano player/songwriter who was being blackmailed by a gangster in Miami.

"A great piece of reporting by the way." Bloomfield smiled.

Sever watched him, feeling like the setup wasn't finished.

"And the little girl's murder in Barbados? Hell, you turned that into a book."

"Jeff, get to the point."

He let out a long breath of air. "Okay, it's the accusations. We want a harder look at Murtz's drug use, his abuse charges and —"

"Come on, Jeff!"

"The disappearance of two girls." Bloomfield slapped his hands on his desk. "In the last seven years at least two young women who were having a relationship with Murtz suddenly disappeared."

"And you think that Danny Murtz was involved."

"We've been getting correspondence for a couple of months now, saying that there is proof of foul play."

"Go to that source."

"It's anonymous. But we believe it's credible information. No hard evidence, okay? But enough questions and concerns to go deeper into the story. I've got another file to share with you."

"Jeff, you not only want me to interview Murtz, but to do an investigation?"

"Murtz is a hometown boy. If we can break the story here in Chicago, it will be worth whatever bonus you want."

Sever stood up and walked to the window of Bloomfield's seventeenth-floor office. He stared down at the Chicago River, watching the colorful boats as they left their wakes on their way to Lake Michigan. He hadn't done a really good story since he and Ginny said goodbye in Miami, and he could use something to occupy his mind. Besides, the money could be very good. If the story played well, the *Trib* would sell it to a number of other publications and he'd share in the profits. His other interview, *American Idol* hopeful Randi Parks, would have to wait her turn.

"Are the cops looking into this?"

"Not officially. We've asked. There have been no charges filed. I don't think they have any reason or evidence. Mick, we may be the only people with inside information. The person who's been writing us wants us to look into it."

Sever gave it a long pause, thirty seconds or more. "You said credible stuff?"

"I said no hard evidence. Whoever is sending us information has their shit together. Dates, times, activities. I'll get you all the information."

"So I'd do the interview —"

"Make a decision if you want to follow up on the missing girls. If you ask the right questions, you just might get a reaction."

Sever considered it. If he thought that Danny Murtz might be capable of murder, then he'd come back to Chicago and start looking into the charges. He had connections with the police, and the *Trib* would certainly turn some of their reporters loose on the project.

"I get to make the decision?"

"You get to make the decision. If you don't think you can make a case, just do the interview and that's it. If you think there's another story, go for it." Bloomfield pushed himself back from the desk and sat with his hands folded in his lap. He didn't take his eyes off Sever.

"There may not be a story there."

"I know. We think there is. And if there is, Danny Murtz has been getting a free pass for a long time. There's something evil about this guy."

Sever studied Bloomfield carefully. "You *want* there to be something evil about him. It's the element that makes your story compelling."

"No. It's all the innuendoes, reading between the lines, and reading the letters from our mysterious source. There's something evil, and I'd like to see him get caught."

Sever gave him a faint grin. "You want to sell newspapers."

"That too."

Sever pursed his lips, running the whole scenario in his mind. "Celebrities get a free pass most of the time. It's just a fact — the O.J. factor."

"Maybe not this time."

He took a deep breath. It could turn out to be nothing. It could turn into a defining moment in his long career. He wasn't sure he needed another one. "What the hell, I'll do it."

A smile broke out on Bloomfield's face. "It might turn into a really good story. You might just give us what we want. You won't regret it, Mick."

Sever shook the editor's hand. He didn't need any more regrets in his life.

CHAPTER THREE

He walked out of the building, pulling his leather jacket tightly around him against the early-April Chicago chill. Despite the cold, a steady stream of people paraded the sidewalk and a cavalcade of noisy traffic prowled the street. Sever's mind was going a mile a minute.

This was the kind of story that he used to share with Ginny. He thought about calling her, but she'd made it clear when she left Miami that she didn't want a relationship of any kind. And why had he agreed to do the story in the first place? Maybe because Murtz sounded like a dirtbag and Sever actually got a perverse pleasure out of putting people like that in their place. But probably because he needed something to get him focused. Focused on anything other than thinking about his ex-wife.

Sever could see a cab about ten cars back and he held up his hand. Chicago wasn't like New York where there were hundreds of cabs on every street in the city. You had to work hard to get one here, and you were damned lucky if they stopped.

He stepped off the curb and heard the engine roar even before he saw the BMW. The driver of the Five Series squealed his tires and Sever watched in horror as the car raced toward the sidewalk. For a split second he froze, the menacing machine aimed squarely at him. Thirty miles an hour, forty miles an hour, the engine roar was louder and louder as Sever stumbled back, spinning and running, three steps, four, five, and six, finally jumping onto the sidewalk and jogging quickly to the safety of the Tribune Building as the white car flashed by, the left front tire jumping the curb before the vehicle shot back into traffic and disappeared from sight. Sever stared after it, his mind replaying the car's accelerated speed and dark, tinted windows. He drew deep breaths, feeling his heart start to slow down.

"Jesus, mister. That guy looked like he was trying to kill you."

Sever rubbed his eyes, barely aware of the little old man in the yellow sweater who addressed him.

Eight or nine people gathered at the spot where the tire hit the curb, shocked by the event that had lasted no more than six seconds.

"Guy was just not paying attention."

"Three martini lunch!"

"I saw him. Short little guy. Those windows were tinted, but I could see him. He didn't look drunk, just crazy."

"You okay, man?"

Sever half listened, agreeing with the *crazy* comment. Obviously someone had lost control for a brief moment. He'd had his life threatened before, but not here. Not in his hometown. Why would someone try to take him out here, in broad daylight? And for what reason? It had to be an accident. What pissed Sever off more than anything was that he'd lost his cab.

CHAPTER FOUR

The jet landed on the oceanside runway on St. Martin. Houses with orange tile roofs climbed into the hills in front of the plane.

"U.S. Airways would like to be the first to welcome you to St. Martin." The sexy-sounding flight attendant was the youngest attendant on the plane. Twenty-something, and she'd recognized Sever in the first-class section.

"You used to be on MTV, right? God, you were so cool." *Were*?

Sever walked down the steps and basked for a moment in the warm sunshine. He traveled light, and with his laptop and one carry-on, he walked across the tarmac to the airport entrance, feeling the heat and humidity already working through his white linen shirt and jeans.

"You don't have to clear customs since you won't be staying on our island," the slender black man smiled at him. "Just fill out the paperwork at the counter. Your plane to St. Barts will be leaving momentarily."

Momentarily was three hours later. Sever kept glancing at the sign by the gate. Wynn Airline, your dependable airline.

The couple in front of him were from New Jersey. It seemed there were nothing *but* couples. Except for him. The middle-aged woman smiled at him. "We usually take the ferry because these planes are always late."

The plane was a twelve-passenger prop and the flight took

twelve minutes. Twelve minutes of breathtaking views of a blue ocean that changed hues one hundred times. Twelve minutes of mountainous, uninhabited islands, and yachts that anchored in secluded bays. Twelve minutes of tiny sailboats and clear blue skies.

And then Sever saw the famous mountains — peaks that formed a deep V — as the small plane, flying high, suddenly nosedived, as if to crash at the foot of the steep land masses. The pilot pulled up at the last minute and coasted between the two monoliths, landing on the very short runway that ran into the beach. The plane pulled to a stop inches from the white sand and only feet from the sparkling turquoise blue water.

The woman in the seat across the aisle shuddered. "My husband's a pilot. He wants to try that sometime, but I won't be with him when he does."

There was no welcome to St. Barts. The twelve cramped passengers shuffled off the plane and walked into the tiny airport. Sever picked up his Budget rental car and the girl handed him a map. He spoke no French, and she spoke halting English, but when they finished conversing, he thought he had a vague idea where the hotel might be. Around the bend and follow the road. Five minutes tops. From the tiny Rover all he could detect were mountains, hills, and rugged terrain. What the hell, the island was small so how lost could you get?

CHAPTER FIVE

"You've got financial forms to sign, Danny." His secretary handed him a sheaf of papers, each with a signature line. "Just sign on the bottom line and we'll transfer the money."

He gazed vacantly at the papers in front of him. Nancy was so officious. Officious and on task. And most of the time he wanted nothing to do with *task*. She was always bringing him papers to sign: order forms and requests. And all he wanted to do was look out the window and gaze down to the ocean. His villa was high in the hills, his view was perfect. From his desk he could see other gleaming white villas, but none as grand as his.

Their orange-tiled roofs tiered down the mountains in a geometric puzzle. And at the end of the tier were the white sand and the crystal clear blue waters of Governor's Beach. Like cocaine powder on a mirror. This was the reward for years of struggling. Years of arranging, composing, and producing the songbook of America. This was the reward for — hell, this was the reward for doing nothing. He laughed out loud. Half the time it made him crazy, half the time he accepted the joke. He lived the best life in the world and did practically nothing to deserve it. He wished the old man could see him now. But the old man was gone. A victim of his own vices.

Murtz stole half the material he'd been given credit for. Stole it. His best songs all copied from other songwriters. Oh, he'd usually added enough changes to get a judge to agree that he was the author, but he'd made a fortune off of other songwriters and producers. And lucked into the rest of it. It was all a sham, a scam, some kind of hoax. As many years as it had been happening, as many years as he'd cranked out major hits — writing the songs, arranging the songs, working with the groups and singers until they had become major stars — he still woke up in the middle of the night, covered in sweat, and panicked at the thought that they knew. Someone had figured it out. It was phony. They would send him back to upstate New York, and he'd end up working on some shit-hole assembly line or digging in some mine a mile below ground level. Or worse yet, he'd be sent to prison, just like his worthless father.

His abusive, leather-belt-strapping father, who lived for drinking other men under the table and beating the hell out of them. And the fucker eventually paid for it with twenty years in a prison cell. When he was finally released, he'd ended his miserable life by his own hand and no one wept a tear. His mother had feigned some regrets, but Murtz knew she was glad to be rid of the abusive asshole. That wasn't going to happen to him. Somebody had once done a story on his career, accusing him of having a charmed life. That's what he dwelled on. A charmed life.

Hell, all Murtz did was record songs for other artists, and the entire world opened up to him like a sliced ripe peach. It *was* a scam. He should have been living his father's life. Instead, the life of a celebrity had kicked in, and there were endless possibilities. And he'd pursued a number of them. Recently he'd come to the realization that there might actually be a *finite* number of possibilities. He was running out of ideas.

Murtz shook himself from his reverie, took a long drink of his second rum and cola of the morning, and picked up the pen. If he didn't sign the papers there would be no money in the bank. If he had no money, his lifestyle on the island would be seriously cramped. And lifestyle on St. Barts was all important.

He sprawled out in the leather chair, his feet splayed on the ottoman. The massive oak desk he'd had shipped to the island sat to his left. He very seldom used it. The big chair was more comfortable, and all he ever really did in this huge office was sign papers. Papers that Nancy brought him. Papers he very seldom understood.

One paper, something about an annuity. Two papers. This one about a stock option. Three papers. Four, five, six, and seven papers. He scrawled his name at the bottom, dated them, and shuffled them to the side. One final paper lay at the bottom of the stack.

He glanced at it. There was no room for a signature. It was simply a double-spaced, typed paper. He stared at it for a second. There was no signature, nor any heading. A simple piece of white paper with a one-paragraph statement.

Murtz glanced up to see if Nancy was in the room or in the hall. There was no sign of his officious secretary. He sighed, resigned to actually reading the letter himself. Christ, you paid for good help, and when you needed them they disappeared.

The letter was in a small font, and he squinted. He still couldn't make out all the words. Murtz reached into his robe pocket, not finding his glasses. He struggled to get up, worked his way around the desk, and reached into the middle drawer. He fished out a pair of reading glasses and slumped back into the padded leather chair.

Picking up the letter, he started to read.

Mr. Murtz,

I understand your prominence in the entertainment world. I understand that people like you believe laws were made to be broken. You act as if there should be no rules in your life. However, I know you killed Jennifer Koenig. I know you did it. I know how you did it. I know when you did it. Thou shall not kill, Mr. Murtz. This is a law that cannot be broken. And if you do, it's an eye for an eye. Read your Bible. It's very clear. My intention is to set the punishment to fit the crime. You and I will meet in the very near future.

Murtz read it again. Nothing changed. He glanced out over the hills to the ocean below and focused on a sailboat, anchored and bobbing in the water. The brilliant sunlight bounced off the craft's yellow sail, sending a shimmering line of light out onto the water. He shook his head as if to clear away the cobwebs. Nancy had brought him the papers.

"Nancy!" *Where the hell was she?*

"Right here, Danny." She stepped from the hallway into his office.

Nancy appeared from nowhere half the time. Pouncing on any situation. He trusted her about as much as he trusted Harvey. Given the right situation, both of them would dismiss him in a heartbeat.

"The letter on the bottom. You put it there. Did you read it?"

"On the bottom? There was just a stack of financial papers for you to sign. No letter."

"Bullshit. This letter!" He waved the letter in front of her. "You put it there!"

"Danny, there were seven papers for you to sign. There were no letters."

He was quiet for a second.

"Impossible. This letter was on the bottom of the stack."

"Danny, maybe you found a letter on your desk or chair. I handed you seven papers. If they're signed, I'll send them out."

"Don't bullshit me, Nancy!" His voice grew louder. "The letter was right here." He clenched his fists. The bitch was lying to him and if he stood up he'd probably hit her.

She let out an exasperated breath, rolling her eyes. Goddamn her.

"Danny, I gave you nothing but papers to sign."

He glared at her for a moment, then handed her the financial papers, studying his secretary of twenty-four years. If not Nancy, who? Who the hell had given him the letter? And why now? Why this Jennifer?

"Damn it. I know what I have in my hand." Maybe he was in the middle of one of those fuzzy moments. They came on him more and more. When the chemical balance wasn't quite right. When he'd had too many drinks or the coke didn't give him the edge he needed or he'd just smoked too much pot. "You didn't do it? Bullshit!"

"Why is this an issue? What's so important about this letter?"

He stared into her eyes, looking for some sign of deceit. "Anybody come to the house in the last day? Anyone who's not part of the group?"

She studied him for a moment. "Oh, you mean Bill?"

"Bill?"

"Bill. Next door. He noticed we were back and wanted to say hi."

"The book collector? The gun collector? The collector? That Bill?"

"That Bill."

Bill something. Some authority on something. He struggled with the name. Bill . . . Timmermeister. That was it. "Timmermeister."

"Yes. Your neighbor."

"No one else?"

"No." She gave him a slight smile, as if to diffuse the situation. "There are some kids out by the pool, but they haven't been in the house."

Murtz shuddered. How could someone have put that letter at the bottom of his financials? And when was he going to meet this person? Was it Bill? He barely knew the man. He collected guns, and his neighbor collected guns. To his knowledge that was the extent of their relationship. They'd talked about ten minutes. It made no sense.

"Will there be anything else?"

Was someone going to kill him? The threat was obvious. Should he hide out or go on with his life? He didn't come to St. Barts to lock himself inside his villa.

"Make me another rum and cola and get some girls together. Call Harvey at the guest house. We're going to Casa Niki tonight. Get me about $5000 in cash. Hell, that should pay for a good party, right?" That should buy ten bottles of Cristal champagne. "Want to go with us? You might get lucky."

She rolled her eyes. "You know I'd like to be five miles away from your attorney at any given time. I don't trust the son of a bitch. I don't trust him at all. And, one more thing, Danny. Harvey wants to fire Jason! If that happens, you and I are going to have some serious problems. And by the way," she glared at him "you can fix your own damned drink." Nancy spun around and left the room.

Murtz wadded the letter into a ball and lobbed it at the wastebasket. The shot went wide. He picked up his drink glass and pitched it at his departing secretary, the glass hitting the tile floor and shattering into sharp splinters. Fucking useless. He pushed himself from his comfortable chair, opened the desk drawer, and pulled out a small plastic bag. Carefully pouring some of the white powder from the bag onto the glass top of the desk, he removed a short straw from the drawer and snorted the line of cocaine. Nancy and Harvey, what a combination! Harvey wanted to fire *the boy*? It was news to him.

Jennifer Koenig. He closed his eyes. The cute little blond. Sexy little wiggle when she walked. Who was she? A backup singer or maybe somebody in a video shoot? He couldn't remember. That happened a lot. The drugs and alcohol. And truth be told, it didn't seem to matter much. He paid other people to organize his life. Other people were paid to remember for him. But he did remember that when this Jennifer had been introduced to him she'd told him she was adventurous. Adventurous. So he introduced her to an adventure. A little more than she'd bargained for, but *he* remembered that adventure. Very intense. He concentrated. Did he kill her? And when? Time and events seemed to blend together and he was never sure when something had happened.

Hell, there might have been something about physical abuse, a little roughhousing, but it had been at least a year or more, and it just wasn't coming back to him. Could someone prove it? Harvey was pretty good at cleaning up messes, but even the savvy attorney might have slipped up.

Harvey might have slipped up accidentally. Or maybe Harvey deliberately slipped up. Maybe Nancy was right. Maybe the little guy couldn't be trusted anymore. And what about Nancy? She'd handed him the letter. And then she had the damned nerve to deny it. A lady who still harbored jealousy in her soul? Still dreamed of a long-term relationship with him after all these years? Maybe she was responsible for a letter that threatened his life? How could she not know it was in the pile? A fucking conspiracy.

The dark wooden blades of the ceiling fan spun lazily above him and he stared at them, hypnotized by the constant rotation. If he couldn't trust his own people, who could he trust?

CHAPTER SIX

Thirty minutes after renting the car, Sever stopped at a small carry-out.

"You can't get lost." The man had a thick French accent. "Just around the corner. It's very secluded." The man pointed, and Sever was about ready to ask him to hop in the car and lead the way. The hell you couldn't get lost! Pretty much the story of his life.

Thirty seconds later, he pulled into the parking lot of the Manapany Hotel and Cottages.

"Welcome. You've come to check in?" The cute brunette had a foreign accent he couldn't place.

Straight out of a movie set, the tiny lobby featured a small wooden desk, two wicker chairs, and a couch. A ceiling fan turned slowly above him, pushing the warm, humid air around. Sever could feel his white linen shirt sticking to his chest and arms.

"Mr. Sever?" She had a shy smile on her young face, her white blouse and shorts showing off her golden tan.

"You know who I am?" It happened a lot. People recognized him from his television appearances, from the dust jacket of his latest book, or from his photo in magazines like *Rolling Stone, Spin*, and *People.*

"A *Mr. Sever* is the only person with a reservation who has not checked in today. If you're not Mr. Sever, you must be at the wrong hotel."

That cute smile. He was humbled. "Yeah. I'm Sever."

"Good. Welcome to the Manapany Hotel. Your room will be at the top of the road." She pointed to the left. "The view of the ocean is breathtaking. I'm certain you will find it to your liking."

He filled out the paperwork, took the key and drove up the winding road. He stopped at the small parking lot, stepped out of the Rover, and turned to the steps leading up to his cottage.

His eye caught the view cascading down to the ocean. Stunning. Maybe even breathtaking. The sun hung high in the pale blue sky and the ocean mirrored the azure color. Tiny waves reflected the sun's golden hue as they lapped the shore far below. He looked up at the balcony he would soon be enjoying. A far cry from the blue-collar neighborhood in Chicago where he'd grown up. A far cry from the row house where his abusive father had died of a heart attack. A far cry from the nursing home in Elgin, Illinois where his mother had starved herself to death at the age of eighty-two. A family of three with very little bond. The few years they lived together was the only glue that even hinted at family. And now, Sever himself was divorced, without any family at all. He gazed up at the room he was staying in. Solo. It was really the only life he'd ever known.

He hung his limited wardrobe in the closet and placed the folded clothes in the built-in drawers. Toiletries were on the sink. Toothpaste, toothbrush, deodorant, a bottle of aspirin, and Nexium. Nexium for acid reflux. Getting old was a bitch.

Sever opened the sliding glass doors to the balcony and stood at the railing, staring at the bay. The sun was still high in the cloudless sky, and he could see the mountains that jutted out from either side of the bay and the craggy rocks that plummeted to the water below. Several hundred feet up, there were villas, with equally impressive views of the ocean. For just a second he turned to the room, where the white phone sat beside the bed. Maybe she'd be glad to hear his voice. He could tell her he'd been in St. Martin. But it was only for a second, then the impulse left him. Don't go there. But he did need to check his answering machine. He'd made a firm decision to avoid a cell phone, but he did need to check in with the real world once in a while. Agents, lawyers, managers, editors all needed to be addressed. Sever picked up the phone, called the international access code, and dialed the number. There was nothing. No answer, no messages. The phone just continued to ring. It was a glitch, obviously. Maybe it was the international connection. He hung up and made a mental note to check in later. There was a slim possibility that Ginny had called. Not likely, but he never dashed the hope.

Sever walked past a personal hot tub to the wet bar, complete with Scotch, vodka, rum, and Jack. He twisted off the top of the Dewar's Scotch and poured a healthy shot into a glass, savoring the first sip. He should have relished the tropical experience, and there was a time when he did. Not now. Now it was just a job. He wanted to finish it and fly home. The problem was there was nothing to go home to. Nothing and no one. He was restless, and there was nothing to focus on. He took another swallow of the Scotch and pushed the thought from his head.

Sever laid the file folder on the wicker coffee table and sat down in a cushioned easy chair. He read from the first page.

> Danny Murtz: Produced 120 albums, 15 that went gold. 11 that went platinum. 3 that were diamond.

Sever was impressed. He had no idea that Murtz had that many successes. Gold meant sales of 500,000 albums. Platinum meant 1,000,000. And Diamond was — he thought for a moment. How many? 10,000,000. This guy was a genius. The artists may have been good, maybe great. But the producer was the overriding factor. The producer was responsible for the overall sound. Sometimes he arranged the music, deciding on the instrumentation. Sometimes he directed the sessions, and sometimes he wrote or rewrote the songs to get the most out of his groups and singers. George Martin produced the Beatles, Phil Spector produced the Righteous Brothers, the Ronettes, and others. Quincy Jones had produced Michael Jackson's *Thriller*, and Boyce and Hart had written and produced most of the Monkeys' hits back in the seventies. William Orbit had produced

Madonna, Bacharach produced Dionne Warwick, all extremely successful producers, but obviously Danny Murtz was a giant in the industry.

The first page listed a handful of the many hit songs that Murtz had produced. Twenty of the songs he'd written himself. Or stolen from other writers. But as his reputation grew, bigger artists sought him out. And Danny Murtz could name his price. Sever turned to the second page. More of the same. Still he read with interest. Songs he'd grown up with, songs that were part of the fabric of his life. And each song title brought back the memory of the time, the place, and the emotion he'd had when he first heard the tune. Murtz had written and produced *Love Gone Wrong*. It was a song that Sever and Ginny had sung along with about one hundred times.

I can't help this feeling
I close my eyes and pray
Every thing I wished for
I've lost along the way
If you go and leave me
I don't think I'm that strong
To live without you baby
To face a love that's gone wrong

He smiled. How lame. But at the time, it seemed like an anthem for the ages. Ginny should have been the girl for all ages. It played on his mind every day.

The slight, balmy breeze caressed the discarded pages, and he set a glass ashtray on the growing pile to stop the papers from fluttering to the floor. Sever sipped the Scotch, reading on.

Murtz liked young girls. He'd been arrested twice for violations with a minor, but never convicted. There were numerous arrest records for drug and alcohol violations but only one conviction. He'd been found guilty for having a partially smoked joint in the ashtray of his car. He got off with a fine. One conviction. Celebrity definitely had its privileges.

Jeff Bloomfield had included numerous press clippings. There were stories about award ceremonies that Murtz attended in his early years, tales of liaisons with starlets, and it appeared that the paparazzi had a field day with all the girls he had dated. Pictures of a restaurant rendezvous, casual hotel visits, photos of Murtz sneaking out of a married actress' house back in the '80s, and headlines from the tabloids cast even more aspersions on the man.

Sever read for half an hour, skimming over much of the material. The details of Murtz's life read like a textbook case of someone who had had too much too soon. Starting with a blue-collar Chicago background, the superstar producer hit it big at age seventeen. Sever'd started stringing for the *Tribune* when he was sixteen. Murtz had found a young, teenage rock group that was as hungry as he was for major success. When Ronnie and the Daytones sold two million singles of *I Remember the Day*, Danny Murtz became a superstar. And with that, he gained major success. And major *excess.* Sever shuffled the papers and laid them on the coffee table. There were scary similarities in his life and Danny Murtz's.

Walking to the railing he breathed deeply, smelling the hint of salty air and sweet frangipani. Palm trees and flowering bushes followed the cottages down the hill. It was idyllic and he should have been at peace with himself and the job. But knowing what lay ahead bothered him.

He bent over and picked up the papers once more, his eyes searching the last three pages until he came to a small copy of a press clipping. The story was from the *New York Post*, and it was dated almost two years ago. He sat back down in the chair and read it carefully this time.

Soap Opera Star Missing

> Actress Jennifer Koenig, a regular on the daytime drama Burma Lane has been reported missing. A representative filed a missing person report with the New York City Police Department on September

> 2nd. Ms. Koenig was to appear on the popular daytime television show last Thursday and Friday but never reported to the New York soundstage. Ms. Koenig had been in touch with the NYPD in August, when the 24-year-old actress reported that her sometimes boyfriend, songwriter and producer Danny Murtz, had physically assaulted her with a pistol. The charge was withdrawn the next day. If anyone has any information as to the whereabouts of Jennifer Koenig, please contact the NYPD.

He stared at the girl's photo. She had a fresh look about her, and the photographer had captured a Mona Lisa smile that played on her lips. A beautiful girl, probably just starting her career. Her eyes looked through him, beyond to something that seemed to amuse her. For a moment he wished he knew her. He'd like to explore that whimsical expression and see if there was any depth behind it.

Sever laid the papers back down and took a final swallow of Scotch. Out loud he said "Jennifer Koenig, this is to you."

Danny Murtz pistol-whipped a reporter then pistol-whipped his own girlfriend. Good music be damned, this guy was a nasty son of a bitch. Something Jeff Bloomfield had said stuck with him. Danny Murtz was evil. Sever thought about that statement for a minute. Evil. Like a son of the Devil. Come on, this was a case of a guy who was handed too much power, and he abused it. Evil? Son of the Devil? That was pushing it. Then he remembered a saying his aging mother used to say when he was growing up. "The greatest lie ever told is that the Devil doesn't exist." So, was Danny Murtz the Devil? Or the son of the Devil? The greatest lie ever told is that the Devil doesn't exist. Bullshit. Sever had told some whoppers in his day. Greater lies than that.

He found the second reference three minutes later. It came from the *Atlanta Constitution*, and was originally buried in the second section, page five. Not a great spot to attract much attention. Almost four years ago.

> Libby Hellman, public relations consultant for Banco de Rio, has been reported missing by her personal assistant, Fred Rea. Rea raised an alarm when the very visible Hellman failed to show up for two interviews in the last week. Hellman, former road manager for British rock sensation God Save the Queen, has been the spokesperson for South American financial institution Banco de Rio for the past two years. She has been romantically linked to a number of A-list celebrities including actor Michael Trump, singer Raul Everly, and most recently, producer and song writer Danny Murtz.

Sketchy. Very Sketchy. Was it enough to conduct an investigation? Sever thumbed through the papers, finally finding a copy of two letters from Bloomfield's unidentified source. They were brief and to the point.

> Mr. Bloomfield:
>
> In the last seven years, at least two young ladies have mysteriously disappeared. They share several things in common. Both were in the entertainment business and both ladies were dating producer Danny Murtz when they vanished. I have sent letters to several law enforcement agencies and I've heard nothing. I will give you the compelling reasons why you should investigate this story.
> 1)Danny Murtz has been charged for numerous assaults on women. (Albeit never convicted.)
> 2)Danny Murtz was dating these two young women at the time of their disappearance.
> 3)Danny Murtz was the last person known to be with these ladies. There is no verification of the exact time they disappeared, but below you will

> see witnesses' statements that place Murtz with each girl within two days of the report of her disappearance.

He pushed the papers aside and closed his eyes. So Murtz had physically assaulted a woman and was mentioned as a partner in the disappearance of another. And an anonymous source had some flimsy reasons why Murtz should be investigated. Sever had been around enough celebrities to know that it was par for the course. He respected Danny Murtz for his tremendous accomplishments in the music business. He thought a lot less of him for the stories of his love life. Beating women? What kind of an asshole did that? Still, it didn't mean he'd killed anyone. If he was afforded the opportunity, he would ask about the two girls during his interview with Murtz, but it didn't seem like there was much of a story here.

He could wrap the story tomorrow, spend an extra day on St. Barts as a company expense, and be home for the weekend. Easy money. But there was nothing at home. Nothing, and no one. It was becoming a point of irritation. Time to move on, find someone who was up for a little fun in the sun. When he was married, he had no problem finding someone else. Now that there was no hope of getting back with Ginny, he couldn't feign an interest in finding someone new. Life was a constant surprise. In reality, a bitch.

Sever flipped over the papers and found the last letter to Bloomfield.

> Mr. Bloomfield:
>
> The final reason you should investigate Danny Murtz is because he tried to kill me.

CHAPTER SEVEN

He always had a gun. Having guns ran in his family. Part of his bad-boy reputation centered around guns. In a rather inebriated state, he'd walked into a recording session, pulled out a pistol, and fired it into the ceiling while his vocal group was recording. After coaxing his scattered artists back into the studio, he'd left the sound of the gunshot on the recording, turning an act of violence into art. Or that's the way the story evolved. Actually, he didn't remember it happening, but it added to his legend, and he got a lot of mileage out of that legend!

Now he needed a gun. You could never be too careful. Someone was threatening him and he had to be *extra* careful. He ran his eyes over the display of handguns lined up in his walnut case. Carefully selecting a small gun, he picked it up and admired it for a moment, feeling the weight in the palm of his hand. Accurate, effective, and German-made. If someone made a move, at least Murtz had a fighting chance. He'd only shot one person. Right here, on St. Barts. But the body and gun would never be found. It was a good feeling to know you could do it, pull the trigger without any compunction. Don't fuck with Danny Murtz.

He stroked the cool barrel of the pistol, the feeling of the smooth metal soothing him. Murtz looked into the end of the barrel, then slowly pushed the end of the gun into his mouth. The roof of the mouth. He could taste the metallic flavor and feel the pressure on his palate. Just for a moment. Having guns ran in his family. Then he tucked the Mauser pocket-pistol into the pocket of his cargo shorts as Nancy walked into the office.

"Danny?"

He shot her a look. "Somebody gave me this letter. I'll handle it."

She looked back. Never backed down. Her blond hair was pulled back, and her green eyes, now looking through narrow slits reminded him of a cat he'd once had. The cat had scratched him one too many times and that was the end of the cat. He was certain that Nancy knew nothing about that cat. Not yet. She turned and left the room, and he watched her hips as she marched down the hall. There was still something seductive about his long-suffering secretary.

He walked out to the pool. Three young girls lounged topless in zero-gravity, canvas-back chairs. Some guy he'd never seen was swimming laps, and Harvey Schwartz sat at the umbrella table, studying his laptop computer screen.

He didn't trust any of them. Any one of them could be the letter writer. He paused and studied his guests. The three girls, all blond, all evenly tanned with smallish breasts and pert nipples, the guy in the pool, who was probably with one of the girls, and Harvey.

Harvey with his long, dark green cargo pants, long-sleeved white shirt, a baseball cap pulled down tight over his pale, bald head, and sitting under the umbrella to avoid a stray ray of sunshine making its way to his fair skin. The lawyer looked up and nodded at Murtz.

"Damned sun. Can barely make out the screen on my laptop."

"I told Nancy we'd go out tonight. Maybe Casa Niki or the Yacht Club."

Harvey nodded. "Enjoy."

"I might call that girl from Atlanta, Michelle what's her name. The one we flew over here. Where the hell did we put her up?"

"The Manapany, Danny. She's at the Manapany Hotel. Can't you remember anything?"

"Then again, maybe there's some local talent we can take advantage of."

"No *we*. I've got things to do." Harvey kept his eyes on the computer.

"No, I want you there. You be there, Harvey."

Harvey kept his eyes on the screen, never acknowledging the demand. Murtz watched him for a moment. The man knew everything. He literally knew where the bodies were buried. At any time Harvey Schwartz could point his finger and it would all be over. Murtz shuddered.

"The television thing. Have you thought it through?" Harvey peered up at him from under the brim of his cap.

"Meaning?"

"Meaning, can you keep it simple? They're liable to ask questions about more than just the music and the job."

Murtz's eyes strayed to the hillside and they followed the incline to the huge expanse of Caribbean water that floated out to the horizon. "I haven't done an interview in what? Fifteen years?"

"And in the past fifteen years you've had drug charges, molestation charges —"

"Goddamnit." He exploded, shoving his finger in the attorney's face as if it were the barrel of his gun. "I don't need you to tell me what charges have been filed. Do you understand that, you little prick? You'll be right there during the entire interview. You'll be there during the little jaunt they want to take with me around the island, when I work with the Indoorfins, and whatever else they have up their sleeves. *You* don't like the way the interview is going, *you* stop it. Do you understand me? Christ, Harvey, it's what I pay you for." He spun around and walked out to the end of the pool. Harvey, reminding him of what a screw-up he'd been. Harvey, like a wife who wouldn't stop nagging. Harvey, who took care of the problems that he couldn't entrust to anyone else.

One of the blonds came up and put her hand on his arm. "Danny, I want to introduce you to Brendon. He's —" he cut her off before she could finish the sentence.

"I don't care who the hell he is. I don't want him here. Get him out of here. Get him the fuck out of here. Right now!"

She stared at him for a moment, appearing confused, frightened, and angry all at the same time.

"Out! Now." He was screaming, and he could feel the fire in his eyes. Cocaine did that to him. Made him crazy. Made him strong.

The girl backed up, grabbing a towel and wrapping it around her as if suddenly aware of her nakedness.

Murtz strode the length of the pool, feeling the heat and humidity seeping into his skin. His hands were clenched and he swore he could feel the tingle of each follicle of the long, ponytailed hair on his head. He pushed wet strands back from his face, now sensing the weight of the pistol in his pocket. That letter was bothering him far more than he thought it would. Murtz stepped through the open French doors into the cool confines of his villa. There had to be a plan. Start with the damned kid in the pool. Somebody had delivered a threatening letter. Somebody with access to his home. It could be the fucking kid. Maybe somebody set him up, paid him to come to the house with the girl. Then, when no one was looking, he slipped the letter into the stack of papers. Damn. It was time to start cleaning house.

He pulled the Mauser from his pocket, walked back to the pool and pointed the pistol at the water. "Get the hell off my property! Unless you don't give a shit about your life."

The young man scrambled for the side of the pool. Pulling himself out, he shot an angry look over his shoulder at the ponytailed man. Murtz starred at him for a moment. The kid bore a remarkable resemblance to *the boy*. Nancy's son, the twenty-five-year-old useless kid who ran the studio back in Chicago. He never remembered his name. Justin, Jason, Jerome. *The boy*.

Murtz followed him, keeping the barrel aimed at his head. He pretended the swimmer was *the boy*. "A little faster, you fucker. Come on. Move it." He aimed just to the right of the young man and squeezed the trigger. With a roar, the pistol jerked in his hand and pieces of deck tile went flying in all directions.

The boy and three girls ran, the boy lifting himself over the fence and taking off across the lawn, dodging between trees without looking back. The three girls were shrieking as they made it to the gate, stumbling over each other as they pushed through and disappeared around the house.

From the corner of his eye, Murtz caught Harvey, standing up, shaking his head. The judgmental asshole was always negative. Murtz was tired of being judged and he spun around, and for a brief second, pointed the barrel at Harvey. For just a brief second. And for that brief second he thought he saw fear in Harvey's eyes. Good. Harvey knew that he was capable of pulling the trigger again. That ought to keep the slimeball attorney in line. Fire *the boy*, but don't fuck with me. He shoved the firearm into his pocket and walked back into the villa.

Walking into his office, he dropped into the leather chair. His notepad and pen were sitting on its arm where he had left them. He picked up the pen, squinting and concentrating on the scene that had just transpired by the pool.

Don't ever play with fire
You'll mess around and stir up someone's flaming ire
Someone who deceives you is a blatant liar
So don't ever play with fire.

It had the theme of a big hit. Maybe the Indoorfins could do it. He'd have to work on it. Steal the melody from some other song, lift a couple of lyrics, he'd have another hit on his hands. It was good to be the king.

CHAPTER EIGHT

She trained the field glasses on the house. The pool was easy to see from her vantage point. It skirted the edge of the mountain, and the pool deck area featured what appeared to be a long teak cabinet cooking area with a built-in stainless-steel grill. His villa was huge. Five bedrooms, six baths, a den, study, living room, and a spacious guest cottage at the rear. She knew the villa, but it had been a long time ago. So she'd gotten some updated information from a real estate agent in Gustavia. A rough sketch of the floor plan lay on a patio table beside her. Her rental unit was more of a cottage than anything else. One small bedroom, an adequate kitchen, one bath, and what could best be described as a wading pool.

The woman pushed her mousy brown hair back from her face with one hand, holding the glasses with the other. She concentrated on the players. She knew who Harvey Schwartz was. She knew a lot about Harvey, but she didn't recognize the others. Some bimbos that Murtz surrounded himself with and a guy in the pool that she didn't know.

Murtz was waving his arms, pointing at the pool with what looked like a gun in his hand. She saw the young man coming out of the pool, then she heard the crack of the pistol as it reverberated down the hill. At first she thought it might be a car backfiring on the curving road that ran in front of the villas. Immediately the boy and the girls took off running, and she realized Murtz was actually shooting at them. My God, she knew he beat people with his pistols, but she didn't know he shot at them as well.

She waited. A minute later he came back out, postured again, then a tall, well-muscled young man walked out onto the deck. He had on what appeared to be white linen pants and a white, open-collared shirt. Untucked. It was the uniform of the island. It had to be a bodyguard. The white-clad man moved to the gate, lay a pistol on one of the tables, and pulled up a chair. Apparently the pool was now off limits. Harvey stood up once but never moved from the umbrella table. He sat down again, glued to his laptop computer. The laptop computer that seldom left his side. The girl had a good idea what was on that hard drive. The files, the information that told a very sordid story. Harvey was seldom separated from that computer.

There was at least one bodyguard, probably two. They changed every other month or so. Murtz probably had someone who would drive his car, and then there was Nancy. Nancy the mother figure. Nancy the bitch. Cold, calculating Nancy. What a combination they all made. Counting Harvey, that made five hired hands. Not quite as many in the posse here as there were in Chicago. Add another ten in the Windy City.

She put down the binoculars and sipped her cranberry juice. Her view of the bay was the same as his. The hillside, the ocean, and the boats below. And if she took the time to admire it, there was bougainvillea spreading an array of colors among the palms, the mango trees, and the assorted brush that spilled down the hill. But this villa was rented for a very short time, and the only reason she was here was because of Danny Murtz and Harvey Schwartz, two villas over. Maybe she'd enjoy the view in a day or two.

Danny Murtz, Harvey Schwartz, and St. Barts. She was reminded of a T-shirt she saw at Le Select, the cheeseburger restaurant and bar in Gustavia. The slogan on the front told it like it was.

ST. BARTS. A SUNNY PLACE FOR SHADY PEOPLE.

There was a lot of time for enjoying herself. A lot of time to see the sights and lie in the sun, maybe take off everything at Saline Beach, or down below at Governor's Beach.

There was time to get drunk and maybe, as Jimmy Buffett said, "roll in the sand with a rock and roll man." But right now, there was work to be done.

She saw movement in the villa next to hers. The big man who owned the home had walked out onto his pool deck, sitting down in a lounge chair with a newspaper and a cup of coffee. He seemed to stare intently at Murtz's villa. The girl wondered if he'd heard the gunshots. How safe was it living next to a crazy celebrity. Did this guy know just who his neighbor was?

She buried her head in her arms, fighting back tears. Stay strong. Stay focused. She had to see this through. It seemed like a lifetime of anonymity, of praying for vindication. She shuddered, trying to shake off the solitude and fear that seemed to creep into her thoughts on a daily basis. It was hell, facing your own insecurities with no one to share them with. Harvey Schwartz had threatened her. Threatened her career, her family, and her life. It wasn't just an idle threat. Harvey had mentioned other prominent figures that had suffered consequences. She'd understood from the beginning that if she reported anything to the authorities, her life would be over. And there was a life worth protecting. She'd lived a life of privilege, of luxury, of overindulgence. She'd lost that existence. But she didn't want to lose her life. The attorney had made it very clear.

She wanted to bring them down, and she wanted Danny Murtz to suffer. It appeared he was starting to slip.

CHAPTER NINE

He called the number he'd been given and a lady answered on the fifth ring.

"This is Mick Sever. I'm doing an interview with Danny Murtz this week and wondered what time we could get together. I usually like to do a preliminary conversation, then meet maybe a day later, and —"

"Mr. Sever, this is Nancy Steiner, Mr. Murtz's administrative assistant. I know who you are." Cold, impersonal. Nothing like, "I admire your work, oh, yes, I've been expecting your call, thank you for taking the time to talk to Danny."

"Well, I'd like to set up a —"

"Danny has a very busy schedule. As you know, A&E is here to do a video of his life on the island and I'm afraid we may not have time to work in the other interview."

What? He hadn't come all this way to be shut out. That was out of the question. Did she have an inkling of what direction this interview was going to go? He bristled, then took a deep breath. This had only happened maybe a couple of hundred times during his career. He could handle this bitch. "Ms. Steiner, it's not imperative that I have two sessions. It's only what I prefer. I can work in the interview anytime you feel works for you. I totally understand your position and the last thing I want to do is make things difficult for you."

She was quiet for a moment. Probably the kind of person who

needed to set the ground rules. Someone who wanted some respect up front. Sever could do that. It was part of the job. He breathed a little slower, feeling his flush and anger abate. He should have taught classes at an anger management school. Sever remembered the slogan: PATIENCE MY ASS, I'M GOING TO KILL SOMEONE.

"Ms. Steiner?"

"Please, call me Nancy. I'll work on an appointment, possibly sometime tomorrow. Give me your number and I'll call you when I have it scheduled."

He repeated the hotel phone number and his extension, then smiled. Still had the Sever charm.

Sever stepped out of the screened porch, walked down the four steps to the paved parking lot, and saw the man from the corner of his eye. His back was to Sever and he knelt down by Sever's rented car.

"Hey, that's my car."

The man jumped, spinning around, a look of fear on his face. Short, dark-haired, probably French. He stared at Sever for a moment, neither man knowing what to say. Finally, he shrugged his shoulders. "Pas de problème."

The short man moved quickly, up a set of stone steps to a dirt path behind Sever's unit. He started running, rounded a bend in the path, and disappeared from sight.

Sever walked to the car, leaned down, and put his hand underneath where the man had been kneeling. There was nothing he could feel. He stood and stared up at the path. The incident made no sense.

He walked down the steep, curvy road, past the lobby, and out to the pool.

Two dark-skinned girls sat at the bar, engaged in a conversation he couldn't understand. He should have studied a foreign language in high school, but writing, girls, and getting high seemed more important at the time.

"Monsieur, what can I get for you?" The bartender gave him a wide smile.

"What's your specialty?"

"Piña colada."

"I'm not really into sweet drinks."

"My friend, you've never tasted a piña colada like the one I will make for you."

A cocky bartender. "Sold!"

"Très bien." The bartender started working his magic with the mixing glass.

"Mr. Sever?"

He turned around. The cute brunette from the lobby had that shy smile on her face.

"You have a message. I saw you walk down this way and wanted to bring it to you."

He took the slip of paper from her. Nancy Steiner had called. He could meet Danny Murtz at one p.m. tomorrow. Perfect.

"Thanks, uh —"

"Natalie."

"Thanks, Natalie."

"If there is anything else I can do for you, anything at all, please, don't hesitate to ask." She turned and walked away. He admired her tan legs as she left the pool.

"Our Natalie makes a wonderful first impression, no?" The bartender chuckled. "She is very good at her job." He set the drink in front of Sever. "Now, if you can tell me this is not a great drink, I will pour you anything you want at no charge."

Pretty confident. Sever took a sip. Fresh fruit, a sweet and sour tang that left his taste buds tingling. He still didn't like sweet drinks, but when a bartender was this good, he couldn't refuse.

"My name is Bertrand. People call me Mr. B. And you are?"

"Sever. Mick Sever."

"And you are from Chicago?"

"How do you know that?"

"The accent. People from the States, I can usually tell where they are from."

Sever grinned. "You're good at a lot of things."

"Mr. Sever, I've been on this island for five years. You can learn a lot on such a small island after five years."

"Then tell me something. Do you know Danny Murtz?"

Bertrand frowned. "I've seen him. I know his reputation. Rum and cola, or Cristal when he's on the island."

Sever shook his head. "You really are good."

The bartender nodded. "He's on the island right now. I believe there is a television production firm about to film his home." He poured freely from several bottles into a stainless mixing glass.

Sever nodded. "Are you a friend of his?"

The bartender looked up from his bar. "A friend? I think not. I've met the man and that was enough. Why do you ask? Are *you* a friend?" Bertrand gave him a questioning glance.

"Never met him."

"He is a very talented man, this Danny Murtz."

"He is."

"However, he is not well respected on the island."

"No?"

"Mr. Sever, we depend on the dollars of tourists for our economy. So it is difficult for us to be critical of the people who supply our income."

"And Danny Murtz is very rich."

"Mr. Murtz helps our economy. But he has a reputation of abusing the people on the island. When he is here he needs to be catered to, twenty-four hours a day. He treats the people on St. Barts as if they owe him, and behind closed doors they complain. There are some things that have happened —" Mr. B. stared out over the pool. "I can't say any more."

Sever was quiet for a moment, hoping for more information. The bartender bowed his head and continued making his drinks. "And money can buy many friends and favors."

Bertrand held up the mixing glass, capped it with a drinking glass and shook the drink vigorously. He poured the orange-colored drink into a tall thin glass. Then, with a long-handled knife he sliced the green-leafed top off a pineapple, and a slice of the pineapple itself. He cut a slit into the leaf and the fruit slice and slid them onto the rim of the glass. A long yellow straw completed the drink, and he handed it to the girl who had just sat down next to Sever.

"Another of your masterpieces?"

He gave Sever a thin smile. He'd taken a couple of deep breaths and was on to being everyone's favorite bartender. "Daiquiri. Just the right amount of sweet and sour. All fresh ingredients, my friend."

"It's delicious. Probably dangerous, but delicious."The girl's eyes drifted from the French bartender to Sever. "I'm Michelle."

"From Georgia, maybe Atlanta." Bertrand winked at her.

"Yes." She smiled

Bertrand glanced at Sever. "Don't be too impressed. She's been here all this week."

Sever couldn't hear any sign of a Southern accent. "I'm Mick. Here's to the Braves and Falcons." Sever tipped his glass to the young lady. "So, do the two of you have any suggestions on a good place to eat?" Sever knew that drinking on an empty stomach was going to cause problems. Two Nexiums tonight.

"La Plage in Saint-Jean, just a short distance from the airport." Mr. B. polished a tall glass.

"Ten minutes?" Sever considered the drive. Maybe this one would be a little easier.

"It's easy to find. They have great food, on the beach, and tonight they will have live jazz. Do you like jazz?"

Sever turned to the girl next to him. Michelle was about thirty, blond hair, blue eyes. She reminded him of Ginny. Recently half the girls he saw reminded him of his ex-wife. Michelle wore a short summer dress, highlighting her bare legs.

"Do you like jazz?" he asked her.

"My boyfriend is coming down in a couple of minutes." She let her eyes linger, holding his gaze.

"Lucky man." Sever signed the check, took another sip of the drink, and put five euros on the bar.

"Mr. B.," the blond gave him a dazzling smile, "I have to use the ladies' room. I'll be back in a flash." She walked away and they both watched her go.

"I think the accent is much like yours — Chicago. The lady says Atlanta."

Sever smiled. "You can't be right all the time."

"Mick Sever, if you have business dealings with Danny Murtz, be very careful."

Mick watched him as he squeezed fresh lime juice into a glass.

"I can usually take care of myself."

"I know someone else who said the same thing."

"And what happened to them?"

Bertrand sat the glass on the bar and wiped his hands on a towel. He picked up the knife and with a flick of his wrist sliced a second lime in half. "I don't know. I'm not certain anyone knows."

"This had to do with Murtz?"

"It did. It does."

"Mr. B., what are you trying to say?"

"I had a friend. He was dating an American girl who knew Danny Murtz. My friend disappeared."

"Pretty flimsy evidence that Murtz was involved."

"It's a small island, Mr. Sever. There are very few secrets."

"You're saying that Murtz killed your friend?"

"There are no murders on St. Barts. No crime. I'm simply saying that my friend is missing."

"No murders."

"Ask anyone."

"And the girl?"

"She went back to America. The day after my friend disappeared."

"Still —"

"I've been here for five years, Mr. Sever. I know the island well. I know the people on the island. Americans, British, the rich French, they buy the expensive properties, they eat at the fancy restaurants and party on expensive yachts. The working class, we work sometimes two jobs just to make ends meet. We work two jobs so that the elite, upper class can have all the services and amenities they want. You see it is not our place to bite the hands that feed us."

"So you're reluctant to go on record saying anything damning about Murtz?"

"There is evil on the island. It's in the air. That I can tell you with certainty." He turned and gazed at the other end of the bar. "Excuse me, I have a customer who is in need of one of my creations."

"Thanks, Bertrand. I'll be careful."

The French bartender turned back. "We've just met, but I like you. I would hate to lose another friend."

Sever watched him as he spread his charm. Don't bite the hand that feeds you. He worked over Mr. B.'s ideas and sipped his drink. Just the right amount of sweet and sour. Bertrand seemed to have figured out the balance. Even if you knew someone killed your friend, you just absorbed the pain, and went on with the perfect St. Barts life.

If you could accept that, then you lived a perfect life — content, fulfilled and happy.

CHAPTER TEN

The music was smooth and mellow, and the female vocalist sounded like a young Lena Horne. The French had a strong attraction to American jazz, and the restaurant La Plage featured jazz five nights a week.

Sever sat at a table on the beach. The Caribbean waters lapped the shore behind him as the last of daylight faded on the horizon. The waitress brought him a Dewar's and soda. Enough of the tropical drinks for now. He took a long swallow and stared into the open-air restaurant. Customers entered from the street level and walked down the stairs to the casual eating area, where the drinks were good, the food even better, and the music drifted smooth and mellow on the air.

He ordered a grouper dinner and was only halfway through the delicate fish when she walked up to his table.

"Well, he didn't show."

Sever looked up, surprised to see the attractive blond. His confusion seemed to trigger her attempt to explain.

"You asked if I liked jazz — at the hotel? I told you my boyfriend was meeting me, remember?"

"Yeah. I thought —"

"I was blowing you off? If I was just blowing you off, you'd know it." She studied him for a moment. "Are you going to ask me to sit down?"

He nodded to a vacant chair, and she eased into it. "I called his cell phone and he told me he wasn't going to meet me. I'm finding out that this guy isn't the most dependable person around. How about you, Mr. Sever? Are you dependable?"

She was toying with him. Cat-and-mouse game. At least it was something to occupy him for the moment. "No. I can give you several references if you want to check me out. All of them will tell you that dependable is not a trait that applies to me." Hell, he'd still be married if he were dependable.

"Oh, well, I have yet to meet a man that is. Anyway, I just wanted some company and something to eat, but if this isn't a good time I can always —"

"No, no, it's a good time, okay? And now is the time for a formal introduction. I'm Mick Sever."

"Michelle Kirkendall."

"Michelle, I'm glad you could come for dinner." He motioned to his waitress. "What are you drinking?"

"Since they probably don't make drinks like Mr. B., I'll just have a gin and tonic."

The waitress headed back to the bar and Sever watched Michelle's face, seeing the pinched frown that wrinkled her brow.

"Chances are he changed his mind and he's looking for you right now."

The black singer's voice drifted out from the restaurant, lingering over the beach like a warm breeze. The song was from a Broadway musical, and Sever couldn't quite place it. Something about *spring arrived on time, only what became of you dear . . .*

"Maybe," she said. "I don't really know him that well. He flew me here to be with him and put me up at the Manapany. I should be happy, but I've been here a week and I've only seen him three times."

Sever nodded, his forgotten plate of grouper now pushed to the side.

"Mr. Sever, please don't get the wrong idea. I just wanted some company and thought maybe your subtle invitation was still open."

"It was. It is."

The waitress set the gin and tonic on the table.

"So you know, this is just for some company."

"Spring Can Really Hang You Up The Most," a song from a Broadway play called *The Boys from Syracuse*. About never finding love. That was the song.

"Sure. I understand." Sever finished his Scotch, feeling the alcohol warming him from within.

"So I'm here, and he's — he's in a house on the other side of the island." She took her first sip of the gin and tonic.

"Why aren't you staying with him?"

She sighed. "He's got a bunch of people staying at his place, and it's all business. He says it's not conducive to furthering a relationship. So he comes to my hotel room or we go out to eat. One time we've been to his place."

In the early twilight her features were soft. She kept pushing the fine blond hair behind her ears, and the breeze played with the summer dress, teasing Sever with revealing glimpses of her fair skin.

"So you haven't been dating long?"

She watched him, stirring her drink with the plastic swizzle stick. "You ask a lot of questions."

"I'm a reporter. It's what I do, ask questions."

She looked away to the jazz group, a sweet smile on her lips.

"No more questions, okay?" Sever put up his hands in surrender.

"Hey, Mick. I've got some questions of my own. Why are you here by yourself?"

"Business."

"And no one to share the Caribbean with?"

It was his turn to watch the jazz group. The dark-skinned singer clutched the microphone close to her body, her dress clinging to her like a second skin.

"Ah, so you don't want to talk about your love life, but it's okay to talk about mine?"

"I'm just not used to being grilled."

"Used to being the griller, rather than the grillee?"

"Something like that."

"Okay. I'll answer your question. No. We haven't been dating long. Off and on for a couple of months. As I said, I don't really know him well. He's, well, he's older."

"So you have something against older men?" Sever gave her a gentle smile.

"Oh, no. And nothing against men from Chicago." She smiled back.

"How do you know where I'm from?"

"Mr. B. told me. And Dan's from Chicago too."

"Dan?"

"My missing boyfriend. Dan Murtz."

CHAPTER ELEVEN

Small world. Smaller island. Danny Murtz looked back at the photograph of the chef. The handsome man with graying hair and a chef's hat stared at him from the ad in the St. Barts *Connection* booklet.

> Frank Simonetti, former New York chef, brings his culinary skills to Confit, the newest hot spot in Gustavia, St. Barts.

Frank Simonetti. Chef extraordinaire, the culinary genius who could turn a simple pork chop, lamb chop, simple white fish, or mediocre cut of beef into a masterpiece of gourmet delight. Frank Simonetti, father of Shelley O'Dell, God rest her soul.

Their paths should not have crossed. Surely Simonetti didn't know the details of the demise of his daughter. Harvey Schwartz was to have taken care of that, how many years ago? Seven?

It wasn't intentional. The stupid twit had been stoned out of her mind, and when they'd consummated their relationship, she'd cried. How was a man supposed to deal with that? Seven years and he could still hear her crying. He'd begged her to shut up, but it didn't register. Things got fuzzy after that. It happened a lot. The balance wasn't always exact — the ups and the downs — keeping an edge, it sometimes collapsed in a rush of confusion. He must have called

Harvey, because the cleanup crew arrived shortly afterward. Harvey said she'd been strangled. Her last breath had been squeezed from her sexy body. To his knowledge, no one ever found that body.

But now, her father was on the island. Coincidence? Maybe. But Murtz was cautious. It bordered on paranoid. Not quite there yet. He was the judge of what was paranoid and what wasn't. Damn it. He was only being careful.

"Danny, I've got five girls to go with you tonight, and Harvey said he's not coming." Nancy stood in the doorway, dressed in her prim-and-proper gray skirt, ivory blouse, and black shoes, her hair pulled up with a clip in back. Today she was officious. Tomorrow, it could be flirtatious. He never knew what to expect. She took off her black-rimmed reading glasses and said, "Do you want me to call that girl you flew over here? Michelle Kirkendall?"

He'd thought about it. Put her on ice for the evening. "No. We'll go with five and Harvey."

"Harvey doesn't want to go. I think he feels your little outings are childish."

He looked at her, trying to shake his brain free from the fog that seemed to creep in daily. Harvey was a given. What did she mean he wasn't going?

"Danny? You asked me to line up some girls and Harvey for the party tonight at Casa Niki?"

He saw the shadow as it cast itself in the doorway. Short and stout, it had to be Nancy's nemesis.

"Danny?"

"Nancy says you don't want to participate."

She folded her arms across her chest, challenging the balding attorney.

"Danny, you know how I feel about —"

"I don't give a shit about how you feel. I need you to be there, and whenever you feel you can do without the exorbitant salary I pay you, you can chose *not* to attend my gatherings. Until then, you will be there."

Schwartz glared at Nancy. "Have I discussed with you the situation regarding Jason? You and I need to talk about the recording studios."

"Another time. I want you there tonight. It has nothing to do with Nancy. You will be there. Understood?"

Harvey Schwartz took a deep breath, frowning at Nancy, then giving his client a shake of the head. Murtz knew Nancy and Harvey were not best of friends, but this bordered on mortal enemies. Something about that type of relationship actually excited him.

"Do you remember Frank Simonetti?" He pointed at Schwartz.

"What the hell are you bringing that up for now?"

Murtz pointed at Nancy, still bristling from the mention of her son's name.

"Well, do *you* remember him?"

She gave him a puzzled look.

"The chef from New York? Fuck it, Nancy! The father of Shelley O'Dell?"

A glimmer of recognition.

"He's here. Has a restaurant in Gustavia."

"Shelley O'Dell? The girl you . . ." her voice trailed off.

"The girl I what? What, Nancy? Fucked? Fucked over? Cheated on?" He refrained from the word kill. "That Shelley O'Dell?"

She glared at him. "It's hard to keep track."

He dealt with her jealousy. You would think that twenty-six years would have put some distance in her feelings, but he still felt her bitterness. And although he knew he should fire her and get rid of her no-talent son who ran Murtz's recording studio in Chicago, there was something that kept him engaged. He'd never quite figured it out.

"Danny," he could tell that a reprimand was coming from his counselor. "Let it die. You don't need to worry about him, okay?" The attorney had stepped into the room, brushing past Nancy Steiner as if she weren't there. "Honest to God, we don't need any altercations while we're on the island." Harvey stood above him, putting his hand on Murtz's shoulder. "It's purely coincidence."

"I say we investigate."

"And as the voice of reason, I say we don't."

"Harvey, I want you with us tonight."

Nancy interrupted the response. "Danny, did you hear me? I told you that Harvey doesn't want to go on the outing tonight. Why do you put up with his crap?"

She always called them outings. Danny hated that. They were adventures. Adventures. An outing was a picnic, for God's sake. He sized up the two antagonists, wondering why he put up with either of them. His life would be a whole lot easier if they both were dead. Maybe that's what needed to happen. They both would die. He didn't trust either of them. Murtz stared at his attorney. "I put up with his crap because I choose to. Just like I choose to put up with yours. He'll be there tonight!" Murtz eased himself from the leather chair, approaching Harvey. "I need you counselor! Do you understand me?"

Schwartz stepped back, extricating himself from the situation. "You need me more than you can possibly imagine, Danny." He turned and walked from the room.

"Danny —" Nancy watched the attorney leave.

"You listen to me, goddamnit! As long as you've been here, you know when I throw a party I expect certain people to be there!"

"Yes, Danny." That condescending tone of voice.

"Hell, I don't trust the son of a bitch, but if he's beside me, how much trouble can he get into?"

Nancy regained her composure and seemed to look through him. She was one of the few people in his life that didn't allow him to gain the upper hand. She knew him better than most, and that wasn't very comforting. But she didn't know the rest of the story about Shelley O'Dell. There were some things that no one knew about. Except Harvey.

"Do you understand me?"

"No one understands you, Danny. No one." She stared daggers at him. "Except maybe me. I know a lot more than you think I do."

He tried to see through her, to her soul. What did she know? "Harvey will be there tonight. You make sure it happens." Murtz pointed his finger at her. He remembered the last handler he'd had. Eighteen, twenty years ago? Rudy somebody. Son of a bitch had walked out on him, and Murtz went after him with a Ford pickup truck. He'd crushed his legs against a concrete building, revving the engine, flooring the gas pedal. Rudy somebody left his employ shortly thereafter, but the lesson was learned. The last time Murtz had seen Rudy, he still used a walker.

She nodded. "Jason called."

"Jason?" Oh yeah. *The boy*. The kid was a noose around his neck. Nancy begged him to save *the boy*'s job. Harvey apparently wanted *the boy* fired.

"He's remixing that new band Lexington Avenue and he wanted you to know it's going very well."

Lexington Avenue. The four guys from Kentucky. *The boy* was useless in the studio. And a nerd in all other aspects of his life. He'd never be able to pick up a groove and there was only one reason Murtz had kept him on the payroll. Because he was Nancy's son. That was it. The kid wouldn't know how to steal a good song, wouldn't have a clue how to rip off an arrangement, and his natural ability was zip. But Nancy was always reminding him of how good *the boy* was. Maybe it was time to clean house.

"Yeah. The money I pay him, it should be going well. And remember, I want Harvey there. Tonight. Do you understand?"

Nancy smoldered. "And I'm not his watchdog, Danny. If you can't control him, fire him!" She walked out of the room, a dark cloud following her.

Murtz walked to the window and again stared down at the water far below. Nancy was bitter. *The boy*, her precious son, was back in the cold April drizzle in Chicago, supposedly running the recording studio, while Mom was in the sunny tropics managing the entourage. Nancy spent far too much time worrying about the stupid *boy*.

Tourists dotted the beach below. People spent their life savings on a vacation to St. Barts. A trip of a lifetime. A yacht, fancy villa, expensive meals, and shopping at some of the most exclusive shops in the world. Did they get enough bang for their buck? Because when you had it all, all the money and power like he did, when it was just a change of scenery and nothing more, somehow it didn't seem to matter. It was harder and harder to make it a big deal. He needed something more.

Some blow, maybe a joint, or just a stiff rum and cola. He reached into his pocket and pulled out the pistol, admiring the blue finish and the sleek lines of the weapon. He rubbed the cool metal against his cheek. It was going to be another line of coke. He wanted to keep his edge.

Murtz reached for the phone and pushed number seven. "Nancy!"

"What now, Danny?"

"Make reservations at Confit. For everyone. We'll do Casa Niki after dinner."

"Confit?"

"Frank Simonetti's new restaurant."

There was a pause. "Is that a good idea?"

Just like Harvey. The bitch acted like his mother. Or maybe a wife. If he needed someone to second-guess him, he never would have left home. One fucking dalliance, God knows how many years ago, and he was still paying for it.

"It's *my* idea. *My* damned idea!" He waited for a retort. There was none. "Do you think you can take care of it?"

"I'll call them."

"You do that."

"Reservations under George Sanders?" It was a name he'd used for years when he checked into a hotel or made restaurant reservations. Much more subtle than Danny Murtz.

"No. This time, Nancy, make sure you tell them who I am." Maybe Frank Simonetti sent him the threatening letter. That made sense. Frank suspected that Murtz had killed his daughter Shelley O'Dell. So he was behind the letter. Yeah. That made a lot of sense. Maybe it was time to start confronting the possible suspects. "I want him to remember." Murtz slammed the receiver down. Hell, *he* couldn't even remember.

CHAPTER TWELVE

It was after nine p.m. Late, but not by St. Barts standards. The girl knew that the clubs wouldn't start cooking until eleven or even midnight. But from her porch she'd watched the two Jeeps pull out about eight, so they must be doing dinner before their nightly adventure. Murtz, a driver, four young girls — no surprise there — the short little bodyguard, and Harvey driving the second Jeep. They were probably going to Saint-Jean or Gustavia, then to the Yacht Club or Casa Niki.

The girl had been there before. It was all too familiar, and the entire experience stuck in her like a knife. She knew that Harvey hated the adventures. She knew he tried to avoid the social scene, but Murtz felt more comfortable with Harvey in shouting distance. He was more comfortable with Harvey in hearing distance, and, better yet, with Harvey in view. She wasn't certain if Murtz *couldn't* function without Harvey or if he just didn't trust him and wanted to keep an eye on him.

One bodyguard at the villa. One bodyguard and Nancy, if she'd counted right. This might be the night. Murtz and crew would be out until three, four in the morning. Nancy and the bodyguard would probably crash by midnight.

She gazed down to the water below, to the beach fading in the twilight. Her gaze rested on the rocks that climbed up the hill to twinkling lights of houses that were scattered like stars. Somewhere in the rocks was the cave where the pirate Captain Monbars, the Exterminator, had hidden his treasure. The Exterminator. One tough pirate.

She walked back into the rented villa, a thin smile on her lips. She hadn't smiled in a long time. She'd dreamed about this moment, plotted for it endlessly. It was all she ever thought of, and she had to come this far to make it happen. And now *she* was about to become the Exterminator. The girl wondered if her legend on the island would ever be as big as that of Captain Monbars.

CHAPTER THIRTEEN

"So, you're going back to the hotel?" She held his gaze, a flirtatiousness in her eyes.

"Where do you suggest I go?" The jazz singer was doing a French number, slow and sultry. They'd had another drink, then a carafe of red wine, and Sever could feel the glow.

"Mr. B. suggested Casa Niki in Gustavia. He says it's a great dance club, and a place to be seen."

"I don't dance, and I don't need to be seen." Sever smiled, thinking that this might be one of the few hot spots in the world he *hadn't* been seen at.

"Aw, come on. It'll be fun."

"Oh, so we're going together?"

"I thought we might."

"And your boyfriend?"

"Fuck him."

Obviously the drinks had had some effect on her as well. "But I told you earlier, I've got to interview him tomorrow. What if he sees us together?"

She reached out and put her hand over his. "Your interview is giving him free press. Don't all celebrities need free press? You're giving him what he wants, so he'll get over it. And anyway, I got the impression he had business to take care of. He's probably back at the villa with his attorney."

Sever studied the situation. "How did you get here from the hotel?"

"The island shuttle." The bus traveled the small island, picking up and dropping off the tourists and locals who needed transportation to and from and didn't want to — or couldn't — drive the treacherous roads by themselves.

"I've got a car. Are you any good at navigating?"

"I can read a map."

Sever pulled a folder from his back pocket. "It's not much of a map, but —" He unfolded the slick folder and laid it on the table. "Here we are, and here's Gustavia.If we can get there, we can find Casa Niki."

"Piece of cake."

"Yeah, I had some of that cake from the airport to the hotel. It took me thirty minutes for a five-minute drive."

"So, are we going?"

Sever nodded. "But I don't do three in the morning. I'm going as long as we make an early night of it."

"Got it."

"And this is just good company?"

"Mick, I've already got one very strange relationship with an older man. I don't need another one. Is that okay?"

Older man. And getting older every second. "I just want the ground rules."

Twenty-five minutes later he parked the Rover along the busy street, and they followed the sign, down the alley to Casa Niki.

A blast of hip-hop hit them as the young security guy opened the door. Sever could tell already that it was going to be busy and loud. The club was much like the Shore Club on South Beach, or Niki Beach, or any number of hot new spots, where private booths were like small bedrooms, cabanas with mattresses, cots, and long couches. Groups and couples lounged on the white sheets, drinking from bottles of Dom Pérignon, Cristal Roederer, and Taittinger Prestige Rosé. Soft, subdued lighting kept everyone's identity muted, but it was obvious that all the customers in the assortment of rooms were at least a decade younger than Sever.

A decade was being generous. Youth was celebrated, and the young girls and guys ignored the old man as they drank, danced, and fondled each other.

"So, what do you think?" Michelle watched the room, a look of amusement playing on her face.

"I think I'm much too old for this shit."

"Oh, come on, Mick. Let's find a spot." She led him by the hand to a vacant sofabed, and they settled in.

Sever wasn't sure whether to lie down, sit with no back support, or lean against the wall. What the hell ever happened to a good, old-fashioned chair?

The waitress approached, a look of feigned boredom on her face. "What can I get you?"

"A Scotch and soda?"

"Sir, if you're going to sit here," Sever now understood he was to sit, "you'll have to order a bottle. Would you like some champagne?"

He glanced at Michelle.

"Sure." The petite blond shrugged her shoulders.

"Champagne is fine."

The young girl nodded, made a notation on her pad, and walked back to the bar.

"So, what do you know about Danny Murtz? Other than his music?"

Michelle squirmed on the white linen sheet, her dress riding up her thighs. Sever figured she must be wanting for a chair as well.

"He's — I don't know, he's demanding. He is used to getting his way. He probably drinks too much, and he and I have done . . ." she hesitated. "You know, it's really none of your business."

"I didn't mean to pry. It's just that when I see him tomorrow, I'd like a little heads up. Maybe you could tell me what his hobbies are. What kind of friends he has? Something I can ask about."

Michelle was quiet, thinking it through. Sever was surprised at her outburst. Here was a new relationship with someone who was an icon in his industry and she started out with accusing him of being *demanding. He drank too much*? What kind of feelings did she have for this man she hardly knew. He thought about telling her some of the things he'd read in his preliminary report, but decided she probably already knew, and if she didn't, she'd find out shortly.

"He called me and said he'd been suddenly called to St. Barts to work with a band. We were supposed to get together while I was in Chicago, and now he was leaving. I got up some nerve and asked him if I could join him on the island. I thought I'd spend more time with him than I have. We've been together a couple of times, but that's no reason for me to bad-mouth him. Let's talk about something else, okay?" Her eyes surveyed the room as if she were looking for someone she knew.

"Like what?"

"I don't know," she kept looking, not happy with what she saw, "maybe talk about your career? Or the latest music group you've covered or something." Her eyes darted to the door, then to the bar, then danced over the room, never making contact with Sever.

"What are you looking for?"

"Dan. I thought maybe he'd be here, and —"

"Is this why you brought me here? You wanted to run into him?"

"Maybe. Are you upset?"

He thought about it for a moment. He'd actually thought that meeting Murtz here would put a unique spin on the interview tomorrow.

"No. In a perverse way, I understand."

The waitress brought a bottle of champagne to the table. "That will be three hundred fifty euros, please."

Sever felt his eyes snap wide open. "What?"

"Three hundred fifty euros."

He shot a glance at Michelle. She shrugged her shoulders and kept watching the door.

"This is a little expensive just to hang out in case your boyfriend shows up."

"So, I'll pick up half the tab." She kept her eyes on the door.

Sever peeled off the paper bills and handed them to the slim waitress.

"It's more than just Danny isn't it?"

"No. It's all about Danny." She looked into his eyes. It had been a while since a girl gave him a soulful look, but this look wasn't about Mick. He knew immediately there was a deeper meaning. It was clear that there was something very personal between Michelle and Danny Murtz.

He poured her a full glass and marveled as she picked it up and drained the icy clear beverage in a couple of swallows. He filled the glass again.

"More than just a romantic fling?"

She spun around and glared at him. "Yeah. It's more than that. I don't know what you know about Danny Murtz, but there's a lot more than just the music."

"Well, I've read some —"

"You don't know shit." The sweet, flirtatious blond's eyes were icy as she leveled her stare. "Here's something you need to know, Mick. He's been known to be a total asshole."

Sever leaned back and observed her, wondering if the quick champagne chugging was causing this effect on the petite girl.

"He can be cruel, vicious, demanding, and he's been known to prey on young girls. Can you understand that?" Michelle lowered her head, leaning into Sever so that he could feel her hot breath on his face. "He's brutal. And I've said way too much." She swallowed half the glass of champagne as Sever studied her, amazed at the transformation.

Leaning farther back he noticed how cold and hard she'd become. The girl kept his rapt attention, and he couldn't help but notice the flare of her nostrils and the way she kept licking her lips. In another situation, he would have found it erotic. Now, it scared him.

"Forget I said anything." Michelle's face hardened and her vacant stare cast over the room and the mass of bodies that swayed to the music.

"Who are you? Really?"

She didn't answer. Instead she stood up and walked away. He caught a glimpse of her through the crowd as she walked in the doorway marked DAMES.

The pounding of the electronic music was giving him a headache, and he searched the room with his eyes for someone he recognized. He dreamed of being anonymous, and when it became a reality, he immediately wanted recognition. The life he led was fucked! He felt the immaturity of a seventeen-year-old, and the body of middle age. Right now he wanted someone he knew to come and save him from this crazy lady. He knew who he wanted. But she wasn't coming back.

When Michelle returned, she smiled. "Mick, I'm sorry for the way I acted. You're probably wondering how to get rid of me."

He was now convinced. She was crazy *and* could read his mind.

"Listen. For right now, Danny Murtz is a boyfriend. He flew me over here for a romantic getaway. That's where it ends."

Sever shook his head. Either she was a serious nut job or she had some of the same information he had. She seemed to know first-hand what her producer boyfriend was capable of. And again he asked himself the question. *What the hell was she doing with Murtz?* "Michelle," he touched her hand as she sat down, "what was that all about?"

"I told you, I'm sorry. It was nothing." She sipped on the champagne and watched the crowd for a moment. "It was the drinks at La Plage. It was the champagne. And maybe it was a little bit of being pissed off at the way I've been treated." Michelle pursed her lips and studied the door, intently watching for someone.

"I guess you've got a right."

"Damn straight! I get flown over here and dumped. He doesn't have time. But that's all it is, okay?"

"So, let's change the subject. Tell me, what do you do?"

"What do you mean, what do I do?"

"What's your profession? What do you do for a living? Are you in the music business like Danny Murtz?"

She shook her head without answering.

"Look, you may have a right to be upset," he continued. "You obviously know a little about Murtz's background, but you apparently signed on for duty."

"I did. What does my profession have to do with this?" The girl turned and gazed into his eyes. He almost lost his objectivity. Her blue eyes misted over and for a moment he thought she was close to tears.

"I was just curious. You know, the reporter in me. So, what do you do?" He pressed.

"It doesn't matter."

"Maybe it would explain your behavior. To me."

Steely again, the eyes hardened in an instant.

"Fuck you. You're someone who came along at the right time. Something to do. I certainly don't have to explain my behavior to you or anyone else. You've got a car outside, Mr. Sever. You can leave anytime you want."

"Does what you do make you this hot-and-cold-running person?"

She finally relented, "I'm a cop from Atlanta. You can make whatever you want out of that."

CHAPTER FOURTEEN

Damned sun was up half the night. That was the problem with being this close to the equator. Too much daylight. The sun was up by six a.m. and didn't go down until well after nine p.m. But it was dark now. She used her binoculars to check the villa, and at about eleven, two lights went out. There was no sign of the Jeeps. They'd be back sometime in the morning.

The girl entered the house and slipped on her Adidas shoes in the cottage's tiny bedroom. Barely enough room to turn around. She glanced at the mirror on the closet door. Looking back at her was a young woman, attractive but not beautiful. With makeup she could probably come close to beautiful. Her short-cropped brown hair hung just over her ears and forehead. Green eyes, a nose that wasn't quite straight, and a faint scar on her right cheek. She wore a pair of gray sweatpants and a dark T-shirt.

She needed to be as invisible as possible, and as fast as she could be. If she had to run, she wanted to be able to move. She strapped a black nylon bag around her waist, gave one last look in the mirror, wondering where her youth had gone, and stepped outside, off the porch, and started a slow, careful walk to the next villa.

She hugged the trees and shrubs that dotted the landscape, pausing and quietly waiting to hear if anyone noticed. There were bird calls and the sound of the tide far below. She heard the occasional car or truck come chugging up the hill and passing on the main road.

Now she was crossing onto the neighbor's property. This was where the big guy lived, the one who stood on his deck and watched the crazy actions at Danny Murtz's villa. The neighbor's terraced deck and pool were dimly lit, almost as if the elevated pool had spotlights from within. Misty blue and white patterns swirled above her over shadowy furniture and shapes she couldn't make out. She tried to blend into the trees. A moment later she was up against the smooth concrete that rose up to the pool, about ten feet above the ground. She hugged the cement wall that elevated the deck, and slowly worked her way around. The moon was just a sliver, but still gave more light than she wanted.

She stopped, smelling something strange. Not the sweet smell of jasmine or overripe mango. Spicy, like smoke. Then she realized what it was. A cigar. Someone was smoking a cigar. She froze for a moment, trying not to breathe.

"You're up kind of late, aren't you?"

She felt herself shaking, and she couldn't speak.

The voice was insistent. "I said, you're up kind of late aren't you?"

She felt sweat beading on her face, under her arms. Where was he? He didn't sound more than ten feet away.

"Late?"

A female voice.

"Come on, you're usually in bed by ten."

"I couldn't sleep. I thought I'd join you here on the deck."

The girl let out a long, slow, controlled breath. The guy who owned the house and his wife. Bill and Susan something. She crouched low and settled in. How long did it take to smoke a cigar? She had business to take care of and this guy was screwing it all up.

CHAPTER FIFTEEN

Murtz watched the assembled guests, all gathered at the round table. Frank Simonetti and staff had prepared a marvelous dinner, and everyone seemed to be having a good time. The little brunette on his right had her hand buried in his lap for half the dinner, giving him every indication that there was more to follow. Sasha? Sandra? It didn't matter. He took a long swallow of his rum and Coke and called the waitress over to the table.

"I asked you earlier to have Mr. Simonetti stop by the table."

"Oui, Monsieur. But he is very busy at the moment."

Murtz smiled and took her hand, squeezing it. He stared into her eyes, squeezing increasingly harder all the time. "I understand, but you listen to me you fucking bitch. You tell Mr. Simonetti that I want to see him. Not in a couple of minutes, but right now. At this table."

Tears sprang to the young waitress' eyes as she tried to pull away. He squeezed even harder, hoping to hear bones snap in her fragile hand.

"Tell him again that Danny Murtz would like to pay his respects."

Finally the girl jerked her hand away, fear in her amber eyes. "Sir, I will report you to —"

"Who? Mr. Simonetti?"

She turned and headed back to the kitchen, her audible sobs wracking her small body.

"My God, Danny, let's not make a scene." Harvey ran his hand nervously over his smooth head, as if to brush back hair that wasn't there.

"Harvey, shut the fuck up. I want to tell Simonetti how much I enjoyed the prawns and the mango salad. You should tell him how much you liked the tuna tartare. I think a chef should be told when he serves a good meal." He poured a full glass of red wine, pouring another for his young playmate. She smiled, and kept her hand where it was.

The door swung open, and the short man with the tall white chef's hat came striding toward the table. Murtz removed the small hand from his crotch and pushed back his chair, standing up.

"Danny Murtz. I hope you enjoyed your meal, and I sincerely hope you'll be leaving soon." He glared up at Murtz. "I don't like demands, and I don't like you threatening my staff."

"Frank, Frank, you never did like me."

"You want to know what I never liked, Murtz?"

"Tell me. In front of my friends here, why don't you tell me." Murtz's voice was loud and abrasive. He spit the words again. "Why don't you tell me?"

Now the restaurant was hushed as diners at other tables heard the raised voices and strained to hear the conversation.

"What happened to my daughter, Murtz?"

He smiled condescendingly. "You know that I have no idea. None."

"I know no such thing."

Murtz leaned into the man, now breathing hot breath in his face. "I don't like threats either, Simonetti. What you *think* you know is of no interest to me." He glanced around the room, noticing the guests who were watching the confrontation. Very quietly, almost in a whisper, he said, "If I find out that you are threatening me, I'll kill you. Then I'll burn down this fucking place you call a restaurant. Do you understand?"

The little man was pale, not quite the shade of his hat and apron, but pale nonetheless.

"Do we understand each other?"

"No, I don't think we do. Goodnight, Mr. Murtz, and please don't come here again." The chef walked back to the kitchen, muttering under his breath and shaking his head.

"Jesus, Danny. You are out of control." Schwartz pushed back his chair, staring in awe at the wild-eyed producer. "Where did you ever get the idea that Frank Simonetti was threatening you?"

Murtz pointed a bony finger at the attorney. "You know so much. Was it you, counselor? Are you the one who is threatening me?"

Schwartz stood up and walked out of the restaurant, never looking back.

Murtz sat back down, pulling the young girl's hand back to his lap. "Well, I think the chef appreciated the compliment."

The girl watched him for a second, then said, "I didn't hear you compliment him at all, Danny."

CHAPTER SIXTEEN

"I think it's about time to leave."

"Leave? We've only had half the champagne."

"I can't afford the half we already had."

"Come on, Mick. It's just starting to get interesting."

The club manager had walked over, introduced himself, and asked if he could pick up the tab for his biggest celebrity of the night. So far.

"Mr. Sever, it was just brought to my attention that you are the famous journalist. We are very honored to have you in the club and would you allow me to pay for your drinks this evening?"

Chicago Tribune expense account or Casa Niki? He could always use the favor from the club.

"Thanks, but I'll pay."

Later on, he might need a favor and besides, the *Trib* could afford this perk.

"Rod Stewart's on the island this week." Michelle put her hand over his. "His yacht sits off St.-Jean. Please, will you stay just a little while longer? I'd love to meet him."

She'd smoothed out, and the flare-up seemed to be history. He was still intrigued by the beautiful cop who didn't want to talk about the guy who brought her to the dance.

"Rod Stewart?"

"Yeah. I've always been a fan."

"And what? You think he comes here every night?"

"There's a good chance. Do you know him?"

Know him? Sever went back to the band Faces in the sixties, with Stewart and Ron Woods. Did he know him? He knew him well enough to not admit to half the things he knew about him. God, those were some nights.

"Yeah. We've met."

He'd done a cover story on Rod Stewart for *Rolling Stone* and the interview lasted a week. He hadn't seen Rod in several years, and he assumed that age was slowing him down. A little. You would never totally slow down the Rodder.

Her eyes kept drifting to the doorway as the revelers arrived. The doorman kept an even flow, singles and couples, blacks and whites, a mix of male and female. Not everyone was welcome.

"You're still looking for Danny, aren't you?"

"No. I'm just intrigued with the people."

"What's a cop doing dating Danny Murtz?"

"I think we've established that what I'm doing isn't exactly dating. Do you see a date anywhere near here? And I'm sorry I told you that I was a cop. It's not important."

The music was loud, an electronic Euro mishmash with a monotonous beat that Sever found almost intolerable. He would have given anything for a good old-fashioned chorus of "Maggie Mae," or "Tonight's the Night."

"Michelle, I really think it's time to call it a night. You can always take the shuttle back."

"I could. Would you abandon me?"

Considering her erratic emotions it was probably the smart thing to do. "I told you it was going to be an early night."

"Can we stay another thirty minutes? Just until one o'clock?"

Sever closed his eyes. Give him back the days with Ginny. They'd grown together, learned about each other, gotten comfortable with each other. Then he'd gone and messed it up.

"Okay. We'll stay until one, but that's it. If Danny comes in, you can introduce me."

She punched him on his arm.

A twenty-something couple passed the couch, the guy staring at Sever in the dim light.

"Holy shit, are you Mick Sever?"

Sever nodded.

"Man, I've seen you on TV like a hundred times. My mom and dad have all your books. This is so cool."

"Thanks." Sever forced a smile.

The young man moved on, talking expressively to his female partner about the encounter with celebrity. Sever was used to it, but there were times when he wished it would go away. There were times when he wished he were just a face in the crowd. And just when it seemed possible, the twenty-something kid would show up. A waitress, a man on the street, a clerk in a 7-Eleven or Wal-Mart, a car salesman would say, "Hey, aren't you?" To have and have not. Hemingway wrote a book with that title. Live with the fame or ignore it. There was no happy ground.

It was going to be a long half hour.

CHAPTER SEVENTEEN

Silence. No one talking, but there was still the aroma of cigar. Her grandfather had smoked cigars. Cuban Monte Cristo cigars. She found the smell hypnotic. Kneeling by the concrete wall, she listened intently. Were they just gazing at the stars? Had they gone to sleep? She glanced at her watch but couldn't make out the numbers. She should have time to move one villa over. And she hoped and prayed that the bodyguard and Nancy were sound asleep. The alarm was probably still on at Murtz's house, but that wasn't going to present a problem. She knew where she was going, how to handle it, and all she needed was two minutes. A little confusion, misdirection, and mayhem and she'd accomplish her mission. If she didn't, then it would be twice as hard the next time. They'd be ready for her.

"Do you want to go inside?"

"Do you?"

"Sure."

"You've been smoking that cigar."

"I'll brush my teeth. Take a breath mint."

"You know, I like cigars, actually."

"I know."

"Let's go inside."

The girl smiled. It felt good. She silently wished Bill and Susan luck, love, and romance and listened to them scraping the deck chairs as they stood up and departed. She waited two minutes before she stood up and silently moved on.

CHAPTER EIGHTEEN

They paraded to the Jeeps, Murtz handing a twenty to the parking attendant.

"You're pushing it tonight, Danny."

"You're playing mother hen, Harvey. The man was fucking with me." Murtz tried to focus, but there was a buzz going on in his brain.

Schwartz opened the driver's side of the second Jeep, pausing for a moment. "Do you ever listen to yourself? Do you ever think about what the hell you are saying? My God, considering what happened, if the chef had a clue, don't you think he should be doing a lot more than just fucking with you?"

Murtz could feel the weight of the Mauser in his pocket. Someday he was going to shove the pistol into Harvey's mouth. He'd push it to the roof of his mouth, and let him taste the metallic barrel. Then see if the Jewish attorney would smart mouth him. Then see if Harvey had all the answers. This wasn't the time.

"Why don't we just tell everyone what happened?" Murtz spun around and staggered back to his Jeep, the young girl walking quickly to keep up.

Two minutes later they pulled up on the street by Casa Niki. Murtz puffed the last of a joint, casually passing it to the young girl. He couldn't remember her name or where she'd come from, but she seemed very friendly, interested, and if nothing better presented itself tonight, he knew who would haul his ashes.

The doorman nodded to Murtz, who passed him an American fifty as they entered the dimly lit club. Danny Murtz refused to convert. Fuck 'em. If they wanted euros, they could go to the bank.

"Danny," Schwartz motioned to him, a serious frown on his face. He steered him to a corner. "All I'm asking is that you stay cool."

Cool? He'd had three lines of coke, a couple of joints, and five drinks at Confit. He was about ready to kill someone. "You get off my case, Harvey. I'll handle it, okay?"

"Well, here's something you may *not* be able to handle. The girl last week." Harvey's eyes were shooting sparks. They were wide, bright, and even in the dim light Murtz could see the attorney's animated expression. Apparently Murtz had angered the usually unflappable counselor.

"What about her? What can't I handle?"

Schwartz glanced around the noisy club, as if looking for concealed spies. "No." Taking a deep breath, "Forget it." He seemed to regain his cool. "This isn't the place. Never mind."

He wasn't getting off that easy. The calm shutdown wouldn't work this time.

"What about the girl? Tell me, now!"

"All right. We know who she is. And we also know who she called from your place that night."

Murtz stared through him, the bald-headed geek who owned his life. Harvey was paid a fortune to clean up the mess, so why was he even talking about this?

"Danny, you need to know. The girl, Randi Parks, was on *American Idol.* She was calling a guy who could screw up your life. Really screw it up. Obviously, we have no idea what she told him, but there's a good chance that she might have mentioned she was with you. And, if she did, it was only minutes before," he hesitated, "the accident."

He shouldn't have pushed the damned attorney to tell him. He didn't need to know this. Wasn't he paying a fortune to have all these problems solved without his being involved? "Harvey, why the hell are you bringing this up now? We're having a party for God's sake, an adventure, and you start telling me about a problem you should have taken care of. You, Harvey. You're paid to take care of this. Now? In this crowded place you have to bring this up?"

"Damn it, Danny, you pushed me. Now listen. You've got to chill. You need to know this. I should have found a better time to tell you, but I'm telling you now. So pay attention. Don't drift on me, Danny."

Drift? That's exactly what he was doing. Listening to his anal attorney, he was drifting.

"Danny? You need to be aware —"

Murtz's eyes tried to focus, but he was slowly losing it. The inside of his head was foggy and Harvey was talking blah blah blah blah. The night had the potential of an all-time high and this asshole, this Jewish prick, was trying to bring him down. Murtz closed his eyes.

"Are you there?"

Of course, he was there.

"Danny, I need you to be sharp here. The guy is on St. Barts. I don't think it's just a coincidence that he's over here the same time you are. We're going to do what we can about the situation. I've got a team working on it."

The chef. Murtz smirked. He'd known it all along. Shelley O'Dell's old man. See, Danny Murtz had it figured out already. Frank Simonetti was on the island at the same time that Murtz was on the island. There was a reason for that. He surveyed the room, his eyes having a hard time focusing. Lights flashed, the steady drone of electronic rhythm pounded in his ears. Steady, easy, one thing at a time. A table of good-looking ladies was giving him a once over. This was good. A waitress in tight shorts was headed in his direction and there were people pointing. There were always people pointing at him.

"Danny! Listen."

Listen? With all the action coming his way? Harvey, shut the fuck up!

"The guy she called —"

What the hell? The girl, what was her name? The one from Atlanta that he'd flown over, Mandy? Mary? Michelle. Yeah, that was it. She was sitting at a table with some older guy. What the hell was that all about?

"Danny, pay attention. That call was to the guy who is interviewing you tomorrow. Mick Sever."

CHAPTER NINETEEN

She was certain there were no alarms outside. She knew there was one inside the house, but she knew the code. She knew what the code *was*. She hoped it hadn't been changed.

She could crawl the distance between Bill and Susan's and Murtz's villas, thirty or forty yards, or she could make the dash. The fingernail moon was still throwing too much light on the ground, but she decided a dash would save time. She took off running, glancing over her shoulder just once to make certain that the neighbors weren't watching from their pool deck.

Slightly out of breath, she reached the fence surrounding Murtz's pool. She slid down the side of the wire fence and rested for a moment. She really needed to get in better shape. The girl closed her eyes and repeated the numbers. 33–45–78. It was simple. 33⅓ r.p.m.records, 45 r.p.m. records, and 78 r.p.m. records. Then you hit "C" for cassette and "CD" for compact discs. So, within twenty seconds she had to punch in 33–45–78–C–CD. No sweat.

She wiped perspiration from her forehead, rubbed her hands on her pants, and stood up. She reached into the canvas bag fastened around her waist and took out the small metal pick and small hammer. A light shone in the shuttered window facing the pool. Murtz's office. Probably just a night light. Just Nancy and the bodyguard. She crouched low and walked slowly to the back door twenty feet from the pool. Nancy's room was on the far side of the villa, and the bodyguard probably fell asleep in the living room or kitchen. Also on the far side of the house. Thank God. He was probably dozing right now, a shoulder holster and pistol strapped to his side. Just for a moment she thought of Nancy and the bodyguard together. Straight old Nancy, getting it on with the good-looking stud. Like that was happening. She smiled, and that felt good.

The lock hadn't changed. She leaned over, carefully positioning the cold metal pick into the key slot. She drew back the hammer and tapped it against the pick. However slight the tap, the sound of metal on metal was loud in the quiet night air. She waited. Then, again. Afterward, silence. One more time. Probably enough noise to wake up the entire hillside. One minute, two minutes, nothing.

The girl gently turned the ceramic door handle. A quarter turn and it stopped. She gave it a little force. With a click it turned and, with her pressure, the door opened an inch with a loud creaking sound. Shit. She reached into her canvas bag and pulled out a small can of WD-40. *Why the hell couldn't Murtz do some simple maintenance once in a while.*

She sprayed the hinges, testing the door by opening it a little farther. The door swung open quietly and she walked in. The alarm let out a soft, high-frequency squeal. Twenty seconds from this very moment it would turn into a siren that would not only waken the entire island, but would alert the police. It could be a while before they arrived, but the bodyguard would be on her immediately.

33–45–78–C–CD. She felt the sweat drip from her brow into her eyes. Her shirt stuck to her torso like she'd been in a wet T-shirt contest, and she ran her hand over her eyes to stop the blurring of vision. She pushed the buttons, realizing she hadn't drawn a breath in thirty seconds.

Somewhere in the villa a clock ticked, the seconds slowly passing by. One. Two. Three. Four. The squeal stopped. Total silence. The girl rested her chin on her chest, straining to hear any noise, however slight. Nothing.

She opened the bag again and fumbled around for a small flashlight. With a flick of the switch, the entrance was dimly lit. The back entrance. Not that impressive. A tiled hall with a bathroom to the immediate right. She was tempted to use it, but decided she could hold out. Farther down she could see one of the larger living areas, and through the glass doors on the far end would be a view of the mountains that climbed even higher.

She walked down the tiled hall, softly putting down each step so as not to wake the residents. When she reached the large living area, with its cathedral ceiling, leather furniture, and wet bar, she turned right.

It would be two doors down on the left. Unless things had changed.

She paced herself. Soft, silent footsteps, now deep into the villa. If something happened at this point, if someone appeared from nowhere to question her intrusion, there was nowhere to go. Nowhere to hide.

Closer to the room. Finally, it was on her left. She stepped through the doorway cautiously, holding her hand over the light. Releasing it, she scanned the area, swinging the beam back and forth. How long had it been? One minute? She flashed the light on the sleek stainless-steel desk, and let out her breath. It wasn't there. In a panic, she swept the beam around the room, looking everywhere. Maybe in a file cabinet? She pulled open the top drawer. Nothing. The second drawer. Nothing. The third and fourth. Nothing. This couldn't be happening. It was all planned so carefully. Harvey's office was empty.

His laptop computer. She knew, maybe she was the only one who knew, that all of the sins, all of the transgressions were captured on that computer. Danny Murtz's life was recorded on that computer. Harvey kept records of everything. So where the hell was all this evidence?

All right, maybe on a disc. A memory stick. Those were small. Surely he had a backup. If the guy were anal enough to take his computer with him to a nightclub, he'd at least leave a backup. Wouldn't he?

She tore open the first desk drawer. Empty. The second and the third. Nothing.

Her heart beat double-time, and her hands were cold and clammy. The son of a bitch must have left the backup in Chicago. Her entire trip was for nothing. How the hell could she have been so stupid? She'd have had better luck if she'd gone to Chicago and burglarized the townhouse while they were all here in St. Barts.

Hot, stinging tears filled her eyes. Had they moved his office? No, there was a plaque with his name on it hanging on the wall and some financial papers on a table. She wiped her eyes, the tears still flowing.

Check the rest of the villa and take a chance of getting caught or go back and regroup? She knew without a doubt the information she needed was on that computer. That computer was in St. Barts. Until Harvey left the island, she had a chance.

"You're up kind of late aren't you?"

She froze, flicked off the flashlight and started shaking. This was the end.

Again, the male voice, more firm this time. "I said, you're up kind of late aren't you?"

"I couldn't sleep." Nancy's voice.

Oh, sweet Jesus. They were right outside the door.

"Would you like a drink?"

Silence. *Somebody say something.*

"Hey, I make a great lemon drop martini."

"Maybe a glass of wine."

"Red? No, white, right?"

"That would be nice."

"By the pool?"

"Not a bad idea." Nancy sounded like a schoolgirl. Almost giddy, breathless, and anxious for a romantic interlude.

The girl didn't breathe. She didn't move. She knew she'd lost ten pounds due to perspiration. They were moving down the hall, toward the kitchen and bar area.

Nancy's faint voice traveled back to the office. "I'll be waiting, Raymond."

Finally, the girl let out a long, slow breath. Now she was cold, the realization of what could have happened washing over her. She shivered. *What the hell? Was everyone having a late night by the pool?* Still, she had to give the older broad credit. The entire event sounded like a planned rendezvous to her.

She took a series of deep breaths and felt her racing heart slow down. Finally she reached into her bag and pulled out an envelope. She dropped it on the floor, and quietly exited the home. As many times as she'd played the scenario in her head, she still couldn't imagine how much the letters were freaking out Danny Murtz. She just knew it would eat at him until he couldn't take it anymore, and it wouldn't take much to drive the producer over the edge. Hell, he was practically there now.

CHAPTER TWENTY

How many jokes started just like this? *So a man walks into a bar* — Sever recognized him immediately. He was huddled in conversation with the shorter bald man as his entourage gathered at the bar. When Murtz looked up, his eyes met Sever's. Maybe the producer recognized him too. No, he recognized Michelle. There was a frown on his face.

"Well, it appears that Danny wasn't so busy after all," Michelle said as her gaze focused on the man and she drummed her fingers on the bed.

"He doesn't exactly look happy to see us."

"Because he got caught."

There was a little blond tugging on Murtz's sleeve, pointing to a table they'd procured. Sever noticed Michelle, focusing on the couple, a frown on her face as she stared at the producer and the young lady.

"The son of a bitch flies me over here, puts me up, then goes out on the town with a bunch of groupies? Look at that twit he's with. She's what? Twenty?"

"Maybe they're business partners."

"Yeah."

The girl kept tugging, and Murtz pushed her off. Sever couldn't hear over the din of the music and voices, the sound of glasses clinking, and ice rattling, but it appeared that Murtz, the girl, and the bald guy were shouting at each other. He watched as Murtz shook his fist at the man, and then with a swing of his right arm backhanded the young girl. She reeled back against the bar, grabbing her cheek.

Several young couples stood up to dance, blocking the view, and Sever looked at Michelle to see if any of this had registered.

"My God. He can be so violent at times."

"Has he ever —"

"No. But I've heard the stories."

More dancers moved in, swaying in drunken revelry to the nondescript music blaring from the ceiling speakers.

"Well, he knows you're here, and he knows you're with someone." He was almost shouting, trying to make his voice rise above the din.

"Hey, I've got the other half of the ticket. I mean, I can fly home when I want to."

"Something tells me you want to see how this plays out."

"I do," she said.

"Even though you know about his temper?"

"What about you?" She looked him in eye. "Now that he's seen us together."

Sever watched the dancers, girls in short skirts, brief tops, grinding against the guys in white linen pants and long-sleeved shirts with sleeves rolled up. He tried to see through the mass of bodies, but more and more people had moved onto the floor.

"I may have messed things up for you. I mean, it's your job to interview him and now that he knows —"

Sever sipped some champagne. Some very expensive champagne. "He doesn't know."

"What do you mean he doesn't know? He just saw us together."

"He knows you're out with someone. I seriously doubt if he knows me. We've never met."

"So you're going to show up tomorrow and hope he doesn't recognize you?"

"I'm going to show up. If he recognizes me I'll tell him you and I ran into each other."

"Well, we did."

"Frank Romano, a mentor of mine, once told me to always tell the truth. That way you don't have to worry about keeping your story straight." He very seldom followed the old man's advice, but it probably would work in this case.

She nodded and poured the last of the champagne into her glass. "Mick, can I ask you a personal favor?"

"You can ask." The answer could always be no.

"If you do the interview, when you do the interview, and if you get any real answers, will you tell me what he says?"

Sever watched the crowd, denser now as more people crowded the floor. "What do you want to know? What's this covert game you're playing?"

"All I'm asking is, that if it's not betraying any confidences, I'd like to know what Danny says."

"You can always read about it in the *Tribune*."

She looked away, frowning.

The crowd was louder now, and Sever watched as attention was drawn, almost in slow motion, to the entrance. The dancers started turning their heads as the noise grew louder. Now there were shouts, and several girls were screaming. A waitress was working her way through the unruly throng, then another, trying to get to the front of the club.

"I hope the girl is okay." Michelle stood, trying to see what the commotion was all about.

Sever stood too. "Knowing Murtz's reputation, he might have hurt her."

Michelle climbed up on the sheeted bed, standing on her tiptoes to see the action. Sever reached up and steadied her, grasping her around her slim waist. Even with the commotion he felt a reaction to the warmth of her skin. He hadn't held a woman like this in a while.

"Oh my God! Mick. You won't believe it." She strained to stand even taller, and Sever hung on, straining himself to see over the crowd. He caught the top of someone's head, a wavy mop of blond hair. Just then the crowd parted. There was no sign of Murtz or his entourage. They had vanished.

"See, I told you." Michelle smiled triumphantly, looking down at Sever as Rod Stewart and his party stepped to the bar.

CHAPTER TWENTY-ONE

His eyes felt like two burned-out holes in his head. His head rang from the loud music and the drugs and alcohol. He found a bottle of pills in the medicine cabinet to calm him down. Downing two of them with a rum and Coke, he sprawled out on the leather chair, waiting for everything to kick in.

Someone knocked on the office door. Someone was knocking at four thirty in the morning. He said nothing.

They knocked again, more insistent this time.

"What the hell do you want?"

Schwartz stepped into the room.

"You don't stop, do you, Harvey?"

"Danny, you're the one who doesn't stop. You go off on these binges, and someone gets hurt." He paused. "Or worse."

"What's she going to do? Sue? Pay her for the bruises and tell her to pack her bags."

Schwartz rubbed his eyes with his index finger and thumb. "Christ, what are we going to do with you, man? You hurt her pretty bad. We just keep cleaning up after you."

"Fuck you. You happen to be the most expensive fucking cleaning lady I've ever hired."

"Danny, you are going to get yourself in more trouble than I can get you out of. It's going to happen."

"You Jewish prick. Let me remind you. If I get into that much trouble, I'm taking you down with me. Do you understand? If I ever get nailed for whatever I've done, you're just as much to blame, counselor. You knowingly fixed all the problems."

"Is that a threat, Danny?" Schwartz barely raised his voice.

"Threat? Nah. It's simply the way it is. All that money I pay you won't do you a bit of good then." Murtz tried to focus his eyes. Harvey was a blur, a big fuzzy blur.

"Settle down, Danny. I've told you over and over again, we've got a good thing going, you and I. Don't fuck it up. Because I want you to make this work. It's a win-win situation. But if you keep up this self-destructive binge you're on, your entire life will blow up before your eyes. Can you understand that? There are only so many times we can get you out of a jam." Schwartz folded his hands, crotch level, staring at Murtz, seemingly looking for a sign.

Murtz could feel the pills kicking in, slowing him down. His speech was slurred, his eyes now just felt heavy and his muscles felt slack. Bald prick. Condescending son of a bitch. Hell, he understood a lot more than Harvey gave him credit for. He understood that Harvey could nail him on several murder charges. Even in his drugged state, he understood that.

Schwartz started to close the door. "I'll pay her, Danny. Nothing will be said. And I want to be there tomorrow at your interview with Mick Sever. If he mentions Randi Parks, if he mentions that he received a phone call from our little *American Idol* contestant while she was at your house, we're screwed. We know she called his phone."

"Even if he doesn't mention her —" he was tired. Sleepy. He could just sleep right here in the chair tonight.

"If he doesn't mention her what?" Schwartz could see Murtz starting to drift.

"That doesn't mean he doesn't know."

"True."

"She only made one call that night."

"Right. And her cell phone had his number on redial."

"You told me back at the club you were working on taking care of it."

"We gave it a shot in Chicago. They almost got him."

"Almost?"

"Hit and run. It didn't work."

"Why not give it a *shot* on the island? Christ, the money I pay you, Harvey. You can't get rid of this asshole?"

Schwartz took a deep breath. He remained calm, cool, collected. He always remained calm, cool, collected. It would be nice to see a little flash of anger or hostility. Something. Instead, Schwartz took that deep breath, let it out, and simply said, "We're looking into it, Danny. We're looking into it."

Murtz closed his eyes. He heard the door click shut, and he took a deep breath of his own. The door opened and he could vaguely make out Nancy's silhouette.

"Is everything all right?"

"What? Does everybody in this house socialize at this hour of the morning?"

"We got a call about an hour ago."

"And?"

"A soft voice, female. She asked for you."

Michelle. Had to be.

"When I told her you weren't available, she said to remind you about Jennifer Koenig. Then she said she'd be looking for you."

"You tracked the number? You got it, right?" *Don't sound panicked.*

"Blocked."

Shit. Get Harvey back in the room? No, just take a deep breath and relax. He hadn't told Harvey about the letter, he'd keep quiet about the phone call as well. He wouldn't put it past the attorney to be behind both of the threats, setting Murtz up for another big payday. He needed to see how this played out. "Is there anything else?" The bitch was always just a little too close, too meddling.

She hesitated, as if there *was* something else. Murtz closed his eyes. He just needed her to go away and leave him alone. "Never mind. Why don't you get some sleep?" Then she was gone.

CHAPTER TWENTY-TWO

She watched them pull into the driveway. A scant hour before, Nancy and Raymond had left the pool, around three a.m. She could see shadows. Even in the dark, the moon was just bright enough. Nancy Steiner. She'd been with Murtz for maybe twenty-four, twenty-five years. Surely the lady knew what an asshole he was. She had to know that Harvey Schwartz was constantly covering up his mistakes. So what kept Nancy with Murtz? She couldn't figure it out. There was no earthly reason other than money that the lady should be working for the man. She had to know that this was a one-man wrecking crew. Nancy had to know that Danny Murtz used his celebrity status to wreak havoc on everyone he touched. Or maybe she was having her own affair with Murtz. That would be beyond kinky. That would be sick. However, stranger things had happened. She knew about some of them. Hell, some of the strangest things had happened to her.

She saw the light in Murtz's office go off. Last one out that she could see. Still she sat by her small pool, watching the villa. There was another way she could solve her problem. If she couldn't get Harvey's computer tonight, there was still time. One way or another, someone was going to pay. Big time. She'd get the evidence, and in the meantime, maybe she could drive Murtz crazy. It wasn't just proving he was guilty, she wanted revenge. Revenge on both of them. She pondered the options and drifted off to sleep in the lounge chair. When the sun finally found her, it was six thirty in the morning. Time to go to bed.

CHAPTER TWENTY-THREE

"Where the hell did you find it?" Murtz looked up from the poolside chair where he'd been nursing a rum and Coke and a king-sized headache.

"My office. On the floor. Did you write this, Danny?"

"No. Did you, Harvey? Because there's no one else in this house who knows what happened to these girls. And it sounds like the letter is referring to the girls. What are you doing? Holding out for more money?" He wasn't going to tell him about the first letter. Not until he'd decided if Harvey wrote the second. Sweat beaded on the attorney's scalp as he shook the paper in Murtz's face. Murtz noticed the man had no cap on. A first. He must really be upset not to protect the precious bald dome.

"What's the point, Danny?"

"Oh, my God. You are doing this for more money. Is that it? You wrote this note to scare me into paying you more?"

Harvey sighed, sounding like the weight of the world was on his shoulders, when all it really was, was just the disappearance of several women. The attorney stood by the pool, shaking his head at Murtz as if he'd been scolding a young student.

"All right, counselor, file the fucking thing." He wanted to mention the first letter, he wanted to mention the phone call that came last night, but it wasn't the right time.

"What's it about, Danny?"

Murtz slowly stood up from the lounge chair. He took a hit off the joint and felt a release inside his head. He grabbed the letter from his attorney and tried to read it himself. His vision was blurred, and the white-hot sun bounced off the paper. He wiped his eyes and studied the words. They seemed to be the same ones Harvey had just read to him.

> Mr. Murtz:
>
> Once again, I am watching you. I know about the girls. Every step you take, I'm paying close attention. You once produced a song called "When it's Time to Go, I'll Know." Your time is coming. Are you ready?

"It's not like it's the first time I've had a threatening letter, Harvey." He tried to remember the song. "When it's Time to Go, I'll Know." Something about knowing when a girl was going to dump him. It usually ended up that he dumped the girls.

"It was in the house, Danny. In the house. Someone is threatening to kill you, and apparently they have access to the villa. I think that's a pretty serious situation."

Murtz crumpled the letter into a ball and tossed it to Schwartz. "It's your job to fix things like this. Half a million here, two hundred fifty thousand there — come on Harvey, do your job." He took another drag on the joint, feeling more and more empowered. "But if I find out it was you —"

Schwartz bent down and picked up the paper. "You're losing it, Danny. You're letting a good thing go to hell, for you and for me."

Murtz approached him, smiling. "Harvey, Harvey," He reached out with his bony hand and grabbed the attorney by the front of his T-shirt. "It's mine to lose, you little prick." His voice was getting louder. He didn't want to scream, but it came out loud. "Don't you tell me what my problems are. If it wasn't for me you'd still be settling domestic disputes in Minot, North Dakota. You're here to fix my problems, not to tell me what they are." Now he was shaking, and he could feel the pressure inside his skull about to explode.

Schwartz staggered, and Murtz saw the surprise in his eyes. He pushed him closer to the pool, feeling stronger every second. Maybe the little shit had written the letter. Maybe Harvey wanted more leverage, more money, and maybe, just maybe, he never had anything to do with the letter. But Harvey was available. He was readily accessible. He was close by, and Danny needed to vent. When you paid someone several million dollars a year, you should be able to take out your frustrations on him. If he'd had a gun he would have shoved it up the lawyer's ass.

"Let go, Danny. You're pushing it." Schwartz was pale, even paler than usual. His upper lip twitched, and even in his drug-induced state Murtz knew the attorney was scared. The sanctimonious prick was afraid. Afraid for his life.

"Maybe I should push it just a little further." Murtz gave him a hard shove, and the attorney fell back, splashing into the shallow end of the pool. Murtz stared at him for a second, then walked back into the villa, letting his joint smolder in the ashtray on the deck table. Two letters in the house. A threatening phone call. He'd been contemplating it for a while. Now it was time to clean house.

CHAPTER TWENTY-FOUR

It wasn't until morning that he found the papers were gone. Every file that Jeff had given him. Totally gone. Sever tore through the drawers, scoured the bar area on the balcony, looked under the bed, and searched under the sink in the bathroom. Everything else was in place. They were gone, vanished, and it appeared that someone had been fooling with his laptop computer. The home page didn't come up when he rebooted.

This put a whole new spin on things. No one else would have any use for the papers. No one except Danny Murtz. Or maybe, just maybe, the girl from last night. Michelle. He couldn't figure out how Murtz had a clue that the questions were going to link back to the missing women. He must have suspected, to have someone break into his suite and steal the papers.

Sever threw himself on the bed, lacing his hands behind his head. He had to go ahead with the interview, but assuming it was Murtz and company that stole the notes, they'd be ready for him. They'd already know what the questions were going to be. The situation was very complicated.

Sever grabbed the phone from the nightstand and dialed the United States access code. Then he called his answering machine number. Nothing. The phone rang, but his machine never picked up. He studied the receiver for a moment then slammed it down into the cradle. He thought about calling Jeff, but there was no reason to concern him at this moment.

He got up, took a quick shower, and drove the car down to the hotel office. Emily wasn't on duty this morning, and the young girl at the desk didn't recognize him. "Somebody broke into my room last night." He pointed to the top of the hill.

"Monsieur?"

"Do you speak English?"

"Très peu. Very little."

Very little. He didn't have the patience to wait for the manager or the night clerk and have them tell him that they noticed nothing. He'd heard the story already. Kids stole once in a while. That was the extent of crime on the island.

"Never mind."

He drove down to Eden Rock for breakfast. The meal, as it was, was served on the beach under the log-framed tent with ten whirling fans above creating a pleasant morning breeze. He started to unwind. Black coffee, a bagel, and for a diversion, he ordered fresh mango with cream. What the hell, live like a native.

If Murtz recognized him today, fine. He'd just say that he and Michelle met at the hotel and she was free for the evening. Danny Murtz was responsible for that. Murtz had stood Michelle up, so what could the man say? And as far as his notes, that was going to be tricky. The background information was one thing. Whoever stole his notes would expect him to have background. They'd even expect the story on Jennifer Koenig. But now Murtz, or somebody associated with him, had copies of the letters to the *Chicago Tribune*. Letters that a woman had written, making innuendoes that Murtz had last-minute interludes with several missing girls. Letters that offered up proof, flimsy proof as far as Sever was concerned, but suggestions that Danny Murtz may have been involved in the disappearance — even the death — of several women. Someone knew he was on a mission to find out about the missing girls.

He sipped his black coffee, letting the caffeine work its magic. A dull headache lay at the back of his skull, no doubt the aftereffect of too much champagne. And what about Michelle? A little of that champagne, or more like a lot of it, and she turned into a crazy woman. A cop? That didn't quite fit Danny Murtz's usual conquest. From what he'd seen, Murtz liked the young starlets. He seemed to gravitate to young girls in show business, not a policewoman from Atlanta. Aside from being drop-dead gorgeous, Michelle didn't seem to be Murtz's type at all. He wondered where they'd met. A cop? It just didn't fit. Did she steal the papers for Murtz?

The champagne, smoke, and late hours were working against him, and he ordered a second cup of coffee. Rod Stewart had insisted on buying the two of them drinks until two a.m. and then wanted to go out for a "bite to eat, mate?" Sever had regrettably declined. He'd heard that the singer's last wife had bailed because Rod wasn't up to the social life anymore. Hell, as far as he could tell, the old man could still party with the best of them.

He wasn't exactly surprised when Michelle sat down next to him. He'd mentioned something about the Eden Rock before they parted company.

"Hey, stranger." She smiled, looking none the worse for the wear.

"He didn't call after you got back to the hotel?"

"No. I didn't really expect him to."

"So it was an uneventful evening."

"I'd say it was very eventful, Mr. Sever. If you hadn't stuck around, we wouldn't have seen Danny and I wouldn't have met Rod Stewart. That was pretty cool!"

The waiter approached their table. "Excuse me. Are you Mick Sever?"

Jesus. Once again, if he didn't get the attention, he yearned for it. But when you couldn't even have breakfast without someone coming up and — "Yeah. Do I know you?"

"No, sir. The gentleman and lady at the table over there," he pointed to a middle-aged couple having breakfast, "they wondered if you might stop by their table on your way out, sir?"

He made eye contact with the man, well tanned with a shaved

head. The lady was streaked blond, and her skin appeared to have had too much sun for too long. She wore a bikini top that accentuated her ample cleavage.

"I'll go over and talk to them." He glanced at Michelle. "Please, get the lady whatever she wants."

"Maybe it's my turn to buy." Michelle smiled, and the crazy lady from last night disappeared. No sign of the rage and insecurities she'd exhibited at Casa Niki.

"Before I talk to my adoring fans . . ." he hesitated.

"Yes?"

"You asked me to share with you anything that I learned from the interview."

"I'd had a lot to drink."

"I know. But do you want to explain?"

"I'm going to. I'm not exactly what I appear to be."

"A crazy cop?"

She didn't laugh. She didn't smile. She picked up his cup of black coffee and took a big swallow. There was a long moment of silence. "I'm here for a different reason. I may be able to help you and you may be able to help me. But I don't think this is the place to talk." She glanced at the couple who were waiting for Sever. "Let's talk about this later. Okay?"

"I look forward to it." He didn't want to push it. He didn't want to blow this interview. "When do you want to talk?"

"Today. After your interview with Danny. Mick, I'm going to trust you and you have to trust me. That's all I'll say for now."

What the hell was that all about? He considered the possibility that Michelle had stolen the notes. All of a sudden she'd admitted that there was more to her story than she had shared. She'd said she was here for a different reason. I have to trust you and you have to trust me? *Why was she here?* Sever reached for his coffee and she smiled.

"Thanks for offering to buy breakfast. I believe you have some fans at the table over there."

Sever walked over to the table, still confused over the last several minutes. He introduced himself.

"Mr. Sever."

"Please, call me Mick."

"Mick. I'm Jordan Clark. My wife and I own a chain of radio stations in Puerto Rico. You used to work for us."

Sever gave him a puzzled look.

"Going back about twelve years ago? Maybe closer to fifteen? You had a syndicated talk show where you interviewed celebrities."

Sever remembered. It ran for two years and the Chicago Tribune Syndicate had sold the concept to radio stations all over the United States. And, apparently, Puerto Rico.

"We ran your show on all ten stations."

"Sure, I remember the show. It lasted all of two years. I don't think our ratings were quite what we wanted."

"This is my wife, Dani." She reached out her hand and Sever shook it.

"Do you come here often?"

"Actually we do. We have a fifty-three-foot Hatteras, and we boat over two or three times a year. The Eden Rock is a great place to stay. We've got a marvelous private suite up those stairs." He motioned to the stairway right off the restaurant. "It's a wonderful view from there . . . or here." He motioned to the beach.

Sever looked out at the shimmering sand and the sun making its lazy climb into the azure St. Barts sky. A young lady was taking her top off, and fastening a towel to her beach chair not twenty feet from him. Wonderful view. Two other ladies were already topless.

When they'd visited the islands or South Beach or any topless beach, Ginny had always called them the brigade of boobs. When Mick, playing right into her hand, would ask if she was referring to the bare female breasts, Ginny would say, "No. I'm talking about the guys who sit there and drool!" When they *had* visited the islands. Past tense. He wished the thoughts would disappear.

"Sometime we'd like to show you the Hatteras," Jordan said. "Have you ever sailed around St. Barts?"

"No."

"Perhaps we can do that. How long will you be here?"

Sever considered the invitation. No, he'd be out of here in a day or two. He didn't know who stole the notes. Michelle? Murtz? This wasn't his forte. This was a job for law enforcement agencies. And his investigation was going nowhere. Murtz was a jerk, but if Sever had to prove that Danny Murtz had been responsible for the death or disappearance of two girls? It was a little out of his league.

"I'll be leaving day after tomorrow at the latest. Maybe another time?"

"Certainly." Jordan smiled and nodded. "It's a date."

Sever walked back to his table. Michelle was chewing a piece of toast.

"You're a popular guy today."

"Why do you say that?"

"Some guy pointed you out and asked the waiter if you were the famous writer."

"What guy?"

"He's gone. As soon as the waiter nodded, the guy took off. Very strange."

"What did he look like?"

"Small," she said. "About five-six, didn't weigh much. Short hair. Very French."

Sever shook his head. "Look, I've got to go back to the hotel. I need a place where no one will bother me for a couple of hours. This interview is coming up and I need a little privacy before I talk to your boyfriend." He was tempted to tell her that someone had stolen all of his notes, but he couldn't be sure it wasn't her. As he thought about it, there was a strong possibility.

"That's very cold, Mick."

"Yeah. It is. But he's the reason both of us are over here, right?"

She studied him for a moment. "I told you last night that I was a cop. I told you today that we need to talk. I think we may be on a similar mission."

"You do?"

She stared out at the ocean. "It's so beautiful that it's almost impossible to appreciate it all."

"Tell me now. What is this mission we're on?"

"Mick, I told you. We'll talk about it later. Okay?"

"Look, you told me for a reason. Or are you just proud of your profession. Which is it?"

She couldn't meet his gaze, continuing to stare at the water. Finally she glanced at him, her eyes immediately focusing on something behind and to the right. Frowning, her forehead wrinkled in an uncharacteristic expression, she said, "It's hard to explain. I majored in social work. I just took it a step further. I decided to go into law enforcement. You know, you and I share some of the same interests. We can work together. But right now you need to meet Danny." She finally stared into his eyes. "Please. Trust me. We're in this together, Mick."

Sever had watched her eyes, drifting from the ocean to the food on her plate, never focusing on him. Finally she looked at him with a laser-like intensity. "What do you want from me, Michelle?"

"I need to get the complete story. You need to get the complete story. When I'm investigating a crime, I talk to any number of people. I interview dozens of suspects, witnesses, neighbors, and friends until I get my story. Isn't that what you do?"

He smiled. "Sort of."

"See? We share a lot more than you realize. I don't owe you anything, Mick, and you don't owe me anything. But together we can get what we came for. Don't ask any more questions, okay? I'll talk to you later, when I've got my thoughts together." She swallowed the last of her coffee and leveled him in her sights. "You get all the answers you can from Danny. He's not the most forthcoming individual you've ever interviewed, but I'm certain that you know that."

So he'd pushed a little too hard. It wasn't the first time. If you did interviews, you probed. You asked questions until you got answers. And that style had become a part of his life. What had Michelle said? You needed to get the complete story. Michelle was a story in herself. If he had the chance, he'd like to explore that story. But the message was clear. Back off until later.

"Listen, I've got some things to do." She pushed her chair back, stood up, and spun around, walking out of the tent. Sever watched her go, her short skirt swinging across her tanned legs. She still reminded him of Ginny. And he wasn't sure that was a good thing.

CHAPTER TWENTY-FIVE

He waited on the sidewalk, watching the small cars as they sped by. He was parked on the far side of the narrow street and the traffic was heavy. Finally there was a break, and he dashed across the street. A small van whizzed by him as he opened the door to his rented vehicle. He turned the key and saw Dani and Jordan Clark across the road on the sidewalk, waving him over. He stepped out of the vehicle, leaving it idling, and ran back across the street.

"Mick, we had a thought." Jordan smiled, motioning to his wife. "Could we possibly interest you in dinner tonight? On the boat? Dani makes a wonderful tuna dish and I mix some fantastic drinks." His eyes were wide open like a puppy dog begging for a treat.

Afterward, Sever could swear he heard a sputter before the huge bang. Almost as if a fuse had been lit. It was a very brief hiss, then a moment of pure silence, followed by a monstrous bang. It wasn't a boom. This was a colossal bang. A sharp bang that rattled the buildings, the trees, the very sidewalk they stood on. And the fiery eruption that exploded from his car singed everything in a ten-foot area. The explosion echoed down the street, inside the Eden Rock, and ricocheted off the walls of every building in the vicinity.

Sever and the Clarks hit the sidewalk, all three covering their heads with their arms as flaming debris rained from the sky. The noise seemed to last forever and red-hot prickly metal fragments landed on Sever, burning his arms and back.

He lifted his head, not certain what had happened or where. His ears rang with the power of ten church bells, and his first view was of a liquid ball of fire that erupted from the hood of the auto, then the entire auto was engulfed in flame. He jumped to his feet, brushing at his arms as if a swarm of red ants had landed on him, all stinging with their venom, and he had to get them off.

In only seconds the intense blaze consumed the car. He squinted as the orange-red fire raged, and he watched the Clarks run to the restaurant for cover. Sever followed close behind, running for his life. The intense heat burned up all the available oxygen and he gasped for breath as he sprinted to safety. This had happened before. In the last several days. Chicago. The car that jumped the curb. *No. It was a coincidence. It had to be a coincidence.*

Obviously the rental car was defective. The agency should have warned him there were problems with this particular model of car. Ducking into the Eden Rock, he had a second thought. *Maybe, just maybe it was this particular vehicle, and only this particular vehicle that had been singled out for this problem. Maybe it wasn't just the model of car.*

The short man who had been kneeling by his car at the Manapany Hotel parking lot. Was he trying to fix an explosive under the car? And Michelle said a short man had asked about him in the restaurant. One of Murtz's goons? How the hell did those gadgets work anyway? Wasn't there supposed to be a device attached to the engine? He was now being paranoid. Sever brushed at his right arm, only now noticing the red splotches from the red-hot residue. His skin appeared to be infected with a rash.

Paranoid? Michelle had described the short French guy who had asked about him just moments before. It was more than coincidence. And then he thought about the girl who had walked out just minutes before. Michelle Kirkendall, someone who professed to be an American cop. She could have stolen the papers and she could have set an explosive device. Hell, you never knew who you could trust.

"Mick, are you all right?"

"I'm fine." He winced at the needle-sharp stings in his back.

"It was your car."

"It was."

"God, I just thank God that we're still alive. If you'd been in that car for two or three more seconds —"

"I should thank you."

Jordan Clark dropped into a vacant chair at an empty table. His wife wandered over and sat next to him. There was no one around to formally offer them a seat. The staff had run to the sidewalk to view the remains. "For what?"

"For asking me to dinner. If you two hadn't called me across the street, we wouldn't be having this conversation."

"Damn. I hadn't thought of that." Clark wiped the sweat from his forehead.

"You saved my life." Sever sat down beside him.

"Well?" Dani Clark put her hand out and touched Sever's blistered skin. "Do you still want to come for dinner?"

Sever smiled. "No. But please, feel free to ask me anytime I'm about to have a really dangerous accident." He motioned to the lone waiter who was holding down the fort. "I don't care how early in the morning it is, I'm buying this man and his wife the most expensive drink in the joint!"

CHAPTER TWENTY-SIX

"The police interviewed you because they handle traffic matters." Jordan Clark sipped his ice-cold beer as the pigeons picked at crumbs by his feet.

"This wasn't a traffic matter. You know it, I know it, they know it." Sever glanced at his watch. Two hours had gone by very quickly, and with all of the activity he was still frustrated. No one on St. Barts took anything too seriously.

"Let me explain this to you, Mick." He motioned to the young waitress who hurried over from the small outdoor bar with another cold brown bottle. She twisted the top and poured Sever a tall glass with a head on it. "Gendarmes would handle this if it were a murder —"

"Or an attempted murder." Sever frowned.

"Exactly."

"And this wasn't an attempted murder?"

"There are no murders on St. Barts. Not in recent history."

Sever took a long swallow, letting the dark brew slide down his throat. "Bullshit."

An overweight American couple next to them loudly slurped margaritas and chewed on large pieces of pizza. The traffic crawled by just a few feet away. Le Piment was bustling with an early lunch trade.

"There are thirteen gendarmes on the island, Mick. Six policemen. The police take care of traffic matters."

"And they're going with the story that the car had a defect?"

"My friend, if there was any suggestion of murder on this island, the tourist business would dry up like a tumbleweed. And the tourist business is all these people have."

"Someone tried to kill me. Right here, in paradise. If you hadn't called me over, there would have been a murder."

"No. People jump from hilltops. People swim out too far in the ocean and drown. People have stabbed themselves, and disappeared on boats, but no matter how they die, they are never murdered."

"The gendarmes would handle murder?"

"They would. Murder and theft."

Sever stared over Clark's shoulder at a huge green pepper on the restaurant's sign. Le Piment must mean green pepper. The clock beside it said eleven thirty. Jordan Clark had already agreed to drop him off at Murtz's place, but with all the morning activity he certainly wasn't going to get any more time to prepare for meeting Danny Murtz. And he wasn't really in the mood to do the interview.

"Just suppose," Sever folded his hands on the table and looked into Clark's eyes, "just suppose that there's a big drug bust on the island. Some American brings in a haul on a yacht. How does that affect the tourist dollar?"

"Technically the PAF would get involved. Police of Air and Frontier. They handle drugs and immigration. However, there are no major drug busts."

"And the reason is?"

"Mick, it's all about money. This island attracts very, very rich celebrities. They bring in drugs. One bust, and it fucks up the tourist dollar. No more celebrities, no more tourists. I can't be any clearer. And you, my friend, were the victim of a faulty rental car. It's as simple as that. That's the official word."

Sever closed his eyes for a second, picturing the ball of fire that shot into the sky. Black smoke hung in the air long after the bang. After the police had done a perfunctory ten-minute interview, a road crew had come to clean up the mess. It was over in half an hour, as if nothing had ever happened. And if he'd been in the car? No murder, just a faulty engine.

"The girl you were with —"

"Michelle? I met her yesterday at my hotel."

"It's fortunate she didn't ride with you. She left right before you did."

"You're right." Any tie to the explosion? He'd thought about it. Probably not. Just pure coincidence. Still, she was in the mix.

"Why don't we drive back to the Eden Rock and you can freshen up in our suite? Then I can drive you to Danny Murtz's villa. We'll have plenty of time to make it by one."

Sever nodded. Another coincidence? Maybe Danny Murtz knew that he was with Michelle last night. Pretty severe warning to stay away from his girlfriend. It really made no sense. No sense at all.

They walked a few steps to Clark's car, a vehicle they had left in plain sight the entire time.

"I'd hate to find out that two cars on the island had faulty engines." Clark gazed at the key in his hand, then inserted it in the ignition and started the car. They headed back to the Eden Rock.

CHAPTER TWENTY-SEVEN

Someone was rigging lights on the pool deck. There were big floods on stands around the water. As if the white-hot sun wasn't bright enough! They'd rolled out tracking with deep grooves and were mounting camera stands with wheels to roll along the track that ran the entire circumference of the pool. The technicians worked with precise efficiency, a well-oiled machine that had followed the same procedure time and time again. She watched with her binoculars, wondering when the filming would take place.

Lines of cable crisscrossed the deck, and two of the men took off their shirts, resting briefly in two of the lounge chairs that were scattered around the pool. Everyone seemed to have a bottle of water, and she watched them wipe the perspiration from their foreheads as they worked.

She caught movement at the neighbors' villa and saw Bill and Susan next door out on their deck, watching the same scene, using their own binoculars. The big-guy and his wife, enjoying the scenery. Ah, the thrill of living near celebrity.

There was no sign of Harvey, Murtz, Nancy, or any of the entourage, but an attractive blond in a yellow bikini was slowly swimming laps. It was almost ten thirty a.m. and it appeared the rest of the household was sleeping in. She put the glasses down on the table and sipped the iced tea she'd made, flavoring it with a squeeze of lemon. It would be so nice to walk over and invite the neighbors in for a drink. She missed the social aspect of her life, the give and take of conversation, gossip, the flirting with members of the opposite sex. She missed the people coming up to her on the street, the flattering remarks. She wondered if she'd ever be able to put it all behind her and live a normal life again. Not that her life had been "normal." But she yearned for the life she used to have. The closest thing she could compare her situation to was rape. Her life had been raped. A good friend of hers had been raped by a stranger and had never been the same again. Always looking over her shoulder. Always afraid of what was around the next corner. God, how could someone live like that for the rest of her life?

A movement caught her eye, and she picked up the glasses again as Danny Murtz walked out to the pool from his office. He wore a pair of cutoff shorts with no shirt, his pale, bloated stomach hanging over the waistband. It was the wealth and the fame that attracted these crazy women. It had to be. She knew it was the wealth and fame, and that only. That's what had attracted her. Physically and emotionally the man was a wreck. The new girl pulled herself up onto the side of the pool and Murtz walked over and hugged her. Through the glasses she watched them kiss, and she shuddered. The thought was revolting.

Another bimbo, another notch in the bedpost, another candidate for a disappearance. She wanted to run to the villa, shout at the new girl to warn her. She desperately wanted to destroy any plans that Murtz had made. But she didn't. Instead, she walked into the cottage to fix herself some lunch. Maybe tonight would be a good time to try plan two.

CHAPTER TWENTY-EIGHT

"What do you want? A drink?"

"It's a little early for me."

"You're upset. I haven't spent enough time with you."

"Last night —"

"Hey, there were no promises." Murtz frowned and eased himself into a cushioned lounge chair. "Have a drink." He picked up a pitcher from the table and poured himself a glass of vodka and orange juice.

She studied him for a moment, and he lost himself in her clear blue eyes. Maybe he should have spent a lot more time with this beauty. "You're here, I'm here."

"That almost didn't happen, Danny." She put her hand on his. "I was lucky I called you when I did. You were taking off for St. Barts, breaking our date, and you weren't even going to tell me about it."

Murtz sipped the screwdriver, trying to remember how many drinks he'd had already. He had an interview with the reporter this afternoon. Probably should go a little easy. Leaving early? Hell, yes. The *American Idol* thing with Randi whatever-her-name-was could have blown up and everything would have been screwed. "Things came up rather suddenly. The Indoorfins were going to be here, and I needed to get over here in a hurry. I would have called."

"Maybe I was a little pushy? But I did want to see you."

"And the idea of visiting St. Barts was intriguing."

"Well, maybe that too. Of course that played a part, but you did too. Thanks again. I can't believe you flew me here."

"Then everything is okay? You're not mad?"

She picked up his drink and took a long, slow sip. "It's hard to be mad when we're here in this beautiful place."

Murtz gave her a long, slow look and silently admired her smooth skin and fine features. Not as young as he usually dated, but very desirable. The minute Nancy had seen her, his secretary had fire in her eyes. She knew this was a catch and she wasn't happy about it.

The bikini-clad beauty glanced up, handed him back his drink, and he wrapped his hand around hers. He could hear the workmen banging around equipment, and for a moment, he lost his concentration.

"Hey, let's go inside. I've got this great custom-sized bed that I think you'd find very comfortable."

"Can't I swim for just a little longer?"

Pleading? Or playing coy?

He glanced at his watch. "I've got an interview with some jackass reporter. Time's tight."

She frowned. As if she didn't want to check out the comforts of his gigantic bed. Plane fare, 5-star hotel, food, and drink — if that didn't buy a piece of ass, he'd lost his touch.

The blond, Michelle something, finally smiled. "Can I get a shower first?"

"Sure."

"Danny, thanks for everything. I know I don't sound appreciative, but I haven't seen that much of you and seeing you with someone else last night —"

He stood up and poured one more drink from the pitcher.

"I'll get a shower too."

Michelle frowned, a questioning look on her face. Finally, "Separate showers. I'll meet you in the bedroom in thirty minutes."

It was Murtz's turn to frown.

"Okay. Thirty minutes. Don't take too much time."

She smiled, a secretive, sexy smile.

"I know, you have some reporter coming to visit you and you don't want to disappoint him."

"Did I tell you it was a him?"

She hesitated. "If it was a 'her,' I'd be jealous."

"It's not."

"Good. Then give me thirty minutes."

Murtz reached back and pulled on his ponytail. It was habit. He wanted to know it was there. No explanation, it was just an extension of him and it needed to be there. He grabbed a towel from the back of his chair and pulled it around his flabby white chest and stomach. He should get into an exercise program, join a gym, do something to get back into shape. Or maybe not. Let the money and the fame precede him and all good things would come. Oh, yes. Life was good. Perfect.

Michelle stood up, exhibiting her stunning figure, and without the help of a wraparound towel headed toward the rear entrance to the villa. There was a shower in the small bath, and apparently that's exactly where she was headed. Murtz smiled. He should just surprise her in the shower. But on second thought, maybe he should do a line of coke, and maybe have one more drink. And he'd promised to take a shower too. One thing at a time. Life was good.

CHAPTER TWENTY-NINE

Danny Murtz took a drag from his second joint of the day. This Michelle was turning into a real tease. She was hot, but somewhat reluctant. The older girls were usually a lot more compliant. This girl was, for lack of a better word, hesitant. He'd spent enough money on her to get laid ten times and she was still playing coy. He heard the water running in the bath down the hall. He should just walk in on her and take her in the shower stall. Time was getting short. Damn appointments. What the hell was Nancy thinking when she booked this interview with Sever? She probably wasn't thinking. Worried about *the boy,* her precious son, and maybe if she'd ever get laid again. The A&E thing was bad enough. They'd wired the entire fucking villa with their microphones and wires and lights and cameras. It felt like he was in some sort of reality show and without the first frame being filmed, his nerves were already frayed.

Then there was this Michelle, who needed to be explored, and now he had to see this Mick Sever. He was familiar with the name, probably had read an interview or two that Sever had written, but that was about it.

He sat in his office, half in and half out of it, trying to decide whether he wanted to take a shower or just shag the girl before he had to talk to the reporter.

"Danny."

Murtz looked up, snuffing the joint in the ashtray on the arm of his leather chair. Always prepared to get rid of the evidence. Whatever drugs he was ingesting, he'd learned how to dump them as fast as possible. He'd actually swallowed joints before to hide the proof. However, this was Harvey. While he didn't like Harvey seeing him do drugs, it wasn't worth eating the joint.

"Danny, Little Jean visited Sever's hotel." The bald attorney stood in the entrance, disapproval on his face. "You've got an interview with Sever in about an hour. Are you up to it?"

"Fuck you. I'm up to anything."

"Maybe not. Jean found a stack of papers at Sever's place. There was a lot of background information for his interview this afternoon. The papers not only contain all the information he needed, but there are some copies of letters to the *Chicago Tribune*." Schwartz folded his arms, body language that showed defiance. Murtz knew what it meant. Harvey was about to crow. Or get in his face about something.

"What letters Harvey?"

"Letters from an unidentified source, some female, saying that you were responsible for the deaths of various women."

Not a good sign. "Credible?"

"Whoever the author is, she claims you tried to kill her."

Why had he snuffed out the joint?

"Can you handle it?"

Schwartz unfolded his arms. "I want you to talk to Sever. Act as if you don't know anything about the background information. You act as if we don't know that he was contacted by Randi Parks. You answer his questions, and if anything at all comes up about missing females, you tell him he's got to talk to me. I'll be there, but I'll set up another time and place for a conversation between Sever and me."

"Damn. Who sent these letters?" More letters. Letters to the newspaper, letters in his villa. That damned phone call. "Why don't you just get rid of him?"

Schwartz's eyes widened. "We've tried, damn it. You do your job, Danny, and I'll do mine!"

"Where are these papers? These letters?"

He wanted to see them for himself. *Who the hell was threatening him? This sounded like the same person who sent the others.*

"On my desk."

"I'll look at them."

"Just do what I ask. If you get in Sever's face, it will just reinforce the fact that we have a serious problem."

"Yeah, yeah, yeah."

"Danny, don't fuck this up." Schwartz spun around and was gone.

Murtz slowly stood up. The water no longer ran in the shower and he wondered if she was toweling off. Maybe drying her soft body with one of the plush guest bath towels. He stretched, rose from the chair, poured himself a rum and Coke from the bar, and sipped it for several seconds. It was time to go down the hall and see if she was ready.

Murtz staggered out the door, walking to the bathroom, noticing the door was wide open. He glanced inside. The glass and tile interior were wet, water dripping from the surfaces. *Where the hell had she gone? To his bedroom. Ideal.* He kept walking down the hall, past Schwartz's office to the spacious living room. He paused, shaking his head to clear the clouds. Harvey's office. Papers. What papers was he thinking of? He bowed his head and stared at the floor for several seconds, trying to remember what it was about Harvey's office. Papers.

He heard a noise. Harvey's office. The bald-headed prick was in there, reading papers. Oh, yeah. Papers that were incriminating. Papers that came from the reporter's hotel room. He should just head to the bedroom, the lovely Michelle-something waiting for him in his customized bed. Huge bed. Soft, monster bed. What was it that the rappers always said on MTV's *Cribs* TV show? Where the magic happened. The bedroom.

Murtz grabbed at the wall, straightening himself, and lurched forward. God he was fucked up. He turned and headed back to the office. No Harvey. He was sure there had been a noise. The office appeared empty. Light-headed, he turned to leave, and then just as clear-headed as sober, he heard it again. A rustle from the corner of the office. He squinted and looked into the dark recess of the attorney's office. Christ. It was Michelle.

"What the fuck are you doing in here? I told you we're headed for the bedroom."

Deer in the headlights syndrome. She was frozen, a sheaf of papers in her hand.

"What the hell are you doing?" Murtz approached her, hand outstretched to take the papers. She stared at him, her blond hair still wet and straggly, a pair of baggy jeans and a white cotton blouse covering her sexy frame.

"Danny, I —"

"You what? You came in here by accident?"

"No. I couldn't remember which room —"

The papers. Harvey had said they were on his desk. Papers that would incriminate him. "You found the papers."

"I didn't even look at them, Danny. I never even —"

He smiled at her, took two steps then punched her in the nose. A hard, fast punch that snapped her head back. As she started to fall, he lashed out with his foot, catching her chest high. She gasped and collapsed on the floor.

"What the fuck were you doing, girl?" She didn't answer. He nudged her with his foot and she groaned. "I asked you a question, bitch. What the fuck were you doing?"

"I told you, it was a mistake."

He drove his foot into her ribs, hearing her gasp and hearing a cracking sound. Bust a couple of bones. Let her know he was serious. Hell, he'd done it before. "Damn right it was a mistake."

"God, Danny." She was crying.

"Danny what?"

"Please, I told you. I didn't know what this was." Sobbing. He hated it when they sobbed.

He kicked her again and she groaned. "Who are you?"

"You know who I am. Don't do this. Please."

Whimpers, sobs, tears, he couldn't deal with it. She was looking at the papers. Papers that dealt with his secrets.

"Who are you?" He kicked her again and she clutched her stomach.

Murtz leaned down, picked up her head by her blond hair, and let it drop to the hard-tiled floor.

"Who are you? Did you write the letters?" He was screaming. "Did you?"

She didn't answer. Maybe too much, too soon. He had a habit of doing that. He looked at her for a moment, then glanced around the room. Nothing of hers. He bent down again and felt in the pockets of her jeans. Three pockets came up empty. The fourth held a credit card and driver's license. He gazed at them for a moment, then walked to Schwartz's chair and sat down. He stared at the blond with the bloody nose and broken ribs. Still lovely, and still alive. He thought for a moment. The guest cottage would be perfect, at least until the reporter left. It was only an hour until Sever arrived. Tie her up, put her in the guest cottage, and keep it to himself. It was perfect.

The phone rang, jangling his frayed nerves. It rang again, and again, and again. Somebody, for God's sake — he grabbed the receiver. "What?"

"Danny?" A hesitant female voice.

"Yeah. Look, I'm kind of busy —"

"Danny." More confidence this time. "I just want you to know that I know where you are, and I know what you did."

A bad attempt at a movie quote? "Who the hell is this?"

"Someone who's going to bring you down, you prick." She hung up.

His head whipped around, searching for an intruder, an observer, someone who had seen him strike Michelle. The windows in the office were closed. No one could have seen a thing. Rising from the chair, he picked up the scattered papers, placing them back on the desk. The whole thing was unraveling and no one was doing a damned thing about it. Except him. Murtz picked up the slight female, threw her over his shoulder, and staggered down the hall to the door. If anyone commented while he was in transit, he'd tell them she overindulged. This time he was taking care of the problem himself. He didn't need Harvey on this one. He'd have to figure out what to do with her later, but the guest cottage was getting a brand new tenant. Someone whose residence was going to be very, very short-lived.

CHAPTER THIRTY

He didn't ask for these scenarios, they just presented themselves. It was like the other girls. He didn't have a death-design on them, it just happened. Shit happened. She was snooping. There was some ulterior motive, and by God she was going to tell him what it was before he finished with her.

He wrapped the extension cord around her wrists as she lay on the bed. The blood from her nose stained the sheets. He was sick of women's blood. The second cord he tied tightly around her ankles. He slapped her face twice, trying to wake her up.

"Michelle. Hey, who are you? What the hell are you doing going through my papers?" No answer. Her breathing was through the mouth, but regular. He'd come back later.

Murtz exited the cottage, locking the door as he left. Because of the papers in Schwartz's office, Murtz knew that Sever knew about the girls. Sever obviously had information on the letters that had been sent to the *Chicago Tribune.* Sever had received a call from Randi Parks, and who knew what else? This guy was here to crucify him and somebody, somebody had to get rid of Mick Sever.

He considered the Randi Parks connection. He had to wonder why Randi Parks had called Sever. Maybe Sever was her boyfriend, but why would the little tramp call her boyfriend while she was balling some other guy? And if they talked, did she tell this Sever that she was fucking Danny Murtz? And was that the reason Sever was interviewing him? Jesus, that was the reason. It made sense.

Murtz walked into his office, taking deep breaths. He needed to calm down and think this whole thing through. He was Danny Murtz for God's sake. He'd jumped dozens of hurdles before, and no two-bit reporter was going to bring him down this time. Son of a bitch. Harvey, the dipshit, had slipped up. Harvey hadn't taken care of this problem. Sever was still alive and walking. After this interview, he'd be alive and squawking. This was so screwed up. And maybe Sever was the one who sent him the letter. Yeah, there was that possibility.

"Nancy!" He yelled into the phone.

"Not so loud, Danny. Some of the late-night crowd have headaches." She stepped into his office. He hung up the phone that she'd never answered. Was she hiding right outside his door all the time so she could surprise him like that? It happened a lot.

"Where the hell is Harvey?"

"I believe he's one of those with a headache." She gave him a cold, hard stare. Her hair was down, not quite to her shoulders, and she had on a pale yellow silky top with a gray skirt. Not too bad today. Not too bad for an older broad. Maybe she was trying to seduce him. Again.

"Get him in here!"

She spun around, obviously irritated with being made the gopher. Any time he mentioned the Jewish attorney she bristled.

Murtz pulled open the center drawer on the desk, taking out the envelope with the pure white powder. He poured a generous amount on a piece of paper, sifted it into a narrow line and sniffed it up with a short straw. Probably not the smartest thing to do, feeling as paranoid as he did, but he needed strength. Cocaine gave him strength.

Harvey wasn't performing as advertised. And that meant the interview was still going to take place. Was Sever going to point-blank ask him if he knew Randi Parks? Was he going to quiz him about the Parks girl's disap-

pearance? Why hadn't Harvey done his job? The son of a bitch had a job. And it wasn't getting done.

"Nancy!"

No answer. What the hell, she could only work so fast. But never fast enough for Murtz.

A few moments later Schwartz stood in the entranceway. "Did you see the papers?"

"Yeah." Hadn't read them, but he'd been a little busy putting out fires. Murtz felt a twitching in his left eye and tried to control it. Then the right eye. He closed both of them and tried to compose his thoughts. Something he wasn't going to bring up but it seemed appropriate. "There was another letter. Another letter. Besides the one you found in your office. Besides the letters to the newspaper that Jean took from the reporter's room. There was another letter."

Schwartz cocked his head and tugged on the brim of that ugly Cubs cap. "You didn't tell me about this. Is this a letter you sent to someone? Or someone sent to you?"

Murtz took a deep breath. "You don't know anything about it, right?"

Schwartz looked at his watch. *What the hell did he have going on that was so important?* Murtz pictured himself with his pistol barrel shoved into Harvey's mouth. The smug, calm attorney would finally show some emotion. There would be fear in his eyes. He relished the idea. Slowly, he pulled the trigger.

"I found a letter on the floor of my office, Danny. Jean found copies of letters to the *Tribune*. Other than that I have no idea what you're talking about."

He couldn't trust Harvey. Could never trust Harvey. If he let his guard down for an instant he'd be a dead man, and Harvey would be the one who pulled the trigger. And yet, Harvey was the only one he could trust. Had to trust. Murtz took a deep breath. "It was another threatening letter. I kept it quiet, but now that there are two of them —"

"Another death threat?"

"Yes."

"Jesus."

"You don't even believe in Jesus, Harvey. And the letters are in addition to two phone calls."

The attorney threw his hands up. "What? Why don't I know about all of this?"

"I wonder the same thing. I just get the impression that things are not being handled. Damn it Harvey, I don't want to do this interview. You should have handled the Sever situation. And I think he's behind the letters and the phone calls."

Now it was Schwartz's turn to take a deep breath. "It has not been handled. There was an attempt — several attempts, but the man seems to be blessed with good timing."

"Damn, Harvey. Damn. What if this asshole was Randi Parks's boyfriend? And what if he knows she was with me? And all of a sudden she's disappeared? She might have told him some other stuff —"

"What stuff? What?"

"Nothing. I mean there was some rough stuff, you know. But maybe that was after she made that call. Shit, Harvey, I can't remember, but this guy is here to bust my balls."

"Danny, get a hold of yourself. You've got to do this interview. We need to know where he's going with his questions. We need to find out what he knows. Do you understand that? You're the only one who can talk to him. I'll be right there."

Murtz felt hot tears welling up. This wasn't good. He needed a couple of those pills he kept in his desk. Get Harvey the hell out of the room.

"Danny —"

"That's all, Harvey. You can go."

The attorney stared at him, wide eyed. "I can go?"

"Yes, you can. Now get out of here."

"You're concerned about a threatening letter, you're afraid that Mick Sever may know that you are responsible for Randi Parks's disappearance, you're upset about a couple of phone calls, and now you cavalierly dismiss me?"

Whatever the fuck that meant. "I do. Whatever."

"You're a nut job, Danny."

Maybe now was the time to shove the gun into the prick's mouth. Murtz knew a few things about what a gun could do inside someone's mouth. The Murtz family had a history of guns. And maybe now was the time to pull the trigger. He was screaming. "I'm a rich nut job, Harvey. A very rich nut job who can do just about anything he wants." Murtz ratcheted up the volume, now sobbing as he shouted. "And right now what I want is for you to leave the fucking room." The screeching sound of his own voice was driving him crazy. He yearned for calm, but his voice got louder and shriller. "Get out. Christ, can't you hear me?"

Schwartz gave it a couple of seconds and tears started running down Murtz's cheeks. Somewhat embarrassing.

"Okay. I'm gone." Schwartz walked down the hall and disappeared from sight.

Murtz wiped his face with the back of his hand, stood up, opened the drawer, pulled out the bottle, and poured two pills into his hand. Walking to the bar, he poured some Bacardi into a glass, topped it with a little Coca-Cola, and washed the capsules down. Shit, Mick Sever would be there in about fifteen minutes.

He picked up the receiver and dialed seven. "Nancy! Nancy!" He studied the doorway, waiting for her to make her unannounced entrance. Nothing. Murtz walked to the hall, his legs feeling heavy and unsteady. "Nancy!"

Spinning around, he saw her through his window to the pool. She was arguing with one of the television techs. She was pointing at the white tile where the cables spread out like pythons weaving this way and that. The tech was shrugging his shoulders, letting her know that whatever was bothering her was beyond his control. Murtz opened the door to the pool, holding onto the two sides of the frame for support. Damn, he was woozy.

"Nancy."

She glanced over at him. "Danny, the black cables are leaving scuff marks on the white surface. I simply asked him to lift the cables and put something under them. He refuses.

"Black scuff marks?" He was slurring his words. He knew it, and could do nothing about it.

"They don't just wash off. Look at this." She knelt down, pointing to a black mark on the white deck.

"Shit."

"Yeah. That's what I thought." She glared triumphantly at the technician.

"No, I meant is *that* what is so goddamned important? I've got an interview with Mick Sever in ten minutes. *That's* important! I'm losing my fucking mind. *That's* important. Somebody is trying to bring me down, Nancy, and it had better not be you."

CHAPTER THIRTY-ONE

He'd pulled over twice, both times against the volcanic hillside, thank God. When these trucks and busses came barreling around the turns, you had no choice. Murtz lived up near the top and, although it might be a wonderful view, it was a bitch to get up there.

The roads were filled with potholes, and the temporary road patches did little to ease the ride. The little car bounced and shook, jarring him to the bone even at low speeds. And these drivers. They knew the roads and careened around the switchbacks like Indy drivers taking the turns at the Brickyard track.

He'd borrowed the Clarks' rental car and promised to return it in a couple of hours. Promise may have been too strong a word. Given the history of his last ride, Sever realized he might never be able to guarantee the return of a vehicle again.

When he finally got on the road to Murtz's villa, he slowed down, concentrating on the individual entrances to each residence. Curving driveways wended their way up steep cliffs to hidden homes that were protected with heavy palm, mango, and papaya trees.

The thick green foliage smothered the landscape with a forest green camouflage.

He slammed on the brakes, looking at the next stone driveway. It was close. If this wasn't it, he needed some directions. He should have talked to Mr. B. Hell, *he* seemed to have all the information. Even on this small spit of land, he wished he had a GPS. Sever started up the twisting, turning drive, relieved that the possibility of a bus or truck coming around the bend was unlikely.

He slowed down, negotiating the curves and watching for the villa. Thirty seconds later he saw it, perched high on a peak. To his surprise the villa, or more like a cottage, was small by most standards, but in a very desirable location. A megastar the size of Danny Murtz couldn't live in this tiny abode. Regardless, he pulled up next to the structure and stepped out, stretching his legs. Sever's right leg was, as he saw it, a *bone* of contention. Every day he regretted being stoned out of his mind that night when he jumped from a performance stage in Toronto with Pete Townsend from The Who and mangled his knee joint. Drugs and alcohol had fucked up half his life. Probably ruined the best relationship he'd ever have. And even though he'd shaken the drug habit, he still drank too much. He blamed it on his abusive father, his submissive mother, and an arrested childhood, but deep inside he knew it was a case of overindulgence. Plain and simple. He knew it. The drug habit was gone for the moment, but the other half was much more difficult to negotiate.

Sever knocked on the door. There was a car in the driveway, but no one answered. He walked around to the small pool, looking down at the beach and crystal blue water. There wasn't a bad view on the island. He rapped on the rear door. No answer.

As he turned to walk back to his car he thought he saw a shadow move quickly through a back room. He turned the door handle and the door swung open.

"Hey, anybody home? I need some directions. Anybody?"

From the rear of the small villa he heard her voice. "What do you want?"

"Directions."

"I'm a tourist. I wouldn't be much help. Now would you please leave?"

Sever stood his ground. "Hey, I just need to know which villa is Danny Murtz's."

The girl stepped out from the room, making no effort to approach him. She studied him for a moment.

"And you stopped here to find out where Murtz lives? Of all the places you could stop?"

She was about five two, with honey brown hair that hung loosely around her ears, cute face, and nice figure in jeans and a Margaritaville T-shirt. A little bit of the girl-next-door, but he saw the potential. With a little prep she could be very attractive.

"Yeah. Look, I'm supposed to interview him in, " he checked his Rolex, "five minutes ago. I've got to be close, I just don't know which drive is his."

"Two more. The second one out of here."

"Thanks."

She stayed her distance.

"Do I know you?" Something familiar. He couldn't put his finger on it. It was usually the other way around. People recognized him. From newspaper photos, MTV, *Rolling Stone* articles, and the like.

"No. Now please leave." She turned and walked back into the room.

He stared after her, trying hard to think what was familiar. Finally he left, getting into his car, and driving back out the winding drive. He hoped Danny Murtz wasn't strong on punctuality. He'd never interviewed a celebrity yet that was, but there was always a first time.

CHAPTER THIRTY-TWO

She was shaking. What the hell had she been thinking? She'd been so careful, cutting and dying her hair, no makeup, jeans and Ts, and then this guy says, "Do I know you?" He'd entered the villa, walked right in. She couldn't pretend not to be home. What if he'd walked through the place and found her hiding? Hell, she had to say something.

The girl poured herself a glass of vodka from the kitchen cupboard and drank half of it in one gulp. Calm, patience. The intruder was fishing. There was no way he knew anything. It was a dumb, stupid coincidence that he'd stumbled on her villa. She could live there ten years and no one would ever visit, but he stumbled onto the place needing directions.

She walked out to the pool and looked out over the landscape, feeling the warmth from the drink spread through her. She needed to finish what she'd started. Tonight was the night. Somehow she needed to take care of her problem. She couldn't live like this any longer.

CHAPTER THIRTY-THREE

He pulled up into the circular driveway, almost blinded by the array of red, orange, and yellow bougainvillea that covered the front of the villa. Nancy Steiner met him at the door with an aloof handshake. She wore a yellow cotton summer dress, and her blond hair hung down almost to her shoulders. With a hint of a tan and some light makeup, she was quite attractive and Sever was surprised. He'd expected a much older woman, with gray hair and a heavy build. He was usually pretty good at figuring people out by their voices. Like Mr. B. But he'd missed this one by a mile.

"You'll be talking to Danny out by the pool. Please excuse the mess. As you know, A&E is here to do a television piece, and I'm afraid they've taken over back there."

They walked through the sprawling home, minimally decorated with leather furniture, wicker and rattan chairs and accent pieces, and Murtz's gold and platinum framed records on the walls. It wasn't a guided tour by any means, and the lady bustled through the villa in short order, taking him out the back entrance to the pool. She pointed to the second pool door to the villa. "That's Danny's office. He'll be out in just a moment. Please wait here." She glared at him, as if she wished he had never arrived. And yet she was the one who had set up the appointment. Without another word, she walked back into the home. Sever had the impression she was very protective of her employer.

He'd been on location with television crews before. He recognized the industrial-strength equipment. This was a top-notch operation.

The door opened again and a thin man wearing a Chicago Cubs cap and sunglasses strolled out, carrying a laptop computer.

"You must be Mick Sever." He offered his free hand and Sever shook it.

"If you're Danny Murtz, you've certainly changed."

The man laid the computer on an umbrella table, never smiling. "I'm Harvey Schwartz. I'm Danny's attorney, among other things. He asked that I be here for the interview."

No emotion. Schwartz almost sounded bored with the whole thing.

"That's fine. I hope he didn't feel he *needed* an attorney for this piece." It was going to be difficult to do any probing with the attorney hanging around. Schwartz sat down in the shade of the umbrella and without another word opened the laptop and started working. Sever no longer existed.

Sever walked to the edge of the pool, looking down the cascading hill as the grass, trees, and flowers seemed to tumble free-for-all in a profusion of color to the beach. Hypnotizing. Mesmerizing. He couldn't really take it all in or appreciate it enough. The view was spectacular.

"The vice president of St. Barts spends time on that beach." The voice surprised him.

"And over to the right, by those rocks, there's a cave where a famous pirate captain supposedly hid a large treasure."

Sever turned around and there was Danny Murtz, the legend, the writer, the producer, the woman-beater. Murtz held out his hand and Sever shook it.

"I don't think we've ever met, have we?"

Sever smiled. "No, I don't believe we have." He waited for a hint of recognition.

"So," Murtz motioned to a table, "let's sit down." The famous writer/producer pointed to a chair and closed his eyes for a moment.

He leaned to the right and Sever thought he might collapse, but he straightened himself, nodded to Sever and said, "Harvey, why don't you join us?"

Sever was surprised by the demeanor of the man. He'd expected a reticent recluse who would be less than friendly. Instead, Murtz seemed to be very open to the interview.

"I've asked Raymond to bring us some iced tea. If you'd like something stronger, just let me know."

After the explosion this morning, something stronger would have hit the spot. But he'd had a couple of beers with Jordan Clark at Le Piment and he wanted to be as alert as possible for the interview.

"So, where do you want to start?" Murtz's eyes looked tired. A little bloodshot and drifting, like he was fighting to stay focused. Sever guessed cocaine. He could be wrong, but the general appearance said he was right.

"Let's start at the beginning. I've got your bio . . ." he hesitated. He didn't have the bio anymore. Someone, probably Michelle or one of Murtz's henchmen, had confiscated it. "But I'd like to hear it straight from you. What was the first sign that you were going to make music your career?"

Murtz glanced at his watch. "I've got one hour. That's about all the time we've got." He turned his head and glanced back at the door as Raymond walked out with a pitcher of iced tea and three glasses on a tray. "One hour. And the best you've got is 'let's start at the beginning?' "

"Danny —" Harvey Schwartz was speaking in a parental tone.

"No, Harvey. If the man has something he wants to ask me, then goddamnit, ask me! *Let's start at the beginning*? Isn't that a little bush league? Have you done this before, Mr. Sever?"

Sever was surprised. Obviously Murtz expected some sort of slant on the interview. Maybe he recognized him from last night at Casa Niki? But Sever bet that it was the papers from the Manapany Hotel. They knew what he knew.

"I don't have a specific question for you. Is there something you want to get off *your* chest?"

There was a twitch on the upper lip, and Murtz started blinking fast. Just for a moment, but he obviously was distraught.

"Danny's had a rough day." Schwartz was on his feet, quickly positioning himself between his client and the reporter. "We had a late night, then the crew from A&E has been disrupting things, he had some company earlier, and now your interview. You know, Mr. Sever, with all due respect, I think the timing here is not good."

Murtz stood up, wild-eyed now, with his hands firmly planted on the glass-top table in front of him. "Don't make excuses for me, Harvey. Don't. I want to know what this fucking reporter wants. Do you have specific questions for me? Is there something you'd like to ask me or would you like to make any accusations?"

"Jesus, Danny!"

Sever stood up and stepped back, stumbling on one of the black cables that crisscrossed the white-tiled pool deck. He caught himself on the corner of the table and felt his knee go weak.

"What? What the hell do you want?" Murtz shoved his finger into Sever's chest.

Sever was seldom caught off guard. He could handle almost any situation and probably had. Not this one. He had one question, and it was to be layered into the interview in a very unobtrusive way. Maybe a little mention about Libby Hellman. *Had Murtz heard anything about her?* Or Jennifer Koenig. *Was she still among the missing?* But now what?

Harvey Schwartz took Murtz by the arm, trying to pull him back toward the villa. Murtz turned on him, strongly backhanding him in his face. "You fucker. If you can't handle things for me, then I'll handle them." Schwartz stepped back, his hand massaging his right cheek. He walked quickly toward the back door to the villa.

"Danny, I don't know where this went wrong, but obviously we should do this another time." Sever started walking toward the same door to the villa.

"No. We'll do it now! Goddamn, we'll do it now. What do you want? You ask me your questions."

"All right. You want a question? Here it is, Danny."

Now Sever was pissed. This overblown needy bastard was being a prick just for the hell of it. Drugs or not, it was time to lay the cards on the table.

"In the past seven years at least two of your girlfriends have come up missing. No one has heard anything from them. They're gone, Danny. Does that have anything to do with you? Off hand, I'd say you're a dangerous date."

Raymond and a short little bodybuilder came barreling out of the back door, and Sever backed up again. At his age he was a little past taking on bar bouncers, although at one time in his life he could mix it up with the best of them. For just a second he thought he recognized the short man. Sever's eyes darted in all directions, but there was no way out. The pool fence was too high for climbing and he definitely couldn't stand up to these two muscle-bound freaks.

Headed right toward him, they veered to the right, picking Murtz up under his arms. The producer tried swinging his arms and kicking out with his legs to no avail. They carried him unceremoniously back to the office door and inside.

Harvey Schwartz walked out, a large purple bruise on the side of his face.

"Mr. Sever. I'm sorry for the display. Danny is rather high-strung, and he obviously thought that you had some sort of agenda today."

"The *Tribune* won't be very happy. I've wasted a lot of their money on a trip to nowhere."

"Let me see if I can reschedule this."

"Do you think that's possible?" Sever pointed toward the office window.

"I think if you can stick around for a couple of days it could be arranged. Can you do that, Mr. Sever? It would mean a lot to me. I'd like to make this up to you."

Sever studied the attorney. For the first time he noticed a trace of zinc oxide on Swartz's nose. The cap, the sunglasses, the zinc oxide, and a long-sleeved shirt. The man didn't take any chances.

"I'll talk to my editor."

"Wonderful. May I show you out?"

They walked silently into the villa and back to the front of the home. There was no sign of the two bodyguards or Murtz.

"Harvey, I'm here for one reason. To interview Murtz. So in that context, I'm trying to explain what happened this morning. Maybe you can help me."

It just came out. His emotions were on the edge, and Danny Murtz had pushed him to that brink. He decided, in an instant, to put everything on the table, right or wrong. "Someone tried to kill me."

"Kill you?"

"Kill me."

"Really?"

"Really."

"They shot at you?"

"No, they blew up my car." From behind Schwartz's mirrored sunglasses Sever could feel the cold stare.

"And you called the police?"

"I did."

"Did *they* think this incident was because you're here to interview Danny?"

"They said it could have been a faulty engine, and they hauled away all the evidence."

Schwartz nodded. "And what do you think?"

"I'm here for one reason. And if someone doesn't want me here, they could just as easily have bought my return ticket to the States. Harvey, I'm not a confrontational person by nature."

"I asked you what you thought happened."

"I bring it to you. I'm here to interview your client and someone blows up my car. Why?"

"What did the law enforcement agents say?"

"I told you, they said it was a faulty engine."

"Maybe that's exactly what it was. A faulty engine. Sometimes, Mr. Sever, things are *exactly* as they appear."

CHAPTER THIRTY-FOUR

Mr. B. made him a simple vodka and grapefruit. To be fair, it wasn't simple. He squeezed the fresh grapefruit, then suggested Armadale vodka. "Armadale is owned by the American singer, Jay-Z. So it is a perfect drink for a man who writes about music celebrities. And I think you will like the finish on this vodka."

Shivering cold, the drink went down smooth, helping him relax a little from the eventful afternoon.

"My friend, you look like someone who really needed a stiff drink."

"Mr. B., you have no idea. My car blew up this morning."

The bartender dropped the knife from his hand. "Pardon?"

"My car exploded at Eden Rock."

"Mon Dieu, are you all right?"

"I had just stepped out of the car."

"Thank God, my friend. A real explosion?"

"A big ball of fire."

"And what caused this ball of fire?"

"The police say it was a faulty engine. I think someone rigged it while we were having breakfast."

"We?"

"Have you seen Michelle?"

"No. Surely you don't think —"

"I don't know what to think. I was delayed by a couple from

Puerto Rico. If it hadn't been for them, I wouldn't be here. And Michelle said that someone asked about me just moments before I went to the car. And she left early. So —"

"It's entirely possible it was a faulty engine, Mr. Sever."

"Yeah. That's possible."

"Seriously, you should not make accusations until you have proof. Even then, it's not always a good idea."

Sever took a long, cool drink. "I've been told that there are never any murders on the island. Is that true?"

Mr. B. poured an amber-colored liquid into a mixing glass, finishing it off with two shots of rum. He smiled at a waitress as he garnished the drink with a slice of pineapple.

"Ah, mon ami, there is nothing here but fun, sun, and rum. No worries, no cares on St. Barts." He gave Sever a big grin.

"But you haven't seen Michelle?"

"No. Perhaps Mr. Murtz decided to entertain her."

Sever took another slow sip of his drink. He leaned in, catching Bertrand's eyes. "Mr. B., what do you really know about her?"

He stared back, a cool, calm gaze. "She would not cause you or your car any damage. And one more thing."

"What? Tell me."

"She is not from Atlanta. She is from Chicago. I'd stake my bartender reputation on it."

Sever drained the vodka and tossed a nice tip on the bar. He made his exit and walked back up the winding road to his room. He probably owed his editor a call.

He'd told Harvey Schwartz he'd try to stick around a couple more days, but it hardly seemed worth the time. Sever figured that if he were a target, it would just give someone more time to find a way for him to have a fatal accident. From the moment he'd accepted the Danny Murtz assignment his life had been in danger. Someone had almost run him over in Chicago, his car had exploded in St. Barts, and he wasn't very anxious to see what the next encounter would be.

CHAPTER THIRTY-FIVE

Danny Murtz sipped a rum and Coke, looking at the sparkling sea through a pair of dark sunglasses. Even with the subdued lighting effect, his eyes hurt. He listened to the water gurgle in the pool as the pump gently hummed.

He'd gotten a little nuts with that reporter, Sever, Randi Parks' friend. And to the best of his recollection, he hadn't found out whether Sever had talked to Randi the night of her untimely accident. But he did remember, quite clearly, that Sever accused him of being involved in the disappearance of two girls. So it was clear, without a doubt, that someone was putting this all together. Someone was trying to get some damning evidence on him. And if the threatening letters he'd received, the phone calls, the letters to the *Chicago Tribune*, and the snooping, conniving bitch in the guest cottage weren't enough, this damned reporter was the icing on the cake. Of course, Sever was trying to make a case. But the writer didn't seem bright enough to figure it out himself. Someone else was responsible. And there was only one person who knew all the facts. Oh, Sever needed to be eliminated, but somehow Murtz had to make certain that Harvey never gave up the evidence. He couldn't be certain that Harvey wasn't pulling all the strings. Harvey brought the second threatening letter to him. Harvey told him about the letters to the Chicago newspaper, and it was Harvey who claimed that Randi Parks had called Sever just before she died. Harvey. Maybe

Harvey was the primary puppet master. Harvey, trying to suck more and more of Murtz's money, his career, his blood.

What if Harvey gave Sever all the information? Maybe Sever was just a stupid pawn.

His head hurt from all the possibilities.

"Jean."

The short, stocky bodybuilder stood up from his chair and walked to Murtz's side. "Mr. Murtz, what can I do for you?"

Jean. Little Jean, who'd been with him for two years. Jean had helped with the Randi Parks cleanup. Murtz wondered what Jean thought about him. Even the little guy knew more than he should. In the long run it didn't really matter. He either paid them off or found a way to get rid of them. Celebrity gets a pass. "Jean, bring me a pad of paper and a pen."

"Right, Mr. Murtz."

"And, Jean,"

"Yes, sir?"

"A rum and Coke. Just a splash of Coke."

Jean walked away quickly. Always in a hurry to do his job. Someone you could trust. Someone who knew his place.

Jean made it back in record time, putting a coaster and a fresh drink on Murtz's table. He handed the producer a legal pad and pen, then retreated to his chair, fifteen feet away. Always awake, always alert, with his gun on the table in front of him.

Murtz took a sip, determined to go slow. Make a list. This Jennifer Koenig — actually he couldn't remember. She'd disappeared, but he didn't remember any accident. Oh, he'd roughed her up. But an accident? If memory served, and his memory wasn't what it used to be, she just dropped out of sight one day. Harvey had said he'd made sure she wouldn't be heard from again.

Of course, there was Randi Parks, the *American Idol* girl, a little too recent to forget. And Frank Simonetti's little girl, Shelley O'Dell. And Libby Hellman. What the hell happened to her? Ah yes, he'd been showing her his gun collection. Lots of blood. That didn't go well at all. He hated it when they bled.

He jotted them all down on the paper in front of him. While he should be concentrating on arrangements, selection of music, and creative ideas for the Indoorfins, he was trying to save his life. While he should be listening to other producers, trying to steal ideas and songs, he was busy figuring out who was trying to sabotage his career. It seemed more important. A lot more important.

And yet, he surprised himself. He was relaxed. He felt like a balance had been reached, one that left him somewhat melancholy. He could reflect without becoming too emotional, remember without becoming attached to the memory. These were the times he liked best. In maybe half an hour he'd need a little booster. He'd have to think about it for a while. Decide what mix would keep him at this blissful state.

One thing that crossed his mind, one thing he kept coming back to, one thing that threatened to destroy the rapture that he'd found, was Mick Sever. Somebody had to deal with the son of a bitch. Harvey had blown it. He'd tried to take Sever out, and the reporter was waltzing around St. Barts like he owned it, throwing accusations at Murtz as if he knew exactly what happened. Harvey had totally blown it. So what could be done?

Murtz picked up the phone and dialed seven. "Nancy!"

"Yes, Danny." She answered the phone this time.

"Get me Harvey. Right now."

She paused. "Listening to the tone of your voice, apparently we have yet another problem with Harvey?"

"Just get him, damn it." He'd figured it out. She wanted the power that Harvey had. And he'd be happier if they both just disappeared. Either the arrogant asshole would get the job done, or Murtz would do it for him like he did one time on the island when a hot-shit twenty-something stud had tried to move in on a young girl Murtz was hustling. The kid mocked him, telling him he was an old man. Harvey refused to deal with the situation, so Murtz dealt with it himself. The kid disappeared in one of the salt ponds near Saline Beach, where the smell of rotting foliage masked the odor of the young man's rotting flesh. Oh, Harvey covered for him. He made certain that Murtz wasn't implicated in the young man's disappearance. But Harvey couldn't handle the deed himself. So Murtz had shot the asshole, about six times if he remembered right. In the chest, and of course in the mouth. Put the barrel of the gun at the roof of the scumbag's mouth and blew out the back of his head. The punk had fallen into the muck where salt was once mined, and was stuck in the muck. Officially stuck in the muck. But Harvey hadn't had the balls to do the deed. And now, he didn't have the balls to get rid of Sever.

A friend of the young man, some bartender at a hotel, had openly questioned Murtz. The fucker had gone to the authorities and made a case that Murtz or Schwartz had killed his *copain*. Killed his good friend. The gendarmes explained to the bartender that no one had ever been murdered on this island. There was no body, no evidence at all. Only Murtz knew where the kid was. Stuck in the muck. That was all, because no one had ever been murdered on the island. Ever. Murders weren't good for tourism.

Schwartz walked into the office, his ball cap still pulled tightly over his bald head as if there was an indoor sun that would burn his flesh to a crisp.

"Harvey, Sever may have sent the threatening letters."

Schwartz looked puzzled. "This was the first time he's been here, Danny. How did he get the letters into the house?"

"Well then, you, Nancy, Raymond, or Jean must have written the letters, because you're the only ones who are always in the house. How about you, Harvey. I think that you are my prime suspect. I mean, if you convince me that there is pressure, then you can demand more money." Murtz took a deep breath. He was exhausted. "How much money do you need, Harvey? Jesus! You don't even have a life, so what would you spend it all on anyway?"

Harvey tugged the brim of his cap. The son of a bitch remained his usual calm, cool self. "Maybe you wrote those letters, Danny. Maybe it's your way to make everyone pay a little more attention to you."

"You crazy fucker. You think I would write threatening letters to myself?"

"Yes, I do." He really meant it.

"Someone sent me two threatening letters. It could be Sever. I don't know how, but it could be." He sat in his leather chair, staring at the pale attorney.

Recognition seemed to dawn on Schwartz. "Did that first letter mention Randi Parks?"

"No. But the writer said that they knew I'd killed Jennifer Koenig. And they were going to deal with their own brand of justice. You heard Sever. He asked if I'd been responsible for the disappearance of—"

"I know, I know." Schwartz let out a long sigh. "You know a little bit about that yourself— dealing with your own brand of justice."

"Damn right I do. He accused me, Harvey. He sat there and said I was responsible for the disappearance of two girls."

The lawyer bobbed his head. Like a fucking bobble doll. It irritated Murtz. "So, Harvey, it makes sense that he wrote the letters. He knows or someone set him up."

"Maybe he's fishing, Danny. And what do you want me to do about it?"

"Did Jennifer Koenig have an accident?"

Schwartz closed his eyes for a moment and massaged the eyelids with his thumbs.

"Did she?"

"Jennifer threatened to have you arrested. She had —" he paused, his eyes wandering around the room, "information on another accident, and if you remember, you beat her up pretty good. We had to do something to keep her quiet."

"Money? Did we pay her off?"

"We took care of the situation, Danny. Have you been arrested?"

"No. But you've always told me you made sure she wouldn't talk. What the hell happened to her?"

"Then why not leave it alone?"

"Because," the smug asshole, staring at him like he was a child, "someone sent me those letters."

"Give me the first letter."

It was Harvey's calm that bothered him the most. You couldn't trust someone who was always calm and collected. You *knew* someone who was emotional, someone who had some passion. You could read them like a book. This sanctimonious prick, this asshole lawyer, just played as judge and jury, and Murtz couldn't take much more of that.

"Danny, where's this threatening letter?"

Where the hell had he put it? In a file? No. He never filed anything. In a drawer? No. Not much in the drawers except his stash. He'd thrown it away. Focus. Focus. Ah, threw it into the trashcan. No, it didn't make the trashcan. He glanced at the floor. Someone had cleaned. The letter was gone.

"I don't have it."

"Shit, Danny. I can't deal with it if I can't see it."

"I can't produce it." Murtz was steaming, starting to boil over. Harvey was at the heart of the problem. "Drop the subject. What about Sever? Are you ever, ever going to do something about that?"

"All right, you fucked up that interview big time. You fucked it up, Danny. But, I'm going to handle it. Here's what we're going to do. I'm going to call Sever."

"And?"

"Your band, the Fins, or whatever they're called, are setting up by the pool tonight. Tomorrow morning A&E, you, and the band will be filmed. It's going to be busier than hell."

"Could we cancel all this shit?"

"No. However, I want to call Sever and have him come over tonight. After the band sets up. When it's quiet and we can just talk."

"Harvey, I'm in no shape to see him. He knows about Randi Parks, and he knows about the *Tribune* letters, and he may have sent me the letters. I can't deal with_"

"That's the beauty of this, Danny. You don't have to. I'll apologize for this afternoon and I'll do the interview."

"You?"

"Me."

"And you can find out about Randi Parks and the letter and all of that stuff." He smiled, breathing a sigh of relief.

"Leave it to me, Danny. But rest assured, it will cost you."

Murtz rolled his eyes, the faint smile leaving his lips. "It always costs me. You're setting this up, aren't you? I was right. You're doing this to get more money."

Schwartz gave him a two-second glance and spun around, walking out of the room.

"Harvey. Get back in here."

He kept walking.

"Get back in here or you're off the payroll, I swear to God."

The attorney stopped, turned, and walked as far as the entrance. "I can't do this anymore, Danny."

Murtz swallowed his pride. Not an easy task. "What do you suggest?"

"You always get yourself into more shit than you can get out of."

Murtz tried to stare him down, but gave up after several seconds.

"When are the Indoorfins setting up?"

"Around six."

Schwartz folded his arms over his chest, looking down at Murtz in his lounge chair. "I'm going to ask Sever to stop by about eight. We'll sit out here. I'll talk about whatever he wants to discuss, and I'll ask the questions that need to be asked. If we've got a problem with the superstar reporter, I'll know. And, I'll find a way to deal with it. Okay?"

"I'm tired, Harvey. Tired."

"Yeah. We're all tired, Danny. Tired of trying to bail you out."

Murtz reached down beside his chair, picking up an FN 9-millimeter pistol he'd laid beside him on the floor, one of the latest acquisitions to his growing collection. He laid it in his lap and squinted at the lawyer. "You prick. If I didn't need you —"

"But you do."

"There are times —"

"You need me Danny. More than you could possibly know."

CHAPTER THIRTY-SIX

A band was setting up on the far side of the pool, overlooking the ocean. Roadies set gigantic speaker cabinets, shiny, chrome microphone stands, and recording equipment on the deck. Heavy black cables and wires were laid down with precision. The girl watched, wondering what new band was going to receive the blessing of the all-powerful Danny Murtz now. The Murtz Magic Show was about to begin.

She was surprised that Murtz had enough sober moments in his day to actually perform his magic. Maybe there wasn't any more of the famed sorcery. Maybe the wizard was no more. He hadn't had a group or a hit in several years. Possibly the drugs and alcohol had finally taken their toll. No. He was a wizard. Everything he touched turned to gold, except his women. They just disappeared. Her friend Libby Hellman was gone. No question about it, she was dead. No e-mails, no text messaging, nothing. The last communication was clear.

> Danny Murtz is crazy. He's threatened me and I seriously think he'd kill me if I gave him a chance. I'm scared for my life!

Every girl Murtz dated should be scared for her life. And scared of the power of Harvey Schwartz.

She trained the field glasses on Murtz's office window, the one looking out over the pool. The other one looked over the hillside, down to the ocean. She'd give anything to peer into the office and see what elixir he was mixing up.

Six o'clock. She may as well take a nap. This time she was going to finish the job, get the computer and try to drive Danny Murtz over the edge. If they caught her, they'd kill her. But they had to catch her first. The girl walked back to the bedroom. She'd probably have to stay up pretty late to get it all done.

CHAPTER THIRTY-SEVEN

Jeff Bloomfield had been disappointed. And, to be fair, somewhat concerned for Sever's well-being. However, he'd asked him to stick it out.

"Let's give it a try, Mick. If his attorney says he can get you back in for a second interview, then stick around until you've exhausted the possibilities."

"It's your money, Jeff."

"We still think we've got a story. You just need to get a better feel for his guilt or innocence."

"Jeff, I don't want to make a big deal out of it, but somebody stole my notes from the hotel."

"What?"

"The file you gave me. It's gone."

"The copies of the letters we received?"

"Those too."

Bloomfield let out a sigh. "I'd say we've been compromised."

"Well, it evened the playing field. Murtz was prepared for the question. He kept waiting for me to drop the hammer, egging me on."

"You're sure they have the papers."

"As sure as I can be. There's one other possibility, a girl I met who is interested in the story as well."

"Mick, are you telling me we have competition for this angle?"

"It's too early to tell. But I think Murtz and company are protecting themselves."

"So, you think he's guilty? Do you think we can get the facts?"

"I think Murtz is nuttier than a fruitcake. He's high on cocaine, and there's absolutely no way to tell what he may or may not have done. Even if they took the file —"

"Work on it, Mick. I know you'll get the job done."

Whatever the job was. Sever hung up and called his answering machine. The phone just rang and rang. No answer. He returned the receiver to its cradle.

When the phone rang an instant later, he thought it must be Bloomfield again. "Mr. Sever, this is Nancy Steiner. I'm calling from Danny Murtz's residence."

"Yes?"

"Harvey Schwartz has asked me to call you and see if you could be free at eight this evening. He would like to reschedule an interview at that time."

Yes. Yes. But, don't sound too eager. This was just a little too soon. Sever had a feeling that something wasn't quite right. "Can I get back to you?"

"Mr. Sever, it is almost six thirty. I'd like an answer now so the staff can make arrangements." Controlling. Demanding. Hell, two could play that game.

"Ms. Steiner, I'll call you back after I've checked my schedule." Sever hung up the phone, hoping he hadn't screwed it all up. Something seemed too pat, too convenient. There was a catch and he wanted to be in charge, not let them make the call.

Sever flipped on the television, caught a Spanish game show playing from St. Martin, watched two commercials that he didn't understand at all, then called Murtz's villa.

"Danny Murtz's, can I help you?"

"Nancy?"

"Yes." Frosty and stern.

"Listen, I can make it about eight forty-five. Will that time work?"

He heard her talking to someone in a quiet, muffled voice. She'd placed her hand over the receiver.

"We would prefer the interview be earlier, but it's all right. If you can please arrive at about eight thirty we would appreciate it."

Sever walked down to the bar, hoping Mr. B. was still on duty. An early dinner crowd was in the restaurant and the bar was packed except for a stool at the end.

"Mr. Sever. Back for some more of the good stuff?" Bertrand gave him a broad smile. He sliced a lemon in half and hand-squeezed the sour fruit into a frothy green libation. Setting the drink in front of a dark-skinned girl who looked fifteen, he immediately grabbed a mixing glass, set it firmly on his counter, and poured from two bottles of rum simultaneously into the stainless-steel vessel.

"Tell me, Mr. B., you said something during our first conversation about dealing with Danny Murtz. You said you knew someone who thought they could take care of themselves and it turned out they couldn't."

Bertrand nodded, busily mixing his next concoction.

"Can you elaborate?"

"As you can see, I am very busy at the moment."

"Did someone die? Was Murtz responsible for someone's disappearance?"

"Mr. Sever, I have a bar full of customers. A roomful of diners. What is it you want? To tell terrible stories about an island of pleasant fantasies? This is St. Barts. I am sorry if I misled you. I'm sorry I misled you about Danny Murtz, about Michelle. I need to, how do you say it, put a filter on my words."

"A filter on your words?"

"Mr. Sever, I live here. It has been brought to my attention that life here is very good. I have nothing left to say."

"What? Someone is threatening you?"

"There is a little man named Jean who reminded me that things can be quite pleasant here. And most of the time, they are." He spun around, wiping his hands on his apron. A moment later Sever saw him talking to a second bartender who immediately came down and started mixing drinks. Mr. B. walked out from behind the bar, around the corner, and disappeared from sight.

By the time Sever left, half an hour later, Mr. B. had not reappeared.

CHAPTER THIRTY-EIGHT

It wasn't cool, but the blistering heat had let up a little, and with the windows open, Sever could feel a slight breeze blowing through the new rental car. Budget had delivered the vehicle, apologizing profusely for engine trouble with the first car. *Engine trouble?* He still couldn't believe the attitude.

The daylight was dwindling, and even though he could see well enough, he turned on the low beams and drove the road slowly, counting the driveways. Only once did Sever pull over when a truck rounded a curve, its headlights blinding him for a moment. He passed the villa where he'd asked directions, still thinking about how familiar the girl looked. The car bounced into and out of the potholes, the beams highlighting gray concrete shells of long-forgotten building projects, weeds and palmettos growing over the construction sites. Murtz's driveway was just ahead and he pulled in.

Nancy met him at the door, a frown on her face. "I would have appreciated it if you could have arrived earlier." Staring daggers at him.

She ushered him inside, marching down the hall. This time she wore a long gray skirt and a white linen blouse buttoned tightly at the neck. All signs of sexy had disappeared. When they reached the pool, she opened the door, let him pass through, and she was gone.

New equipment was set up on the pool deck. Amps and speakers, microphones and guitar stands. He tried to think what band Bloomfield had mentioned Murtz was working with. Fins? Indoorfins. That was it. That was the reason that Murtz had come over, to work with this new group.

"Mr. Sever."

"Mr. Schwartz, we meet again."

"Hopefully on better terms." Schwartz reached out and shook his hand.

"Danny's had a little time to calm down?"

"Actually Danny has some other obligations. Tomorrow is a big day with the television interview and the band will be —"

"Then what am I doing here?" Sever had been outmaneuvered.

"Hopefully you're going to get an interview."

Sever watched the attorney's eyes, looking for some sign of deception. "But you just said —"

"You're going to interview me. I can answer most of your questions and those that I can't answer I'll take to Danny. We'll get back to you in a couple of days."

Sever shook his head. "It's bullshit."

"But it's the best you'll get."

"I should leave. Now."

"But you won't, Mr. Sever, because you've got a lot of questions, and without Danny here we can actually discuss some of those questions in a very sane and civil manner. I'm afraid that's something you wouldn't get if Danny were here."

"Can I quote you on that?"

"I'll deny I ever said it."

Sever couldn't help it. He smiled. Schwartz had it all figured out. "What the hell, let's go for it."

Schwartz glanced back at the villa. "Jean. Could you bring us a couple of Dewar's and sodas?"

"That's my —"

"I know." Schwartz gave a tug on the bill of his cap. "I thought it would be a perfect way to start the evening."

Two hours later they stopped talking, after three Scotch and sodas, and more dialogue than Sever could document. It was the first break in a conversation that wanted never to end. The interview was almost a bond, where two strangers found they had so much in common that they should have met years ago. Schwartz knew the business, and understood the power of celebrity. He approached his job with a strong dose of reality, even though he admitted that his client did not. The situation was comfortable, friendly, and Sever somehow wished they'd met years ago. But they hadn't. They met because Sever was charged with getting a confession, of sorts, from Danny Murtz, and as yet that hadn't been accomplished.

The moon was up, the night air still humid, but Sever preferred it to a frigid air-conditioned room. "Mick, I want to ask you something off the record. Will you honor that?"

"Sure."

"You asked Danny if he was responsible for the disappearance of several girls he'd been dating."

"I did. He was pushing me, and that was one of the questions I wanted to ask."

"First of all, did you really think he was going to say yes?"

"I didn't expect an answer. I expected a reaction."

Schwartz tugged on the bill of his Chicago Cubs hat for the twentieth time. "And what kind of a reaction did you get?"

Sipping the last of his Scotch, Sever gave the answer plenty of time. Finally he said, "I think there's something to it."

"You've got balls, asking the question, then telling me that you believe it's true. I can tell you, you're wrong. I can tell you that with total certainty. I basically live with the man, sometimes," he gestured to the house with his arm, "sometimes twenty-four hours a day. What you heard, or thought you heard today, was our boy with a head full of cocaine, a belly full of booze, and probably a couple of joints before you showed up. I told you I'd be truthful. But don't ever print that, Sever. It's off the record." He stood up, again tugging on the brim of the cap. "There is no admission of guilt. Not a hint."

In the moonlight, Sever tried to read Schwartz's face.

"So we're clear on that?" The attorney pressed.

It was at that moment that Sever felt certain Murtz was guilty. The interview, without Murtz, had been a sham. And it was at that moment, even though he could feel the Scotch in his veins, in his brain, that he felt certain someone associated with Danny Murtz had tried to kill him. Someone in this organization had tried to blow him up. And maybe someone in this organization had tried to have him run over in Chicago. And other than his interest in the disappearing girls, he didn't have a clue why they wanted him dead.

"Mick? I asked if you understand how serious I am about this."

He'd been through this before. An agent, a manager, a handler would try to spin the interview, sometimes almost pleading for the direction of the story. It was time to bail. He stood up, carefully stretching his bad knee. Reaching out his hand, he took Schwartz's limp hand and shook it. "Thanks for the interview. I really need to be going."

Deck lights had come on, casting eerie shadows over the pool area. The attorney held his hand up. "Let me ask you something. Do you think you know something?"

"What?"

"I sense that you feel you've got some information, something maybe you can share with me?"

"Look, Harvey, I've got my job to do and you've got yours. We may be at odds here but —" Sever wanted to bring up the stolen papers. He wanted to tell the smug attorney that they shared the same information. But he couldn't. It was all so strange. Harvey Schwartz knew exactly where Sever got his information, but they both had to play the game.

"What makes you think that Danny is responsible for the alleged disappearance of a couple of women?"

Alleged. Lawyer talk. "Harvey, I came here to interview your client. Obviously, that's not going to happen. You talked me into the interview we're now having. I feel compelled to at least broach the subject when I write the story."

"You're an asshole." For a little guy, Schwartz was the one with balls. He walked up to Sever, clearly four inches shorter than the journalist, and shoved his finger into Sever's chest. "Sever, if you allude to the fact that Danny may have been responsible for the disappearance of anyone, anyone at all, we'll sue you, we'll sue the *Tribune*, we'll come down on you like a ton of bricks."

Sever pushed him away, wondering where the even-tempered, demure man of just a moment ago had gone.

"This was a hatchet job, plain and simple!"

"Maybe if your client hadn't gone berserk during our interview we could have had a civil conversation and a good story."

"Forget it." Schwartz shut down. His head dropped, his previously flaying arms were at rest by his side. "Please, forget all of this." The lawyer collapsed into his chair, his chin resting on his chest. For a moment it appeared he'd passed out.

Sever smiled. It was forced, but it was a smile. "I think it's time I left." Christ, eleven o'clock.

"Mick, he's my client. My friend. I can't defend everything he does, but he's not someone who is a murderer." Schwartz's voice was cracking and Sever thought there was a chance he was going to break into tears. "He's not involved in the disappearance of anyone. Please, understand. Off the record, he's a little kid. Danny has never had to grow up. Everything he's wanted since he was a teenager has been provided. So I protect him. That's my job, one of many, but it's also something I feel I need to do."

Sever edged toward the door. Get through the pool door, into the house, through the maze of rooms, and out to his new rental car. That was his goal.

"Please, let's not have a negative story out there."

Sever kept moving toward the door. Schwartz followed.

"Tell me you're not going to use that as part of your story. Tell me."

"Harvey, I have no idea at this time what I'm going to write about. Let me consider everything we've talked about. I need time to reflect."

"Reflect? Okay, Mick. You *reflect*." There was a bitterness in his voice. "We had a nice conversation. However it turns out, nothing personal, okay? Go on, reflect."

A threat. Sever recognized it. Possibly Schwartz didn't even realize he'd said it, but there was the threat. Hell, he'd been threatened before. There'd been attempts on his life. He'd survived. But a cat only has nine lives and he was afraid his lives might be running out.

CHAPTER THIRTY-NINE

Murtz knocked softly on the door with the thick roll of packing tape. More for amusement than any concern for the person on the other side. "You up?" Opening the door, he walked into the room and was somewhat relieved to see her eyes wide open.

"What the hell are you doing? What is wrong with you?" She'd become a little feisty since the last time he'd seen her.

Murtz shook his finger at her in a scolding fashion. "Is this the lady who said 'Danny, I'm sorry. I didn't know what these papers were. Danny, I didn't see anything?' Now it's 'What the hell is wrong with you?' "

"Look, take these cords off of me, let me go, and I'll never mention this again. I promise you, Danny. Please, let me go."

"It's tempting, but I don't think so. You're part of this conspiracy, and I can't let you go. Sorry."

"What conspiracy? What are you talking about?"

He tore off eight inches of the heavy tape. "You call me and beg me to bring you here. Then you find a reason to go through my papers. Personal stuff, Michelle."

"Danny, it was a mistake. There is no conspiracy."

"But I was out by the pool, enjoying the sunshine, the blue sky, and all of a sudden it hit me."

"What? What hit you? Tell me."

"The other night at Casa Niki. You were there."

He saw the raw fear in her eyes. Caked blood smeared on her face, her nose swollen, and her eyes as big as saucers. She knew he'd figured it out. "Danny, I —"

"You were with the reporter, Sever. The two of you are trying to take me down, Michelle, and of course, I can't let that happen."

"My God, he's just a guy who's staying at the hotel. That's all. You were out with your little group and —"

He bent down and stretched the tape over her mouth, pushing the edges over her cheeks as she twisted and turned. "Now, you think about it, and the next time I come back here I want to know who you are, who you work for, and what you and Sever are trying to accomplish. And maybe you'll even tell me if Harvey is setting all of this up. I will get the information. Do you understand?"

She gurgled and moaned as he walked out of the room. It was too bad about the situation. She was a cut above the girls he usually dated, and he would have enjoyed seeing where this relationship was headed.

He didn't trust any of them. Not even Nancy. A wild fling and a lifelong relationship. Maybe she still resented his rebuff of their romantic spree, and was trying for the ultimate payback. Could be. Hell, he'd supported her for twenty-five years and pretty much given *the boy,* her precious son, a lifetime career. But you just couldn't trust anyone.

Tomorrow he had to work with the rock band, deal with the A&E team, and keep his sanity. That seemed a real priority. It seemed to be slipping away fast.

CHAPTER FORTY

He stepped out into the warm, humid, evening air. Harvey Schwartz had left him with one more word of caution. Hell, it was one more threat and no less than that. Sever was afraid to start the car. He almost felt like a kid again. When he was a teenager, there were many nights he was afraid. Afraid to go home. Afraid to open the door. Not for something he'd done, but because of his father's alcoholic rages. The old man was a mean drunk, and most nights he came home with one too many drinks in his system. So Sever stayed out late, letting his docile mother take the punishment. He'd try to slip in under the radar, either late at night or during a loud parental argument. Sometimes it worked, oftentimes it didn't. When it didn't, his father would assault him, verbally and physically, and after all the years of adult life and uplifting accolades from his peers, he often felt like that young teen who was afraid of opening the door.

He cautiously walked down the cobblestone driveway, taking deep breaths, letting his anxiety evaporate. For just a brief second he caught a movement from the corner of his eye. Off to the left, twenty feet, something darted. It was behind a palm tree, one of the three-trunk ornamental trees. Big enough to be a deer or a big dog. Small enough to be a short man, like the one he'd seen kneeling by his car at the Manapany Hotel. Like Murtz's short bodyguard.

Sever stopped for only a brief second. Then he continued his brisk walk, approaching the car. He walked to the driver's side, ducked down, and still in a crouch, stepped to the rear of the automobile. His bad knee ached as the tendons stretched. He could now make out the outline of a person, crouched as well, behind the palm. The first thought that crossed his mind was that someone was trying again to kill him. He paused. If this person had a gun, standing up would make him a prime target. Even in the dark, his silhouette would be easy to see. Sever measured the distance. He was twenty feet from the tree. Reaching down, he found a large round pebble. He threw it off to the left, then started running as the stone hit the ground. He was close enough to see the other person whip his head around, following the sound of the stone. By the time the figure had turned his head again, Sever was on him.

Sever leaped at his stalker. Wrapping his arms around the person, he pulled him down with a thud, immediately startled at the tiny body, the slight figure, and the almost weightlessness of the person under him.

"Stop. Get the hell off of me." A girl.

"What are you doing here?"

"It's none of your goddamned business."

He slowly let go, rolling over, and trying to stand up. His knee had cramped up and he couldn't straighten it out.

The girl pushed herself up, towering over him. She leaned down, offering her hand, and he took it as she pulled him up. Now she was at least a foot shorter than he was.

"Thanks." Sever brushed himself off.

"What the hell was that all about?" It was the girl from the other villa. She was speaking in hushed tones.

"You're slinking around, hiding behind the trees, the shrubs —"

"I'm . . ." she stammered, "I was —" she looked into his face. "You're the reporter. You're the one who came over here to add another layer to Danny Murtz's already stellar résumé. And how did that work out?"

Sever stared back at her. He knew the face. Somehow he knew that face. "Changing the subject?"

"Fuck you. You had no right to jump me like that."

"I'm sorry. I *am* a little jumpy. Someone tried to kill me since I've been here, and I thought that maybe —"

"What? That I was going to kill you?" She stepped back, as if trying to melt into the dark shadows.

"Are you a singer? Were you with a band? You were weren't you? You had a hit record?"

She took three more steps back, then turned and disappeared into the trees. He seriously considered going after her, but he knew where she lived. What had she been doing sneaking around Murtz's property? It was going to come to him in the middle of the night. He'd be sleeping and all of a sudden he'd bolt straight up and remember who the young girl was. It was important to remember. He wasn't sure why, but he knew it was important.

He started the car and just for a moment thought about jumping out and running as far as he could. If this one exploded, the rental company needed to look at getting a whole new fleet.

CHAPTER FORTY-ONE

She emptied the drawer into her suitcase. Screw the folding, the sorting, the meticulous way she packed. Her eyes darted around the small room. An alarm clock. She chucked it into the open luggage. Rummaging through the closet, she crumpled up the four or five tops, a ragged pair of jeans, and a couple pairs of shorts. Piling them into the suitcase, she forced the top down, zipping the bag closed. Nothing else came to view.

She took the carry-on and walked into the bathroom. A razor, hair dryer, toothpaste, and brush. Some basic makeup — a girl still had some pride — deodorant and her birth control pills. Why did she take these things religiously? What the hell had she been thinking? That she'd need them? She'd met one person from the time she moved into the cottage. The reporter. Chances were slim she'd have sex with him.

Finally she'd cleaned the place out. Not much to clean, but she didn't want anything left behind. She gave the small bungalow one final glance and walked out to the car. She opened the trunk and tossed the luggage into the open space.

Now what? Go home? Leave paradise and call it quits? This was her life. This was her future, her past, her present. Everything in her life revolved around what happened here and now.

She could sleep in the car, clean up in a public restroom, and still keep an eye on the place by parking just up the road. There were two or three villas that never seemed to be occupied. Owned by rich Americans or French or Canadians, these palaces were obviously very vacant. The worst that ever happened to them was that some teenage kids from St. Barts would break in and steal some of the decorations.

It was a plan.

The son of a bitch reporter had blown her previous plan. Now she was on the run. She could picture him knocking on her door, trapping her inside the villa, and forcing her to answer his questions.

She started the engine and tried to picture the road and the driveways where she knew no one was home. Actually, there was a large villa just two residences away on the other side of Murtz's. She'd scoped them all out and this place had shown no signs of life. She pulled out of the driveway, saluted the cigar-smoking neighbor's residence, and drove down the road past Danny Murtz's palatial home. Cautiously, she pulled into the driveway about a quarter of a mile from Murtz's villa. There was no sign of anyone living there. Hell, maybe she could break in and live in the lap of luxury for a few more days.

No cars in the circular drive, no lights, no sign of anything or anyone. Chances were that the owner either rented it out or had gone home at the end of season. It was April and they probably wouldn't be back until next November. She sat quietly, waiting for some sign of life. Finally, she opened the door and stepped from the car. She'd decided. Break a window and go inside. If an alarm sounded, she could get out long before the cops arrived. If no alarm sounded, she'd stay for a couple of days. Just long enough to accomplish her mission.

What had the reporter asked her? Did she have a hit record? Was she in a band?

Obviously he recognized her, but boy was he confused. A hit record? No way. She remembered her father telling her that she couldn't carry a tune in a bucket.

CHAPTER FORTY-TWO

He thought about stopping at her villa, but it was late. There were a lot of unanswered questions and it seemed to Sever that she could answer some of them. *Who the hell was she?*

He swung out of Murtz's driveway and made a right turn, heading back down the mountain. He felt a little more comfortable with the roads than he had just yesterday. Three Scotches had gone to his head, and he felt just a touch of being out of control. He turned up the radio, an oldie station out of St. Martin owned by some expatriate from the States. They were playing a Gideon Pike tune, with Pike's piano backed by some lush, 1970 strings.

If you had to choose, which one of them would lose
Whose heart would you break? Which one would you take?

Two Hearts. He'd heard it one hundred times. He'd stumbled on two women in the short time he'd been on the island. Michelle and the mysterious lady from the villa. He needed to know more about both of them. It was strange that both women had a connection with Danny Murtz. Very strange. But, as Mr. B. had told him, it was a very small island. Apparently a lot of things and people dovetailed.

Sever slowed down, going into the first curve cautiously. Jan and Dean, from the sixties, sang about sliding into the curve with a Jaguar at "Deadman's Curve." Sever saw the car behind him, coming up fast. Slow down, asshole. I'm not a native, and obviously I don't know the roads as well as I should.

Sever negotiated the steep curve, then straightened out and gave the little car some more gas. Now the lights in his rearview mirror were brighter, closer, and pushing him. He heard the horn as the car came up along side of him on the inside. Sever was on the open side, where a turn of the wheel would send his little car over the edge, careening down to the ocean. He clung to the wheel, trying to maintain control.

As the car passed him, the next curve appeared, his dim headlights barely picking it up. The passing gray sports car swung back into the outside lane as headlights from around the bend flashed onto the road. Sever braked, trying to negotiate the turn and not run into the rear of the car that had just passed him.

The vehicle in front of him slowed down, and Sever once again applied the brakes. On the straightaway the auto in front of him drifted back, and Sever floored the small four-cylinder vehicle and went to the inside, passing the strange driver. Finally, he was in the lead. If this guy was drunk, he wanted to get the hell out of his way. He drifted back into the right lane, comfortable now with his position. The straightaway lasted for twenty seconds and he was once again negotiating a hairpin turn. He let up on the gas as the rear car came up fast, hitting the left lane at the steepest part of the curve. Jesus. If there was another vehicle coming around the bend —

There wasn't. And the faster car hung in the left lane. It stayed even with Sever and as Sever slowed, so did his counterpart. As he speeded up, so did the other car. This guy wasn't drunk. There wasn't room for two cars, and any approaching vehicle would not have been able to find room to hide.

Now the offending car eased to the right, bumping Sever's auto. He gasped, then thought about the rental company. They were going to be so pissed. The sleek gray car hit him again, a gentle bump, metal scraping metal. It was as if the other driver was testing Sever's resistance. It stayed even and when Sever braked so did his rival. The other car came over harder this time and bashed the small rental. Sever felt himself drifting to the edge of the road, certain to spill down the mountainside. He swung the wheel hard to the left and hit the sports car. Not a gentle hit, but a hard, crashing hit that threw the other car against the side of the mountain.

That had to be the final blow. Sever left the other car behind.

The lights surprised him. Goddamn, the other car was coming up fast. The lights were on bright, blinding Sever for an instant. His nemesis ran into the passing lane, pulling away quickly. With barely a foot clearance, the car pulled in front of Sever, slamming on his brakes. Sever slammed his brake pedal as well, turning to the left to avoid rear-ending the phantom auto. As he did, the car in front drifted slightly to the right. Brake lights still blazing, the car's wheels slipped off the edge of the narrow road. The gray sports car hung on for several seconds, and Sever could see the shadow of the driver as he frantically turned the wheel, trying to pull back onto the road. Four seconds, five seconds, six and the auto shot out over the side of the hill and plummeted down the cliff.

Sever braked hard. Squealing to a short stop, he jumped from his vehicle and staggered to the side of the road. The car was still careening down the mountainside, at one point flipping end over end, and in the dim light Sever could see it land on its top.

Surely the driver couldn't have survived the tumultuous crash. Sever thought about trying to traverse the hill, maybe pulling the driver from the wreckage. He thought about it for all of two seconds. Then the explosion destroyed all of those thoughts.

With a yellow ball of hot fire, the car exploded, the sound roaring across the valley and ricocheting off the mountains. He could feel the heat even at his distance.

Again, someone had tried to kill him. He needed to get the hell off this island, and back to the safety of Chicago. What the hell, they'd tried to kill him in Chicago too. What he really needed to do was find out why someone was trying to take his life. The answer was with Murtz, Schwartz, Michelle, or the strange girl from the villa. He was convinced of it.

CHAPTER FORTY-THREE

Sever watched the lights on the other side of the bay, twinkling in the humid evening air. He'd poured himself a Scotch, then another, as he sat on the porch, listening to the hot tub gurgle. Other than the banged-up side of his rental car, there was no proof that he'd been involved at all with the car going off the side of the mountain. He took his clue from his last car explosion. The authorities didn't seem to care at all how something happened. It was an innocent accident and that's all there was to that. So, he didn't report it. A driver was dead. All Sever had done was protect himself. It was surprising how objectively he could look at it, the death of another human being. However, it could have been — should have been — him. The Scotch was working its magic.

He plugged in the laptop and gazed at the screen as it slowly came to life. There were three mysteries on the island, and if he wanted to stay alive, he had to solve each one of them.

Was Danny Murtz responsible for the disappearance of one, two, or even three different girls? Who was the mysterious girl who lived in the villa next to Murtz? Who was Michelle Kirkendall?

And, possibly the fourth mystery was Mr. B. He'd been extremely cryptic the last time Sever had talked to him. He'd mentioned something about a friend who'd disappeared and insinuated that Danny Murtz was responsible.

One mystery at a time. They all seemed to have strong ties to Murtz.

Sever brought up Google and typed in *Michelle Kirkendall.* The list unfolded. A sixth-grade teacher, a customer service rep, someone who ranked ninety-sixth in the Lake Havasu poker tournament. Interesting, but this wasn't getting it. He added Atlanta beside her name. It didn't help. Someone named Miriam Kirkendall had a restaurant and Tom Kirkendall had an accounting business, but no Michelle. Sometimes a search engine worked, sometimes it didn't.

Michelle Kirkendall Atlanta Police. He hit Search. There was a Brian Kirkendall married to a Michelle Bender. Nothing. It had been worth a try. Then in the upper left corner he saw it. *Did you mean Michelle Kirkendall Chicago Police*?

He clicked it. There it was. A Michelle Kirkendall in Chicago worked for the police missing persons bureau in Chicago. Was it the same Michelle Kirkendall? She said Atlanta. And what was it Mr. B. had said? He could tell accents and he thought Michelle's was a Chicago accent like his, not an Atlanta one.

Sever scrolled down the list. Not much information, just the name. No picture, no age, no description. Just that a Michelle Kirkendall worked for the Chicago Police Department in the missing persons bureau.

Sever went into the suite and pulled a business card from his wallet. Jeff Bloomfield's home number was scrawled on the back of the business side. He dialed the international code and Bloomfield's number, and after a long pause he heard it ring. Glancing at his watch he noticed the time was one a.m. Jeff would be so pleased.

One ring, two rings, three rings, four, and he heard the sleepy voice.

"Yeah?"

"Jeff, it's Mick Sever. I need some information, and I think I need it right now."

A long pause. "It's, jeez, Mick, it's . . . what time is it?"

It wasn't important what time it was. Sever had done some of his best work in the middle of the night. He'd also gotten into most of his trouble in the middle of the night. Just because nighttime was synonymous with dark-time didn't mean you couldn't do business. It didn't mean you couldn't do some damage. And when you followed the entertainment scene, all of the interesting stories happened in the middle of the night.

"Jeff, write this down."

"What? You think I've got a pen right here by the — oh, here's a pen. Okay, what?"

Sever could hear Bloomfield's wife asking him what the problem was. "Michelle Kirkendall. She's a Chicago cop."

"Uh-huh."

"I need as much information as you can get. Picture, age, description, how long she's been on the job."

"Sever, this had better be related to your story. If I'm chasing down a woman for you at one in the morning just so you can score —"

"Oh, and one last thing, Jeff."

"Yeah?"

"I want to know if she's working this week. I want to know if she's in Chicago, out of town, or on assignment."

"On assignment. Okay. What would be the assignment?"

"I want to know if she's tracking down a missing person."

Bloomfield was waking up. The newspaperman was starting to put things together in his head. "Missing women in particular?"

"I'll give you more information once you get me what I need. It's possible I'm not the only one over here who is checking up on our friend Danny Murtz."

"A missing persons cop?"

"Maybe. And Jeff, there's a young girl over here who is staying in a villa near Murtz. I found her tonight kind of sneaking around Murtz's property."

"And?" Bloomfield had a reporter's mind. Always another question.

"She looks familiar. A singer from a couple of years ago maybe. I think she's stalking Murtz. It's just a feeling I have."

"You don't know who she is?"

"I thought maybe if I told you about her it might jog my memory."

"Now that you've destroyed any chance of my getting to sleep, anything else you want to share?"

"I had an interview with Harvey Schwartz, the handler, slash, attorney. He's a piece of work. He's protecting the hell out of Murtz." Sever took a swallow of Scotch and relished the warmth as it went down.

"Considering you think they stole the papers, that sounds about right. And your feeling is?"

"I left him, giving him the impression I was going to explore the story about Murtz and the missing girls."

"I imagine he wasn't too happy about that."

"He tried to kill me, Jeff."

"What?"

"It was either Danny Murtz and Harvey Schwartz or this little girl I caught on the property."

"Jesus, Mick. Maybe it's time you came home."

"Somebody tried to kill me in Chicago too. I've got the players over here, so it's probably better to stay and find out why someone wants me out of the way."

"I'm not going to pretend to understand that, but, my God, please be careful."

"Personal concern or afraid the paper will get sued?"

He heard Bloomfield chuckle on the other end of the line. "If my wife wasn't lying beside me I'd tell you to go fuck yourself."

"All right, Jeff. You can e-mail me whatever you find out, but I could really use some information on this cop by tomorrow."

"Shouldn't be a problem."

"And, Jeff, I really do think Danny Murtz is involved in the disappearance of those girls. And possibly someone else on the island."

There was a pause. "Uh, Mick. Remember the girl you were planning on interviewing for MTV? The *American Idol* contestant? Randi something?"

"Sure. Randi Parks. Did she call? I haven't been able to retrieve my messages from here. What, is she pissed off because I took another assignment?"

"No. She never called at all. We've run the story two days in a row. She's disappeared, and no one — not her parents, the *American Idol* producers, or her best friends — has any idea where she's gone."

CHAPTER FORTY-FOUR

Blind drunk. That's what they called it. But it couldn't be blind drunk because he could still see. Things were extremely blurry, but he could see. He'd sent the bodyguard Raymond to take the two girls home. He'd thought about seeing if the girl in the cottage was still alive, but right now he didn't really care. Murtz had loaded his system so full of shit that it was coming out of his nose and eyes and mouth. Like small snakes, oozing from the pours of his body. He shuddered. Life would be better at this point if he just passed out, but his senses were on high alert and he needed some air.

He glanced in the mirror that hung on his office door and immediately looked away. His eyes burned like coals and his blotched face was covered with a course two-day growth. Even in the dim light and with his blurred vision he could see that his red nose shown like a neon light. His long, tangled matted hair hung over his ears and he pulled it back into a disheveled ponytail that hung limply from the back of his head. Not a pleasant sight.

Murtz staggered to the pool area door and jerked it open, holding on for balance. The room was spinning and he knew he was going to throw up some very expensive alcohol and cocaine.

A thick blanket of clouds hid any light from the moon, and he strained to see beyond to the pool and the parameter fence. Tentatively he took one step, then two. He grasped for a deck chair and took in a lung full of St. Barts air. The deep breath had a negative effect and he felt another wave of nausea as he eased himself into the chair. He sat there forever, breathing shallow breaths, trying to put the demons inside his body to rest.

Forever. He'd written a song called "Forever" once. He'd pretty much stolen the melody from some one-hit-wonder named Sammy Beach, but the song had made Murtz about ten million dollars. How the hell did it go? He concentrated. Forever something something —

Forever, the world cannot hold us forever
But we'll hold each other the promise is strong
The way that I feel with you all night long
Forever our passion will last through the years
The world may explode but through laughter and tears
We'll stay together. Forever.

What a pile of crap. His life, reduced to sappy love songs and heavy orchestrations. His legacy to the world. Danny Murtz, known forever as someone who sold slick music. Someone who stole almost everything he produced. Fuck 'em.

The voices were soft, coming from the other end of the pool. It was too dark to see anyone, but he could make out the soft whispering voices. The conversation was soft, the tone of the conversation somewhat combative. Sharp utterances, like fingers being pointed. Murtz shrank back into his chair, more than a little paranoid. His stomach rolled and he shivered in the warm night air. Who the hell was arguing at this time of night?

The voices were close now, coming around the side of the pool. He wanted to stand and go back to the confines of his office, his bedroom, his thirteen-million-dollar villa, but he couldn't muster the strength to lift a leg. God, he was so fucked up.

And then he saw the silhouettes. Two shadowy figures coming right at him. One of them lifted something high above their head, maybe a thick pipe, a small tree limb, he couldn't tell. The darkness, the blurry vision. He ducked his head, buried it under his arms, and opened one eye, barely getting a glimpse of the raised object. And then, as if in slow motion he saw the person swing down, with what seemed to be brutal force. Silently, Murtz screamed, praying that whoever it was wouldn't strike him. His short prayer, "Lord, don't let it be me," was the last thing he remembered before he mercifully blacked out.

CHAPTER FORTY-FIVE

Breakfast at the Manapany even at the early hour of seven a.m. included the march of the topless French lasses down to the pool, across the deck, and down the stairs to the beach.

He'd stayed up until three, trying to sleep but continually flashing back to his near demise the night before. Everything was quiet at the hotel, and the dining area next to the pool was sparsely populated at this hour of the morning.

He kept expecting some authoritative figure to approach him and bring him in for questioning. Maybe more than that. Handcuffs, jail, but Mr. B. said there was no crime on the island. At least none to really speak of. The accident would be written off as just that. An accident.

He'd been set up by Schwartz. He was sure of it. And, by now, Murtz's lawyer had to know it hadn't worked. Sever walked back to his room, nursing a cup of coffee. *Get the hell off the island, or confront the son of a bitch.* Obviously he couldn't prove anything, but if he put it to the bald bastard, if he made an accusation, they might think twice about doing anything else until he could get off the island.

Sever picked up the phone and called Murtz's number.

"Mr. Murtz's residence." A male voice he didn't recognize.

"Harvey Schwartz please."

There was some mumbling as if someone had put his hand over

the receiver. Finally a response. "No one is taking any calls. There's been an accident."

"What kind of accident?" Christ. They'd found the car. Could they prove he was involved? Had they identified the driver? Well, of course, they had. They knew who was on the road trying to run him down. And what was he worried about? He'd only tried to defend himself. Of course, he should have called the police or gendarmes or whoever. He hadn't. Sever stared at the receiver and thought about just hanging up.

"Someone drowned in our pool last night."

Sever froze. Not even close to the response he'd expected.

"Hello?"

"Drowned? How? Who was it?"

"I'm sorry. That's all I can say."

The line went dead.

The girl he'd tackled last night. A strong candidate for someone who might have drowned. Casing the property at that hour in the evening? Or maybe Murtz himself. Sever could see him, stumbling around the pool with a head full of coke.

He finished the coffee and picked up the car keys. He had to know who it was, and since they weren't going to tell him on the phone, he'd have to ask the question in person.

CHAPTER FORTY-SIX

He'd had an aunt who lived somewhere near Rockford, and although she'd only visit his family in Chicago once a year, Sever was closer to her than he ever was to his dysfunctional parents. It wasn't because she brought him the latest records, although he appreciated them greatly, and it wasn't because she was younger and closer to his age that he found himself so fond of her. It was the fact that he instinctively knew she was just as fond of him. She was the only person he felt truly close to in his formative years. Once a year, as if the time was compressed, they picked up their relationship and shared stories, songs, and memories, and although twelve years separated them and even though she was his mother's sister, it was an entirely different family experience. He was more connected to her than to his own parents or friends.

Sever thought about her as he negotiated the same dangerous curves he had faced the night before, this time climbing the winding St. Barts roads that led to Danny Murtz's villa. Linda Lewis was attractive in a dowdy way. Bowl-cut brown hair, scuffed up shoes, and usually wearing a sweater and jeans. It didn't matter. She was the sister he never had, the best friend that eluded him in school, the confidant that he needed.

And then, one day he came home from school to find his mother crying. Linda had been found at the bottom of a public swimming pool. She'd slipped, banged her head on the concrete, and gone into the water before a lifeguard could get to her. He thought about her now, wondering if she ever knew how much her nephew had depended on her for his life lessons.

He turned another tight corner as a small truck passed him, the driver puffing on a big cigar. There were times that he was afraid he'd have to pull over when a larger vehicle was coming at him. He cringed when he thought about the banged up driver's side of his little rental car. Sever sped by the spot where the car had gone off the road, and he didn't slow down at all. He was certain someone had found the remains, but he wanted nothing to do with it.

Who drowned? And why wouldn't they tell him? At least he finally had a story to take to the *Trib.* Not necessarily the story that Jeff Bloomfield wanted, but a story nevertheless. A death at Danny Murtz's villa in St. Barts.

St. Barthélémy Island is a dependency island of Guadeloupe, which in turn is an Overseas Department and Region of France. As such, St. Barts Island participates in French elections. It has its own mayor, who is elected every seven years, a town constable, and a security force consisting of six policemen and thirteen gendarmes. Four gendarmes were clustered at the entrance to the compound with three squad cars. Sever assumed at least two more were waiting inside or by the pool.

"Mr. Sever?"

"I am a —" *What the hell was he?* "a business acquaintance of Danny Murtz. I called and was told that someone was found —"

The uniformed military man crisply finished his sentence, "in the pool. I understand." The lead gendarme glared at him. His attitude said *another fucking American.* "Sever?"

"Sever."

"We have several questions we need to ask you, Mick Sever."

"What?" He was the one who asked the questions.

The gendarme tapped the handle of his sidearm as he watched the surprised expression on Sever's face.

"Mr. Sever." The English was flawless. "We've had a discussion about you."

Was it about the car crash? Or did they seriously think he'd had something to do with somebody drowning in the pool?

"Mr. Sever, you have been a frequent guest here at Mr. Murtz's villa."

"Twice. I wouldn't call that frequent."

The gendarme ignored his comment. "You were here last evening."

"I was."

"Could you tell me what the purpose of your visit was?"

"I was here to interview Danny Murtz."

"And that was all you did?"

Sever was pissed. This asshole was avoiding the major question. *Who the hell was at the bottom of the pool?*

"No. I ended up interviewing his attorney, his handler, Harvey Schwartz."

The gendarme turned his head, making eye contact with his counterpart. "Mr. Schwartz?"

Sever nodded. "Who the hell died last night?"

"Mr. Sever. There is a report that you had a heated exchange with Mr. Schwartz."

Oh, jeez! A heated exchange? "He wasn't exactly happy with the way I was going to write my story."

"And did he threaten you?"

"If you're insinuating that I'm a suspect in a committed crime, I can assure you that I'm not. My understanding is that someone died at the bottom of a pool. I had words with Harvey Schwartz, with Danny Murtz —"

The gendarme interrupted him. "Mr. Murtz? You had words with Mr. Murtz?" Again he exchanged glances with his partner.

"Yes."

The military officers looked at each other. "Mr. Sever, we will need to take you to Gustavia for further questioning."

"What?"

"Would you please come with us?"

The hell he would. He'd go if they told him who was at the bottom of the pool. "No. You tell me who was found in the water, then maybe — maybe we can talk."

The gendarme tapped his sidearm once more then walked up to Sever. With physical prowess, he took him by the arm, twisted it behind his back, shoved him face forward into the side of the gendarme's vehicle, at the same time kicking his legs apart. As Sever's face cracked against the surface of the car, he shook his head and tried to right himself. The second officer pulled his other arm behind him and through the excruciating pain Sever could feel and hear the handcuffs being snapped on his wrists. He'd felt that kind of pain once before, when he'd jumped from a stage with Keith Moon into the front row of seats at a Who concert. He'd bent his knee in a most unusual position. His arms, shoulders, and wrists felt that same pain now and he saw bright lights as stars flashed in his brain. His head rested against the vehicle, and he took deep breaths.

"Mr. Sever, we have some serious questions for you at our headquarters."

What happened to leaving the big-spending tourists alone? What happened to the story that no one has ever committed a serious crime on St. Barts? Sever took a deep breath and exploded. He kicked his legs out, aching knee and all, and brought his cuffed hands up as hard as he could. He could feel the impact as he caught one of the soldiers under his chin. He spun around, head-butting the second guard, and knocking him to the ground. He'd had enough of people taking him on. His frustration, his temper, was getting the best of him, but damn, his patience had been tested one too many times. Sever turned to confront the next Frenchman and felt the cold steel barrel of a gun pressing into his temple.

"Wait a minute." Another gendarme approached the group. Two of the officers were on the ground, one staring up at him and another not moving at all. "Let Mr. Sever go, please." One of the standing gendarmes grudgingly put his key into the handcuffs and immediately removed the metal manacles. Without a moment of hesitation, they let him go. Sever shifted his shoulders, trying to ease the pain. "This is a very famous American journalist, Mr. Mick Sever. Officers, we need to be tolerant of this gentleman."

Sever stretched and thought for a second. His car was only thirty feet away and all he had to do was walk, jog, or run to the vehicle. He didn't trust this guy or the ones who tried to take him in for questioning. But St. Barts was a small island and they'd find you, no matter where you decided to hide.

"Mr. Sever, you have been here before?"

Sever thought about "*good cop, bad cop*." A popular police procedure where one cop pretended to be tough and the other cop pretended to be a friend. This was the good cop.

"Sure. I've been here." He rubbed his wrists, bruised from the hard metal cuffs.

"And you and Danny Murtz had some problems?"

"Problems? We had a disagreement."

"You and Harvey Schwartz had some problems?"

Sever had an idea of where this was going. "Yes, we did. It doesn't mean I would kill either of them. I didn't throw someone in the swimming pool. I would never do that."

Sever took a deep breath. "I'm a reporter for God's sake. The only reason I'm here is to report. I'm not here to shoot, stab, or kill anyone in any fashion. Are we clear on that?" And then it hit him. The reason he was being let go was that he *was* a reporter. These guys couldn't afford any bad press. Someone had done some homework and realized that Sever had a reputation. He might actually write a scathing column about how poorly he was treated in St. Barts and with his reach, his readership, his popularity, he might actually influence some people not to travel to the tropical paradise.

"I'm sorry for the inconvenience, Mr. Sever. You can understand our concern. We have yet to determine the cause of death and we are looking at all of the possibilities."

Sever nodded. He still wasn't sure he was safe. "So you can tell me who was in the pool?"

"No. I can't. The next of kin have yet to be notified and there must be some preliminary fact finding before we announce the deceased's name."

Announce the deceased's name? "So I'm free to go?"

"With my blessing." The uniformed officer extended his hand, and Sever kept his by his side.

"I'm still having trouble understanding the way you treat people on the island."

"Mr. Sever," he withdrew his hand. "We were overzealous in our actions. For that I apologize. I will make it up to you in any way I can, but I ask you to be forgiving. Any time there is a death on our island, we want to make certain that we explore all possibilities."

So his celebrity played well on St. Barts. He smiled at the officer, still not offering his hand. "I'm sure this encounter will appear in print somewhere back in the States." He couldn't keep from saying it. The sons of bitches deserved to have their faces rubbed in their own smugness. If he was going to be treated like a common criminal, he wanted a little revenge.

"Mr. Sever, before you go, I have one more question for you." The man ran his fingers over the dented, scratched surface of Sever's car. "How did you get this damage on a rental car?"

"I didn't get far enough over coming around a curve." Not exactly a lie.

"Were you aware there was very bad accident just a short distance from here last night?"

Sever feigned his best innocent look. "No."

"There was. A young man was killed. These roads can be treacherous if you are not familiar with them. I would suggest that you be a little more careful."

CHAPTER FORTY-SEVEN

Doug Druckemiller had found the bloated milky white body. The guitarist for the Indoorfins had come in early to check the sound and equipment. By the time the rest of the band had shown up, the gendarmes had already sealed off the area.

Nancy had pounded on his door and kept pounding until he unlocked it. What the hell could be so important as to wake someone up at such an ungodly hour? Christ, it had been a gruesome night. He tried to remember going to bed, and couldn't. Something about the pool and a couple of people arguing. Oh, God, he must have passed out.

"Danny! Danny!" She was shouting from the hall. He'd blearily opened his eyes and studied the clock. 7:28 a.m. Hell, it was time to fire the bitch. His secretary, after this many years, should know better. And her son — *the boy* — he was history. Waking him up at this fucking hour, this went beyond any normal employee-employer relationship. He'd find another secretary and find another recording engineer. Harvey had been right. Fire the stupid boy. It wasn't like there weren't dozens of them out there. He'd seen a résumé just yesterday from a kid, Josh Morgan, who qualified as a recording engineer. Kid had done a two-year school, interned for a couple of studios — and he could put that kid into his system for half of what he was paying *the boy*. The kid would be elated, working with the world famous Danny Murtz.

He threw off the bedcovers and staggered from the bed, pulling on a thick bathrobe and opening the heavy oak door. "What the hell do you want, and it had better be a damned good story!"

"Doug from the Indoorfins came in early —"

"I don't care."

"You will." She forced herself into his room, filling the immediate entrance space. He had a moment of panic. They'd found Michelle, the blond, back in the guesthouse. If she was still alive, she'd nail him. He hoped it wasn't that. And he hoped she was dead. God, that would be a lot easier to deal with.

"Get the hell out of this room." Murtz backed up, letting Nancy fill his space.

"Doug was here and found a dead body in the pool."

"A what?"

"A dead body."

That was insane. Michelle was in the guesthouse, not the pool. And if it wasn't her body, why would someone put a dead person in his pool? He thought back to last night. A little fuzzy. A lot fuzzy. "It's still there?"

"It is." Her eyes were riveted on his, boring a hole in his brain. Nancy was a witch. "We've called the authorities."

Murtz shook his head back and forth. He needed to clear it of all influence and he couldn't seem to do that. Booze, drugs, they colored his perspective.

"Danny, we have to have a plan of attack and a plan of defense."

She was right of course. Defend and attack. Against whom?

"You're right. But —" What was the question? Deny he had anything to do with the body. The body. Oh, hell, who was the body?

"Nancy, who was in the pool?"

She glanced at the doorway, as if someone would enter and stop her testimony.

"I know this sounds horrid, but I can't say I'm sorry, because I'm not."

Murtz frowned. "Just tell me who it was, damn it."

"Harvey. They found Harvey's body."

Jesus, Harvey.

"Danny, did you have anything to do with this?"

Of course not. He'd thought about it. Dreamed about it. Schemed and calculated the risks. But *would* he actually kill Harvey? *Could* he actually kill Harvey? "Of course not. What kind of a goddamned question is that?" The bitch had the nerve to accuse him?

"You've said you didn't trust him, and I know you've thought about getting rid of him. I was so afraid that —"

He couldn't remember last night. Every *last night* became a blur. And last night was no different. The entire idea behind *last night* was to have a party that you could not remember the morning after. He'd succeeded.

Schwartz's body had been transported. To where, he didn't know. If the attorney had been alive, Murtz would have put him in charge. Talk to the authorities, take care of this mess. Whatever it costs, just get rid of it. As it was —

"Mr. Murtz, I understand you are surprised by this death, but we want to make certain we cover all possibilities."

They were sitting at a table by the pool, the scene of the death. Murtz wondered if they could make a chalk outline on the water where the lawyer had been floating.

"Can you please tell us when was the last time you saw Mr. Schwartz?"

The uniformed man kept asking him questions. Questions and more questions. Where the hell was Harvey? Harvey took care of this crap.

"If I may," Nancy interrupted. "I saw Mr. Schwartz at about eleven thirty p.m. I believe that Danny had already retired for the evening."

Retired? He tried to remember. Hell no, he'd gone out to party. He must have rolled in about four in the morning, but it was just too fuzzy. He couldn't remember if he'd seen Harvey. Harvey'd had a meeting with the reporter. That much he remembered.

"Yeah. Harvey had a meeting with a reporter last night. I remember that. The guy wanted to talk to me, but he was an abusive, pushy bastard, and I told Harvey to talk to him."

"His name?"

He struggled for a moment, drawing a blank.

"Sever. Mick Sever." Nancy answered for him.

The gendarme wrote the name down. "He was physically abusive?"

"I heard him yelling at Harvey. They had an exchange of words, I do know that." Nancy nodded at Murtz, as if to make sure he was on board with the story.

"Do you know where this Mick Sever is staying?"

"I do. The Manapany Hotel."

"We will want to ask him questions. We'll want to question anyone who had contact with Mr. Schwartz."

Murtz watched his secretary with a newfound appreciation. She was filling in for Harvey very nicely. Maybe *the boy* could stay in his position for a while. At least until this Harvey thing went away. He half listened as the gendarme droned on, talking to Nancy and taking notes. Harvey was gone. Whatever threat there was had been eliminated. Sever was still a threat. Harvey had failed again in his attempt to kill the reporter, and Murtz was more certain than ever that Sever knew about the girl from *American Idol.* Randi somebody. She'd called Sever that night, from Murtz's house, and Sever had put it together. Time to get rid of all the evidence. All of it. Time to do it right now. He gazed at the pool, the water shimmering in the early morning sun. Did he, Danny Murtz, have anything to do with Harvey's death? There was a nagging suspicion that he might have been by the pool last night. Something about the pool and confrontation. Something. But it slipped away in an instant and it was as if his mind was completely empty. Void of any recollection. He couldn't remember. Maybe if you didn't remember something, it just didn't happen.

CHAPTER FORTY-EIGHT

His head throbbed, the blood pounding in his temples. A more circumspect person might have let the gendarme's words go, but Sever had almost been arrested for a crime he didn't commit. He knew he had a temper, but did he have a killer instinct? Depending on the circumstance, yes. One night he tried to kill his father. He'd had enough of his verbal, mental, and physical abuse on him and his mother and he'd beat the shit out of him. Almost killed him. It was justified, but the point was, he thought he could have done it. He had bad dreams about the incident, but he could have killed him. There was absolutely no doubt, he could have killed him.

Sever jerked the wheel, narrowly missing a lumbering truck as it struggled up the hill. The next time he damaged the car was probably going to be his fault.

He could still remember the gun battle at the strip club in Miami, lying on the hot pavement, shooting at a man who held Ginny hostage. He'd killed him. Given the proper motivation, he'd found out he *could* kill a man. He pounded his fist on the steering wheel, venting some of his anger. The radio station from St. Martin came out of a commercial about some sort of lavender soap, and he heard the familiar strains of the Roberta Flack song, "Killing Me Softly With His Song." No one would ever believe it. He was pretty sure the producer of songs was killing people. And he was pretty sure he'd kill the producer or his henchmen if it meant saving his own life.

Sever spun around the corner and started down the narrow drive to the hotel. And what about last night? Did he have motivation? He thought for a moment. Schwartz had sent someone to kill him. When that happened, Sever had wanted to go back and finish the job.

Yes. There was no question in his mind. If the situation called for it, he could kill someone. He *would* kill someone. Any time, any place. He wasn't entirely happy with the revelation. How did you deal with the fact that you could be a cold-blooded killer?

But there was a comforting factor. If someone fucked with his life, or the life of a very important person in his life, he would not have any question about solving the problem. He could solve the problem.

CHAPTER FORTY-NINE

She couldn't see Murtz's property from this new villa. This new villa with the huge pool, the outdoor kitchen, the fully stocked bar, and ceramic tile floors. This villa with the four bedrooms — a master with mirrors on the ceiling. My God, mirrors on the ceiling. She'd done that once in her life, made love with mirrors on the ceiling. A very long time ago. The villa had a workout room with state-of-the-art equipment, a gourmet kitchen to die for, and a stocked refrigerator. Steaks in the freezer, lobster, crabs, and so much more. If she had to break into a house, this was the one. She'd hit the jackpot. But she couldn't see her target. It was impossible to see Danny's house from this property.

The phone rang, a shrill, vibrating ring. The girl froze. A ringing phone should be answered. It rang again and again. Five times and each time she wanted to walk into the kitchen and pick it up. Contact with the outside world would be welcome. The fifth time it rang she heard the voice.

"I'm sorry."

Her eyes quickly darted around the spacious family room. No one.

"No one is home at the moment." She breathed a deep sigh of relief. "Please leave a detailed message at the sound of the beep and we'll get back to you as soon as possible." Beep.

"Hey, Scottie, we're going to be on the island this weekend and would like to hook up with you two. Call me."

So she couldn't stay here long. The residents were expected back by the weekend and they'd be somewhat upset to find out she'd set up camp in their villa. There could be worse people. Actually, they should be thankful it was just her.

The girl considered the options. To see Danny's villa, she could walk two properties over, stand on the border, and have a perfect view of Danny's pool. At this hour of the morning, and with the reporter knowing what she looked like, that probably wasn't a good idea. Here at the villa, even though she was still looking out over the water, on this gorgeous patio with teak furniture, marble tile, and an outdoor movie screen, she couldn't see around the bend to Murtz's property. She couldn't see the results of the aftermath of her encounter last night. She was still shaking.

Harvey's computer. She had to have it. At first she thought she could just get a copy of the files. Now, it was her mission to take the entire computer. Who knew what else she might learn? Maybe other girls had been threatened. Maybe other girls were in hiding. She was pretty sure that information regarding her friend Libby Hellman would be on that computer. Maybe she could get all of that information. That computer was on the island and there was no question she was going to get it. She wouldn't leave the island unless she had that computer. And she was going to get it tonight.

And then it occurred to her what she was thinking. She wouldn't leave the island without that computer. Which might mean she wouldn't leave the island. At all.

CHAPTER FIFTY

Harvey had drowned. The gendarmes had left it at that. They were investigating, looking at the body, trying to decide if it was accident or murder. Who knew? Maybe he'd been murdered, but Murtz had been living on the island long enough to know that no one ever admitted that a murder had been committed. So, even if he himself had had some involvement, even if he had killed Harvey Schwartz, they would never admit it was murder. A blow to the head — they'd say it was caused in a fall. A gunshot — they'd say it was self-inflicted. If Harvey had been strangled or beaten to death, they'd have an excuse for it.

Murtz leaned back in the leather chair, holding a glass of single malt Scotch tightly and remembering a record executive in New York, some guy who had been around in the early years. Name was Rueben somebody. Rueben had accused Murtz of stealing some of his material. Songs, some riffs, some actual tape. If he recalled right, he *had* stolen the material. One hundred percent. He was young in the business and full of attitude and bluster. It was the way you got ahead on the South Side of Chicago. You took what you could not afford. But this guy came in, full of piss and vinegar, and accused Murtz. So Murtz waited for him two nights later.

This Rueben had gone to his car, parked in a marked area of the company lot. A Ferrari or some outrageously expensive vehicle. He climbed into the Italian convertible and Murtz had split his head with a crowbar. It was the way things were done on the South Side of Chicago. He bet himself that they never got all that blood out of the leather seats. Two blocks away he tossed the crowbar in a dumpster and that was the end of that. He remembered that incident well because he was sober that night. Lucid. Determined to pay the son of a bitch back. Recent accidents he didn't remember as well. Take for instance this Jennifer Koenig. Subject of the threatening letter.

He didn't remember killing her. And he didn't remember doing anything to Harvey Schwartz. But he'd thought about it, planned it a dozen times, and just maybe —

No. He was sticking with his first thought. If you didn't remember it, then it didn't happen. And that was that!

Now, he had to plan the demise of the reporter. Mick Sever. Best to be lucid for this one. Maybe he'd do just a little blow to give him some courage, but he wanted it done right. Christ, Harvey had tried to get the reporter run over in Chicago, tried to blow his car up over here, and last night had tried to have him run off the road. One of Murtz's bodyguards, Little Jean, had died because of that. They were dropping like flies. First Little Jean, then Harvey. Now it was down to just one bodyguard and Nancy. And all because of Sever. Because Sever knew what he had done to that singer. Sever knew what Murtz had done to Randi Parks.

What a waste. All because this fucking reporter had talked to a girl who had taken a tumble off of his balcony in Chicago. Randi Parks had called Sever right before the fall, and she'd probably told Sever where she was. May have even told him that she'd slept with Murtz, and that he'd been a little rough. Forceful. It's the way the game was played, and if you were a player then you had to be prepared to play.

Sever wanted an interview. Well he was about to get his wish. If the gendarmes let him go, if Sever wasn't in jail for the murder of Harvey Schwartz, he'd probably chomp at the bit to do the definitive interview with Murtz. Murtz would promise him everything. Promise him names, dates, and places. But this time, Danny Murtz would handle every detail. No Nancy, no Harvey, no bodyguards.

He'd set it up himself. Shit. He was capable. This empire, this fortune he'd built, this kingdom hadn't been constructed by any of the people on his staff. He'd done this by himself. The wealth, the glory, the honor had come from his creative abilities. It was simple to him, but it generated billions, yes billions for others. He was capable of doing anything he set his mind to, and the most important thing he could do at this moment was save his own ass.

He sipped the Scotch, staring at the window that looked out over the pool area. No A&E, no Indoorfins, just a bunch of lights, electrical cords, amplifiers, and equipment. Sever had fucked up the entire day. Sever — and Harvey.

"Danny?"

She surprised him. She was always doing that, just appearing when he least expected her.

"That Michelle that you flew over here —" Disgust in her voice. Still jealous after all these years?

"What about her?" Oh, Christ, had they found her in the guest cottage? Instinctively he looked over his shoulder, toward the cottage. He had the only key. There was no way. "What? Tell me what."

"Her return flight is the day after tomorrow. I assume Raymond is driving her to the airport."

There was no way she was ever going back.

"Sure. Yeah, go ahead and make the plans."

Leaning back in his leather chair, his robe loosely wrapped around him, he studied Nancy Steiner, framed in his doorway. Still attractive, in a matronly sort of way. He tried to picture her twenty-six years ago, soft, sexy.

"She was here yesterday. Raymond picked her up, but he didn't take her back."

Oh, shit. He tightened the robe and straightened up from his slouch.

"A friend. Somebody she met on the island took her back to the hotel." And then it came to him. A way to take care of all his problems.

"Nancy, make dinner plans tonight in Gustavia. Maybe Carl Gustaf."

"How many people?"

"Two. I'll pick up Michelle and take her to dinner."

She nodded. "I'll make the call. Is there anything else?"

"No."

He smiled. He had to think this through, but it was a great plan. He could get rid of Michelle, the little sneak, and it all worked right into his plan to get rid of Sever.

"No. There's nothing else for now. But stay close. You never know. You just never know when something might come up."

CHAPTER FIFTY-ONE

The phone was ringing when he walked into the unit. He grabbed it.

"Mick Sever?"

"Jeff?"

"No. This is Danny Murtz."

He was taken aback for a moment. He'd been sure it was Bloomfield with the story on Michelle Kirkendall.

"Is this a good time to talk?"

"Yeah. Sure. I understand you had a drowning at your place this morning."

"We did. My attorney, Harvey Schwartz. You talked to him last night."

Sever felt a tightening in his chest. What was the producer going to do? Accuse him of the death?

"Any idea how it happened?" He was going to get as many questions in as possible. He couldn't believe that Danny Murtz was calling *him*.

"Look, Sever, we got off on the wrong foot the other day. I'd like to set up another interview with you tonight."

"And?" It was too self-serving. Schwartz was gone, and now Murtz wanted to make sure the record was set straight. Maybe he wanted to settle the score. He knew they were out to get him, but he wasn't sure how they were going to do it the next time. Maybe this was the next time.

"Eight p.m. I'm going to give you everything you wanted. We'll talk about whatever you want to discuss."

"And what's changed?" Longtime reporter skepticism.

"It's time I got some things off my chest."

"Eight?"

"Yeah. I'll be the only one home, so either knock at the rear by the pool or just come on in. The back door is never locked on the island. I'll see you then." He hung up.

Sever sat on the bed, staring at the receiver in his hand. Everything was back in play.

He walked down to the pool, contemplating the change in Murtz. Mr. B. was setting up his bar for the lunch crowd.

"Mr. Sever, it's good to see you. Here, sit at my bar. I trust your adventures on the island have been kinder to you than the last time we talked. No more accidents with your car?"

He sat down, hesitating, not certain whether to tell Mr. B. about the car chase. "No, things are good."

The sun beat down on the tiled deck and bounced off the artificial blue pool water.

"Coffee?"

"Yeah. Black." The bartender poured him a cup and set it on the bar.

A yapping poodle broke the morning quiet, chasing around in the shallow end of the pool where an overweight woman waded through the water, her black bathing suit bulging everywhere.

"There was a drowning at Danny Murtz's villa last night."

Mr. B. dried a martini glass, then held it up to inspect it, the sunlight sparkling off its surface.

"In his pool?"

"Yeah."

"I'm sure it was accidental. There are no killings here in Paradise."

"That's what everyone keeps telling me. But you have a friend who went missing after he crossed Danny Murtz."

The bartender dried his hands, then placed them on the bar,

leaning toward Mick. "I do. I did. I told you we shouldn't discuss this."

"Did someone threaten you?"

Mr. B. glanced at the exit. Sever half expected him to leave again, but instead the bartender drew a deep breath and looked Sever directly in the eyes. "I tell you this because I fear for your life."

"Mine?"

"Yours. No one has ever found the body of my friend, so —"

"So no murder."

Mr. B. gave him a tight-lipped smile.

"Understand that I have no proof."

"I lied about having no problems. And, I do have proof, but I don't think anyone will want to hear it." Sever kept his eyes on the French bartender. "Someone tried to run me off the road last night, Bertrand. Right after I had an interview with Danny's attorney."

Mr. B. pursed his lips, pausing. "My friend, you may have crossed a line. You may have gone too far with a very dangerous man."

Sever sipped the coffee as the bartender turned. He reached into a drawer under the bar. Rummaging through it, he finally pulled out a bar towel wrapped around a hand-sized object.

"Take this."

"What is —"

"No." Bertrand looked in both directions. "Don't open it here. Put it in your pocket and take it with you. You can return it when you are ready to leave the island."

Sever could feel the outline of a pistol under the towel.

"Hey, I don't think —"

"Mick Sever, the problem is, you are not thinking. Someone doesn't want you to leave this island. Luck may not save your life. This," he pointed to the towel-wrapped pistol, "this will even the playing field."

Sever shoved it in his pocket, put five Euros on the bar and walked away. Just drop the gun off before he left the island. Assuming he left the island. Alive.

CHAPTER FIFTY-TWO

It was all coming together. Murtz called the Tropical Hotel in Saint-Jean where the band was staying. The lead guitarist answered the phone.

"Doug! Man, I'm sorry about what happened this morning. You having to find the body. Must have bummed you out."

"Dude. Like, in my entire life I've never — you know?"

"Yeah. Tough. Harvey was more than an attorney. He was a damned good friend."

"Hey, Danny, I'm like really sorry about Harvey and everything, but, dude, are we going to lose the shot with A&E? National television, man, it would have been very cool."

Spoken like a true rock promoter. Too bad about somebody dying a tragic death, but let's get on with making our career a reality.

"Doug. I'm going to call A&E and ask them to reschedule. Stop by about 7:15 tonight and we'll discuss. Cool?"

"Cool."

Murtz wrote it down. Clearly this was going to be a made to order plan. The Indoorfins' guitarist would show up at seven fifteen, and he'd be gone by seven forty-five. He'd tell Doug that he had a date with Michelle in town, and cut the meeting short. Then, Sever at eight. And that left Nancy and Raymond. How could he get Nancy out of the house? He'd give her the night off, but hell, she had nowhere to go. She'd been coming to the island for twenty-six years, but she always stayed in the villa, rarely ventured outside, and knew no one. A couple of times she'd brought *the boy*, but even then she'd stayed in most of the time. Went out with some American doctor named David once, but that went nowhere. An orthopedic surgeon. That sounded exciting. So she ran the place and it was almost like if she left, things would fall apart. Well, she hadn't left and things were starting to fall apart anyway, so maybe it was time to push the bird from the nest.

Murtz stood up, poured himself another shot of Scotch and walked out the office door to the pool. Raymond, the bodyguard, was lounging poolside, deep in sleep, his feet propped up on a stool and his pistol and shoulder holster lying on the table in front of him. Murtz's number-one bodyguard Little Jean was dead, killed in the car accident when he tried to run Sever off the road, so this sleeping beauty was the only barrier between Danny Murtz and some deranged fan or enemy who decided to kill him. Rather frightening.

Murtz stepped to the table and quietly pulled the gun from the holster. Pointing the pistol at Raymond's head he kicked the stool out from under the big man's feet. The bodyguard lurched, his eyes snapping open.

"Guh, who, what the hell?"

"What the fuck am I paying you for?"

"Danny, jeez, put down the gun. Man, you —"

Murtz put the gun to Raymond's temple, pressing the barrel into the soft skin and bone. A little louder now. "What the fuck am I paying you for? Naps?"

"Oh, God, Danny. Please. It was just for a second."

"I what? Surprised you? You know, Raymond, it's obvious you're doing me no good here."

"What do you mean? So I drifted off for a couple of seconds." The big man seemed to gather his courage. "Come on. It's not like we had an intruder or anything."

Big and dumb. Where did these guys come from? Murtz pulled the pistol back and aimed squarely between Raymond's eyes.

"It's not like what, Raymond? It's not like Little Jean may have been run off the road and killed? It's not like Harvey ended up at the bottom of this pool and no one knows why? And you sit sleeping on the job? Christ, you're useless."

"Danny, I'm sorry."

Murtz threw the pistol back on the table.

"I've got a job for you." It galled him that he actually needed this son of a bitch. He would love to have fired him on the spot. The useless, no-good piece of crap should have been cut lose right now. He should have smacked him a couple of times with the pistol, but that would have to wait. Maybe tomorrow would be the perfect time.

"Anything, Danny. I'm really sorry. It won't happen again."

"Tonight I'm taking Michelle Kirkendall to dinner. I need you to be at the restaurant."

"Sure, man. I can do that."

"Seven thirty, Carl Gustaf in Gustavia."

"I promise, I'll be there. Got it."

"No, you don't. Not yet. I want you there, but I don't want you at the table. So, I want you to ask Nancy to go as well."

The bodyguard shifted his eyes, looking at the villa for a moment. "Take Nancy?"

"The two of you, we'll get another table. You have dinner with her. That way you're nearby. A lot of shit's gone down, and I don't trust anybody on this island. I need protection. Do you understand?"

"I ask Nancy to go to dinner?"

"More like, you tell her. It's better than having you sit there like some fucking idiot, drinking a Coke at the bar by yourself, and watching Michelle and me eat. Or falling asleep on the job."

"You're the boss."

"Keep reminding yourself of that."

"And you're coming to meet us?"

"No. I'm going out drinking and carousing. You're an idiot, Raymond. Of course I'm meeting you." Murtz shook his head. "I've got Doug from the Indoorfins coming here at seven fifteen for a short meeting, then I'll pick up Michelle and meet you about eight thirty."

Raymond had stood up, cowering as if afraid he may get struck. Murtz was pleased and surprised with his own restraint, but he was on a mission, and that mission meant he had to keep some civility in his manner.

Murtz spun around and headed back to his office. Nancy had better not give him any shit about this. He had a strange suspicion that she had a thing for the dumb, beefy bodyguard, so maybe she'd accept the invitation without an argument. He walked to the walnut gun case, studying it for a long time. Maximum damage, something that would put someone down immediately. His eyes rested on the Colt .45 semiautomatic. The thing would do the trick. He pulled it from the case, balanced it in his hand, picked up a chamois and started polishing. Quite a history, this one. From 1911 through Vietnam, the Colt .45 had been a hero. He released the clip, checked it and smiled with satisfaction. Every one of his guns was loaded and ready for action. Murtz slowly inserted the barrel of the gun into his mouth. He closed his lips on the metal, wondering how his father had felt the second before he'd pulled the trigger on his gun.

CHAPTER FIFTY-THREE

Sever called her room. No answer. He tried again. Nothing. His eyes drifted to the balcony and the fully stocked bar and hot tub. The bar was a good idea. The hot tub was wasted on him. The phone rang.

"Mick."

"Jeff. Any luck?"

"Check your e-mail. I'll hold."

Sever clicked on his computer and tapped his fingers on the keyboard, waiting for it to boot up. Finally the familiar Windows chimes played. He ran through the usual spam and found Bloomberg's message and attachment.

"Got it. Hold on." He opened the attachment. Michelle's picture flashed on the screen, a shoulder and head shot. "Damn, it's her."

"Read on, friend. If this lady is on the island, I think we can make a good case for why she's there."

Sever scanned the story that followed. Michelle Kirkendall operated as an investigator with the Chicago Police Department and the missing persons bureau.

The story detailed some of her successes in missing children cases, highlighting a forced prostitution ring that had kidnapped a number of young women.

"It's what I needed." Sever smiled. The picture was dead-on. "But what leads you to believe she's here looking for Danny Murtz's missing women?"

"It's not so much in the story. I called a friend of mine on the force."

Probably the Chief. Jeff was well connected.

"He was guarded but said that she was 'on assignment.' "

Sever shut the computer down. "Which one is she looking for?"

"Find out."

"This is one tricky lady, Jeff. Supposedly she got Murtz to fly her over here on the pretense that they were boyfriend-girlfriend. Only they haven't seen much of each other since she got here."

"Murtz flew her over? Maybe Danny Murtz knows who she is and he's going to take her out too."

Sever rolled it over in his mind.

"Honestly I don't think he's figured it out. Jeff, they've tried to take me out twice. As far as I know she's been left alone."

"You should come home, amigo. This doesn't sound healthy."

"I know. But I've got a one-on-one with the man himself tonight. It's got to go better than the last interview."

"Be careful. Jesus, if they've tried twice who's to say they might not try again?"

"Actually, I think they tried three times. Someone tried to run me over in Chicago." Sever patted his pocket. "But I've got some protection. I don't know how much good it will do me, but I'll take my chances."

"Anything else you need, let me know."

"Thanks, Jeff. There'd better be one hell of a bonus at the end of this story."

"I'll see to it."

"Oh, and Jeff, if something does happen, and I'm not suggesting it will —"

"Yeah?"

"Make sure Ginny gets everything. I know that sounds weird, but I want her to know that whatever is left, it's hers. I've got no family, and hell, I owe her a lot more than that."

"Come on, Mick. This doesn't sound like you."

"I know. But I'm not going to live forever."

"There was a time when you thought you would."

"Maybe it's a sign of maturity?" Sever pulled the towel from this pocket and unwrapped the gun. He studied the Walther PPK. A German model made famous in the Bond movies.

"You? Mature?" Bloomfield chuckled. "Never."

They said their good-byes and Sever tried Michelle's room one more time. Now the question was, what was he going to tell her? That he knew the situation? That he suspected she was using him to find out more about Murtz? No answer.

He went out to the dinged-up rental car and climbed in, not certain exactly where he was going. Sever turned toward St. James, and in five minutes pulled up in front of the Eden Rock.

It was almost too easy. The man he was looking for was right there, sitting at the bar, in animated conversation with the bartender. Sever tapped Jordan Clark on the shoulder and he spun around, breaking into a wide smile.

"Mick. Undamaged and alive. Sit down, my friend. Let me buy you a drink." He signaled the bartender. "The best for my friend Mr. Sever."

"Vodka and grapefruit." The bartender looked disappointed. There was something about the bartenders on St. Barts that smacked of adventure. Don't give them run-of-the-mill drinks. Give them something with a challenge. Exotic, romantic.

"So, Mick, what brings you here?"

"Jordan, I need somebody to watch my back."

"Your what?"

"You'll be here tonight?"

"We're here until the weekend. My wife and I have extended our stay."

Sever sat down beside the man, the slow moving fans above swirling the warm air with a gentle breeze. "Look, I almost got you killed when that car exploded."

"It wasn't your fault, man."

"Yes, it was. I put myself in a position where someone needed to get rid of me."

Clark smiled. He toyed with his colorful yellow and orange drink, swirling it around in the glass.

"In Puerto Rico, we aren't exactly immune to crime, corruption, and death threats."

"Jordan, I've got a real problem. I'm not sure you want to get involved."

Clark held his hand up. "A long time ago I realized that I thrive on challenging experiences. Let me tell you a story before you tell me what you want."

Sever nodded.

"In 1997 my radio news team came to me with a story about a hotel. It turns out the Paradise Beach Hotel was owned by a mob guy in Pittsburgh, named Dominic Baronie. A number of crimes were attached to this guy and his brother, Tony, and our news team ran a series of stories about them."

"Really? A mobster named Tony Baronie?"

"Bad news guys. They threatened us."

"You ran them out?"

"They tried to make good on a couple of threats."

"But you hung in there?"

"My wife was kidnapped."

"Jesus."

"Jesus. I prayed to him every day."

"You prayed, but you took matters into your own hands?"

"She's alive. She's with me. And I did what I had to do. Let's go no further with my participation. However, in April of that year Dominic pleaded guilty to helping his brother hide money skimmed from a bunch of Indian casinos, a chain of Ramada Inns in New Jersey, and our hotel in Puerto Rico."

"And Tony Baronie?"

"He's doing time. In a wheelchair."

Sever stared at his new friend with respect and a little fear.

"And your point is?"

"My point is, we were all scared to death. Hell, our lives were in danger. And because we were doing what we felt was right, we were exhilarated. It was the thrill of a lifetime."

"So you're telling me you look forward to life-threatening experiences?"

"I thrive on them."

"Well, I've got a great one for you!"

CHAPTER FIFTY-FOUR

Nancy had agreed to dinner. She'd even stuck her head in his office door, giving him a wry smile. "So we're chaperoning you tonight?"

"You can always stay here and eat cold pizza."

Murtz leaned back in the leather chair, a drink in his hand and a slight buzz going on in his head. He'd dimmed the lights, and the room had a ghostly quality to it.

"No. I'll go."

He watched her silhouette in the doorway, her hair down around her shoulders. Sometimes the stern, officious, matronly manager of his empire, sometimes a seductress. An aging seductress, but a seductress nonetheless. "What have we heard about Harvey's drowning?"

She hesitated.

"You know it might not look good, all of us going out for dinner on the day of his death."

"I thought about that. I'm not certain there's a strong clamoring for a mourning period."

"What's that supposed to mean?"

"You wanted him gone. You were afraid he was going to fire your boy. I had my own issues with him."

"But how will it look?"

Murtz knocked back a slug of rum and Coke, going very well with the cocaine he'd snorted ten minutes before. Didn't want to get too far out of whack. There was a lot going on tonight.

"Danny?"

He caressed the cold glass, drawing a pattern in the condensation on the outside. "It will look like we're going on with our lives."

"You know this is a small island. People will talk."

"When has that ever bothered me before?"

She shook her head. "I talked to one of the officers earlier and he said it appears that the drowning was an accident."

"An accident." Big surprise.

"There was a large gash on the back of his head, but they believe he probably slipped, fell, hit his head on the side of the pool, and drowned."

"Is that what you believe?"

"What?"

"They would never admit that Harvey was murdered, would they?" He sipped the rum drink, rolling the sweet mixture in his mouth.

Nancy walked into the room, standing squarely in front of Murtz.

"What the hell are you insinuating?"

"What if someone killed him? What if someone came onto the property last night and killed Harvey?"

"Why would someone do that?"

He sat still for a moment in the semidark study, thinking it through. The logic was a little fuzzy, but so was everything else.

"Mick Sever was trying to accuse me of being responsible for the disappearance of several girls I dated."

She was quiet.

"No comment? Oh, come on, Nancy. Let's not pretend you don't have questions too."

She was quiet. Eventually she'd have to go. They all had to go. She'd walked out on him for six months after her first year. When she came back, he knew it couldn't be forever. That was twenty-five years ago. He couldn't trust her. He couldn't trust anyone.

"No comment?" he asked again.

She frowned. "Go on, Danny."

"He and Harvey had the interview last night. I think Sever threatened to do some investigative reporting —"

"And?"

Another swallow of rum and Coke. "And I think Harvey threatened to stop him."

"Danny, that's ridiculous."

"Ridiculous? Nancy, Harvey came in to see me after the interview. He said he'd given Sever a veiled threat, and now he was concerned that the reporter might take matters into his own hands."

She shook her head. "It was an accident. Officially an accident. I believe we leave it right there. If we don't, they might start looking at you."

He couldn't remember. Something happened last night but it wasn't registering.

"Watch your back, Nancy. We continue to be surrounded by people we can't trust."

She gave him a quizzical look. "I've got to get ready for dinner." She stomped out of the room.

Murtz sipped the last of the drink, cocked his arm, and tossed the glass after her. She didn't even turn as it landed behind her and broke into dozens of fine, sharp splinters.

CHAPTER FIFTY-FIVE

The phone rang at seven fifteen, just as he was about to walk out the door. He looked down at the parking lot and saw Jordan Clark standing by his car. Maybe this was just a bad idea, having backup for an interview. He didn't trust Danny Murtz or anyone associated with him, and putting Clark in harm's way was dangerous. However, there was no one else. Maybe Mr. B., who had his own axe to grind with the famous producer. But that didn't make much sense either. Besides, Clark had been almost giddy with the prospect of being part of the plot.

"Hello."

"Mick, it's Jeff."

"More information?"

"Listen, they found the body of Randi Parks."

"Body? Not good."

"No. No identification, no clothes, nothing. So it took them a while. She'd been gone over thoroughly by somebody who didn't want her identified. Bleach, peeled off skin on her fingers, broken teeth —"

"Man! But they're sure it's her?"

"DNA thing. Don't ask me to explain it."

"Thanks for the update."

Sever shuddered, remembering the attractive redhead, the tall slender body, and those soft eyes. He'd anticipated the interview. Now . . .

"There's more."

"I'm a reporter. I know there's always more."

"Stay away from Danny Murtz."

"Why?"

"We've been doing some homework on Miss Parks. Danny Murtz had a couple of dates with her."

Sever stared out at the ocean. The sun hanging low in the sky sent shimmering golden waves across the pounding surf. Three boys rode the waves in, precariously balancing on their brightly painted surfboards until, like dominoes, they spilled from the boards and were lost for the moment in the frothy sea. When you put yourself in a dangerous situation, you take your chances.

"Mick? Do you hear me?"

"It doesn't mean he killed her."

"No. But what if it means that's why he's trying to kill you?"

Sever walked out onto the patio and motioned to Jordan Clark, still pacing the parking lot. "Jordan, we're going to be a couple of minutes yet. Come on in and pour yourself a drink."

"Mick," Bloomfield measured his words, "you were in touch with this girl —"

"Almost daily. She called me everyday for two weeks, bugging me to set up the interview."

"What if she called you that night? Got a little drunk, out of control, and decided to call you and talk about the upcoming interview?"

"I never got that call."

"It doesn't mean she didn't try."

"Jeff, come on."

"What if Danny Murtz caught her calling you? Maybe got jealous? Maybe was afraid that she told you she was with him."

"You're stretching things, Jeff."

"Somebody did a job on this girl. Her head is bashed in, her limbs are broken. Damn, Mick."

"She never called and told me she was with someone. It wasn't like that. It was strictly business."

"Mick, I'm asking you not to do that interview."

"Covering your ass?"

A long pause. "You're a friend. Your life has been threatened. For God's sake fold it up and come home."

"You know I can't do that."

"You're an idiot."

"I'll get you your story, Jeff. I have never walked away from a good story."

Sever could hear a radio somewhere in the background playing a country tune.

"Mick, don't become the story. Okay?"

He'd become the story so many times before. It was part of his fame. Books, movies, he didn't even think about it. Woodward and Bernstein had become a part of the story back in the Watergate days. It was part of investigative journalism.

"Jeff, I'll be careful. I'll call you tomorrow and let you know how everything came out."

"You're meeting him tonight?"

"I am."

"I don't care what time it is, you call me tonight. Understand?"

"Jeff—"

"Goddamnit, I'm paying you good money, Sever. You call me or I'll hold your bonus hostage. Understand?"

Sever smiled. Jordan Clark watched him, sipping a glass of the Manapany's finest Scotch. "Got it, Jeff. I'll wake your ass up at three this morning. Don't worry about it. Everything is going to be fine." Sever heard the click on the transatlantic call and knew Bloomfield would stay up half the night waiting.

"Drink up, friend." He nodded at Clark. "We're already going to be late for my big interview."

"Bad news?"

"I shouldn't tell you. My editor back in Chicago has a dead body he's attributing to Danny Murtz. He thinks I should cancel the interview and get off the island."

"What do you think?"

"Jordan, I've been in the line of fire before. It doesn't scare me. It probably should, but it doesn't. I want this story."

"Good for you."

"But you've got nothing invested in this. You've got a wife, a business, a boat, and you're putting yourself on the line for absolutely nothing. Remember," Sever walked off the patio, Clark following close behind, "I'm getting paid."

"Good point."

They got into the car, Sever hesitating before he started it. One big bang and this conversation would be pointless.

Clark stretched his legs in the compact car. "At this point, would you do the interview if you weren't getting paid?"

No hesitation. "Without a doubt. No question. I want to nail this son of a bitch."

"That's what I thought."

Sever checked his watch. He was going to have to push it to make it by eight. "When we get there, you stay in the car. If I'm not out in forty minutes, come looking for me."

"Wouldn't it be easier if I came in with you?"

"No. I don't want him to know I've got backup. If you hear a gunshot, screaming, come running, man! Come running."

"Okay. I'll wait. You know, it's too bad."

"What's that?"

"The guy seems to have so much talent. He's had so many hits. I mean, this guy could have just about anything he wanted."

"So far I think you're right. He's had everything he wanted, including immunity for murder."

"What is it about fame, Mick? Celebrities get away with murder. Literally. They never have to pay."

Sever was reminded of a line from a Thompson Brothers song. *Pretty faces pay no cover.* "That's about to change."

Sever reached out and touched the pistol lying beside him. He stepped on the gas as he rounded the first curve and started climbing the hill.

CHAPTER FIFTY-SIX

"I've got a dinner engagement, Doug. I think we've wrapped everything up here."

The Indoorfins' young guitar player stood up from the lounge chair, running his fingers through his long black hair. He once again surveyed all the equipment by the pool. "Man, it was so strange this morning. He was bloated, you know, and you could see the top of his head was caved in. God, it was just —"

Murtz glanced at his watch for the tenth time in half an hour.

"Gotta run, Doug. Let yourself out. I've got a lady waiting for me and I've got to meet her at eight."

"Thanks, Danny. The guys appreciate what you're doing. You want us here tomorrow at ten?"

With everything that was going to happen, tomorrow at ten would never happen, but for now he'd say whatever the long-haired kid wanted to hear. Just get the hell out so tonight's drama could unfold.

"Yeah. And we'll see how much the guys appreciate it when they become best-selling artists. It's easy to forget who got you there."

"No, dude. We're solid, you know."

Doug walked out through the house and Murtz picked up the drink glasses, taking them to the kitchen, and putting them on the granite-topped counter. He waited until he heard the guitar player's rented car start up. Then he entered the study and picked up the

Colt .45. The handle felt clammy, the ivory custom grip almost slipping in his hand. Humidity. It must be. He eased into the leather chair, and for just a moment thought about the entourage at the restaurant. Nancy and the dumb, burly bodyguard, Raymond. They'd be waiting. Waiting for a rendezvous that wasn't going to happen.

He thought about checking on his guest, but Sever would be along shortly and he didn't want to miss that. He wondered who Michelle really was. Did she work with Sever or was she on her own? Maybe a private detective? Murtz couldn't even remember where he'd met her, probably in a bar in Chicago. But when he found out he was being exiled to St. Barts for a brief time, he'd immediately thought about lining up someone to pass the time with, and out of the blue, she called. The problem was, he didn't really know her that well. She wasn't the run-of-the-mill dumb blond that he was used to. She wasn't someone who was involved in the entertainment business. She wasn't the kind of girl he usually chose for his excursions.

And maybe that was a bad thing. If he'd stuck to the bimbos, he wouldn't have a trussed-up prisoner in the cottage right now. Later tonight, after everything settled down, he would take a trip with her. To Saline Beach. The boggy salt marshes hid one of his victims already. Tonight would be number two. Stuck in the muck.

Murtz slowly eased the barrel of the gun into his mouth. He toyed with the trigger, his index finger on, off, on, off. He pulled it out and laid the pistol on his desk. One more line of coke. He sniffed it up and checked his watch. Five after eight. Damn. They'd be waiting for him, so this had to happen fast. He needed the timing to be damn near perfect.

What was the noise? He'd expected Sever's car to pull up in the driveway, and he hadn't heard a car. But there it was, a faint, barely perceptible noise from the back entrance. He'd told Sever to come in that way, even left the pool gate open. It was time. Murtz walked out the door, down the hall, and quietly stood just shy of the opening to the living room. Murtz could hear footsteps. Closer. Closer. He didn't need to see the victim, just fire through the center of the hall. Someone was breaking into his house. He had to defend himself.

Murtz spun into the opening, spreading his legs and holding the pistol with both hands. Just like a ponytailed cowboy, defending the ranch. Without hesitation he squeezed the trigger once, twice. Bang, bang. The explosion was deafening in the confined space, the gun bucked in his hands and the shadowy figure dropped like a stone. Don't fuck with Danny Murtz. Breaking and entering. Someone had to pay.

Murtz walked to the body, knelt down, and his head started to spin. It wasn't Sever. Oh, Christ. It wasn't the reporter. Some slight little girl. He stared for thirty seconds, playing scenarios in his muddled brain. He grabbed the wall to steady himself. Was she one of the girls from last night? Maybe she left something. Or maybe it was the girl he slapped around a couple of evenings ago. Harvey was supposed to have paid her off. Goddamn, Harvey wasn't around to handle the situation. He needed Harvey. Finally he rose and flipped on the hall light. He turned her over and almost jumped when the body twitched. Damn. She was breathing. He stared in horror at the face, shocked for an instant out of his drug-induced stupor. He knew that face. Jennifer Koenig, complete with the facial scar from that pistol whipping he'd given her. He was suddenly more sober than he'd been in a long time.

The phone rang, the shrill ring assaulting his brain. Ignore it. He had guests waiting in Gustavia. He had a girl in the guest cottage and a severely injured girl bleeding in his home, and Sever was already late for an interview that never was supposed to happen. Sever, the intruder, should be dead by now, the gendarmes should have been called. Instead he had another victim on his hands. Holy shit, could things get any worse? Murtz buried his head in his hands.

He lifted his head, and sat on the floor, gazing at the far wall, listening to the girl's labored breathing. She appeared to have been hit in the shoulder, blood spreading over her T-shirt and staining his white-tiled floor. Finally he rose, grabbed her legs and pulled her to the hall closet. He opened the door and shoved her inside. He had to think, and having a dying girl lying on his floor didn't help.

The doorbell broke the stillness, shaking him, and he pushed the Colt into the rear waistband of his jeans. Should he answer the door? Sever. That was it. Sever, breaking and entering. The bell rang again, cascading tones that used to sound so musical. Tonight they jangled, reminding Murtz of a cowbell he'd used on several songs by a band called Ironwood. Blood streaked the floor and he thought about toweling it up first. Hopefully there would be more blood, so he could wait until Sever's was spilled as well.

What the hell. How many more things could go wrong tonight. Murtz slowly approached the front door. Damn it, he'd told Sever to come in the rear. It would look a lot more like the reporter was a burglar if he used the back entrance, but what the hell. He turned the handle and pulled the door open quickly. The big man filled the entrance, a frown on his face. Bill from next door. The collector. Guns, cars, cameras.

"Mr. Murtz. It's good to see you again." He stood there with his hand outstretched.

Murtz looked at his own right hand. Blood stained the palm from where he'd dragged Jennifer's body into the closet. Ignoring the offered hand, he glanced back at Bill, saying nothing. God, he needed a drink. A joint. A hit of something.

The phone rang, and Murtz took a step toward the kitchen as Bill started to step into the house, his imposing figure threateningly close to the entrance. "I don't mean to bother you, but as you know, we're in the villa next door. My wife, Susan, and I were out by the pool and we both thought we heard gunshots. Two of them, maybe inside your house. Well, you know, I thought I should stop over and make certain everything was all right. I mean —"

The nagging phone kept ringing. He had to get rid of this guy. Murtz let the phone ring, stoically blocking the entrance to his home, his blood-covered hand now behind his back, feeling the grip on his Colt .45.

"So, can I come in?"

What? He barely knew the man. There was blood on the floor and a dying woman in the closet. Of course he couldn't come in.

Bill stuck his head in and looked back and forth. "Mr. Murtz, is everything all right?"

He tried to smile, but the corners of his mouth refused to respond. Too much going on. Too much to think about.

"Yes. Thank you for your concern, but —"

But what? What had caused the two loud bangs? A pistol. Murtz slowly pulled the Colt from his back, gripping the handle tightly. He'd have to clean the blood off later. "I was cleaning this, and —"

"You're sure you're all right?" Bill's eyes were on the Colt.

"Really, it was nothing."

"It's a nice piece. Do you mind if I hold it?"

Son of a bitch wouldn't back down. Blood on the handle, he couldn't let Bill touch it.

"I mind. I'm very, uh, protective of the collection."

The big man frowned again. "Sure, I understand." He stood on the porch, looking beyond Murtz. "Well, if you have any problems or need anything, please, let me know."

Shoot him now? Or use him as part of the alibi? Murtz just wanted him to go so he could pour himself a stiff Scotch.

"I was checking out the gun. I think somebody tried to break into my house in the last several days and —"

"Oh, my God. And the drowning of your attorney. I don't have to tell you that these things don't normally happen on St. Barts."

Only to Danny Murtz.

"Got to go, Bill. I've got dinner with a young woman in town and I'd hate to disappoint her."

He felt a tremor shake and chill his body. He had to get rid of Bill. Please leave, please! If he didn't go, he'd shoot him. Right there on the porch.

Bill gave him a sad look, then walked down the steps and headed toward his villa. Where the hell was Sever? The guy had practically salivated over the interview and it was now almost eight forty-five and he hadn't appeared. Christ, the entourage, as it was, would be sending out the gendarmes to look for him. He could call the restaurant, but he was afraid it would look too setup, too convenient. He wanted to call afterward, not before.

He watched Bill disappear around the bend. Damned busybody neighbor. Murtz walked back into the living room, entering the guest bathroom. He yanked a towel off the rack and wiped the blood from his hands and the gun, then knelt down in the hallway, sopping up the sticky red blood. It had already stained the grout. There was a soft moan from the closet and he considered opening the door and finishing the job. Put the girl out of her misery. Then he heard the handle turn on the rear entrance door.

CHAPTER FIFTY-SEVEN

They coasted into the driveway, and Sever cut the engine. "It's not too late to say no."

Jordan shook his head. "I'm with you, Mick."

Sever smiled. It was late, and he hoped Murtz had waited. Surely he didn't have any other plans for a while. An interview was going to take at least half an hour and if Murtz was fair, he'd have set aside a couple of hours.

"I know, Mick. I stay in the car. If there's any sign of trouble, I either come to the rescue or drive out of here and get help."

"If it comes to the help part, we may be in this by ourselves." Sever stared straight ahead at the villa.

"I don't know anyone on the island who would give us a hand."

Sever opened the door of the rental. He was to enter from the rear, by the pool. He stepped out and stretched his tender knee. Regardless of whether he was in the warm sunshine of the Caribbean or the bitter, windy cold of Chicago, it always hurt when he'd been in confined spaces. He reached in and picked up the Walther PPK, stuffing it in the waistband of his khakis. Sever pulled his blue linen shirttail over the weapon and headed toward the villa.

"Good luck, friend."

Clark stepped out, walked around the car, and took his place in the driver's seat.

It was at that very moment, as Jordan Clark settled his bulk into the cloth seat, as Sever walked five steps toward the pool entrance, that they both heard the two loud explosions. Sever froze.

"Mick!" Clark was yelling. "What the hell was that?"

Fireworks? Sever glanced at the horizon. It was still light outside and fireworks made no sense. The sound had come from inside.

"Gunshots."

"I said I was game for anything." Clark shouted at Sever as he started the engine.

Sever turned and headed toward the car.

"I lied. I'm not game for live ammunition."

Sever opened the passenger door and climbed inside.

"Neither am I. Pull out and let's drive down the road a couple of houses."

"Then what? You're not thinking about going back in there?"

"Give this thing time to play out."

He thought about his options. *Go back in five minutes and act as if nothing was wrong. Go back to the Manapany and take Jeff's advice, grab the first plane and head for home. Call the gendarmes, or, if he had a damned cell phone, call the villa.* As it was, he didn't know the number and had no cell phone.

Clark drove down the road slowly, not familiar with the terrain. A flatbed truck rounded the first corner and almost forced him into a ditch. Clark swore and slowly continued. Two driveways down, he pulled off.

"Is this good enough?"

"Fine. Let's just give this a couple of minutes. Chances are it was nothing. There could be a lot of explanations for a sound like that."

"Name one." Clark still clutched the steering wheel, his fingers wrapped tightly around the vinyl.

Sever couldn't.

"Mick, I really think you should consider the danger here. From what's already happened, this could be an attempt on your life."

Sever hadn't considered that. Someone may have been firing at his car. It was a cinch that the crew at Murtz's villa knew what his car looked like. Hell, they'd tried to run it off the road last night. He got out and walked around the vehicle, looking for bullet holes. There was nothing. Just the deep scrapes from the fatal road chase.

They both sat silently, staring at the large villa in front of them. No one seemed to be home.

"We'll give it a couple more minutes."

"And then?"

"I'm going back. I've got to find out what happened."

"Mick, somebody has a gun!"

"Yeah. And you know what?"

Clark shook his head. "No. What?"

"So do I." Sever pulled the Walther from his waistband and held it flat in his hand.

"Jesus. You're crazy, do you know that?"

Sever made eye contact. "Do you want to leave? I told you before, I feel guilty even having you here. I never should have asked."

Clark met the contact, smiled and said, "I'm not leaving. I'll admit that shots fired at close range scare the hell out of me, but I've had a chance to catch my breath. I'm in, Mick. I'm in."

"You're sure? What about your wife, Dani?"

"I think she'd want me to see it to its completion. I told you before, I almost lost her to the bad guys. I owe it to her, and to me, to stick this out and see if we can get this asshole."

"All right. Then let's drive back to Murtz's. I'll act as if nothing ever happened. Whatever disturbance there was, it's had time to settle down. I'll tell him I'm late because we got stuck on the road or something."

Clark put the car in reverse.

"Have you ever used a gun before?"

"I have."

"Are you any good?"

Sever stroked the black metal. "I don't have a clue what I'm doing."

"So you really don't know how to use the thing?"

"I shot a man once."

"You what?"

Sever was silent. It was kill the guy or the guy would kill Ginny. There really wasn't any choice. It still felt funny to admit that he'd taken someone's life. Tom Biddle. Even though he felt justified, and Ginny walked away unscathed, the act would haunt Sever for the rest of his life.

"Could you do it again? Tonight if you needed to?"

Sever wasn't sure he could. You never knew until the situation was in your face.

CHAPTER FIFTY-EIGHT

He heard the soft chimes of the clock in the living room. Nine chimes to be exact. His timing was way off. The door handle turned and Murtz froze. It should be Sever, but you could never tell. There was a dying girl in the closet, a suspicious, prying neighbor just leaving his house and, hopefully, a nosy reporter coming through the door. Holding the pistol in front of him, Murtz walked to the hallway. The lights were off, and he saw the shadowy character turn and pull the outside door shut. He blinked, trying to make out the person.

"Danny? What the hell are you doing?"

Murtz froze. The voice, the authority in the voice. It reminded him of a nun he'd had in sixth grade. He'd had a thing for her, but she was a bitch.

"Danny, answer me."

The nun. That was who she reminded him of. All these years. That's who she was. Nancy glowered at him from down the hall. What the hell was Nancy doing back here? Raymond had strict instructions.

"Danny, put down the gun. My God. Where have you been? I got tired of waiting and decided to see if you had some problems. Raymond is back at the restaurant, waiting, just in case you got there. Why didn't you answer the phone? Now put the damned gun down."

He could make out her severe outline, hands on her hips, and he wanted to pull the trigger. He wanted to start over. No Harvey. No Nancy.

She reached for the wall and flipped on the lights. Her pale, drawn face wore a serious frown. Things were falling apart quickly.

"Danny, give me the gun."

She walked up to him, holding her hand out. Murtz's arm quivered, his index finger twitched as he stroked the trigger. "Danny." The voice was firm, tough, and he felt tears sting his eyes.

Nancy took three steps to him, her arm outstretched. She grabbed the barrel, the smooth cool barrel of his gun, and gently pulled it from his grasp. He felt himself go limp and he slumped against the wall.

"Now, what the hell is this all about?" She walked to the grand piano and laid the pistol on the white lacquered wood.

The moan came from the closet, louder than before. Murtz buried his head in his hands and tears ran down his cheeks.

"What the hell? Who's in the closet?"

Murtz was silent. His voice had left him.

"Danny, I can't help you if you don't tell me what's going on. Do you have a girl in the closet? Is that why you didn't show up for dinner? Jesus, Danny."

Murtz looked up at her, studying her questioning face. Harvey would have handled it. Harvey would have taken care of everything. He desperately needed someone to take care of the situation. Where the hell was Harvey? He'd abandoned him in his hour of need. He opened the door and Nancy gasped.

"Who . . . what . . . what is *she* doing in there?" Then she gasped again. "She's covered in blood. Jesus, Danny, what did you do?"

Backbone. He needed a little fortitude. He held up an index finger.

"Wait. One minute." Murtz quickly walked back to his office, laying out a line of pure white powder and inhaling it through a straw. He put his head back for just a moment, then fixed himself a rum and Coke at the bar. Coke and more coke. He'd read once that Coca-Cola had originally used cocaine in the drink recipe. Should have left it alone.

When he approached the hall, he saw that Nancy had pulled the girl out of the closet and seemed to be tending to her wound. She knelt by the girl who took shallow. gasping breaths. Her pale face was the color of talcum powder, or maybe the powder he'd just ingested.

Nancy glanced up with a grim look. "You've got a habit of doing this, don't you?"

His eyes widened. "And where does that come from? What the hell are you insinuating?" Mother Superior, with that attitude. "She broke in. After what happened to Harvey and what happened to Jean, I wasn't taking any chances." He took a long swallow of his drink.

Nancy wiped at the blood with a towel from the hall bathroom.

"Do you know who this is?"

Murtz nodded, standing above the two women. He needed some perspective. Harvey wasn't here. Harvey wasn't coming back for a cleanup. And Sever still had to be dealt with.

"Danny," she looked up at him, "she's alive. Now, we can get some medical help or I suppose you can do what you've done before."

"And what the hell does that mean?"

"Come on Danny, you and I go back. Way back."

"So you have the right to accuse me of shooting people?"

He gave her a wide-eyed stare. Throw the blame back on the accuser. It was part of his arsenal.

Nancy held the towel, soaked with the blood from the girl's wound. It was obvious from her tone of voice that she wasn't buying any denial.

"Do you finish the job or try to save her?"

Save her? Breaking and entering. And what if Sever were to walk through the door right now? Well that would certainly fuck everything up. Certainly.

"Danny, what do you want me to do?"

He walked to the piano and picked up the Colt .45.

"Sever's supposed to be here. I scheduled an interview."

"You what? What about dinner, and that Michelle and —?"

It was so far out of whack. He couldn't believe it had gone so wrong. Counselor, I take it all back. You were a genius at solving all of my problems. Hell, it's a lot harder than it looks. Why the hell did you fall into that pool and leave me?

"Danny, I need to know."

Murtz squinted, focusing on Nancy's face. She knew. He could tell that she knew.

"You know. You know exactly what's happened, and what's about to happen. You know about Randi Parks, don't you? Did Harvey tell you? Were you both trying to get more money out of me? Were you trying to drive me fucking crazy?"

Holding the gun at waist level, he pointed it at Nancy Steiner's head as she knelt by the girl.

"Randi Parks? Who the hell is Randi Parks?"

"The girl, the singer who called Sever. You know."

She looked genuinely confused.

"You know, damn it, you know. Did you deliver the letters? Trying to make me lose my mind?"

"Danny, point the gun somewhere else. I do know this is Jennifer Koenig. You beat her up pretty badly and she threatened to go public with it. She wanted you behind bars, and I do know that Harvey stepped in and saved the day. As much as I hated the bastard, I know he shut her up. We almost lost a good thing, Danny."

A tremor shook his hand, and he tightened his grip on the pistol.

"But I didn't kill her, did I? I knew I didn't. There were others, but not her."

"Time will tell. She may be dead by tomorrow. I don't think she's doing that well at the moment. Please, put the gun down."

"No. The gun stays where it is. This girl, this Jennifer, was breaking and entering. I'm well within my rights. Now, tell me how Harvey shut this girl up."

He was feeling a lot more confident. In control, and it felt good.

"Can I stand up?"

"No. Stay there. And tell me."

She frowned. He wondered what he'd ever seen in her years ago. She was a conniving bitch, a power-hungry ball buster that he should have fired years ago.

"You pistol whipped her and she had the scars to prove it. This girl wanted to hand you to the authorities. Plus, she claimed she had information that would tie you to at least one disappearance and a possible murder. The murder of some girl you dated named Libby Hellman."

Murtz remembered the story. He remembered that Jennifer had threatened him. He should have killed her. He beat her, slashing her face with the barrel of a pistol. Couldn't remember which pistol. Should have taken care of the problems as they surfaced. Instead, he let it fester. And now she was in his hallway, her blood staining his clean white floor.

"Harvey retaliated." Nancy knew the story much better than Murtz. "He had a couple of his friends in Chicago visit her in New York. They roughed her up, convinced her that her career was over, threatened her with her life and the lives of her family, and she immediately disappeared. As far as I know no one has heard from her until now."

"So *we* didn't know if Harvey's goons had killed her or not? All this time we never knew if she was dead or alive?"

"No." She started to rise and Murtz shook his head. "Danny, I only talked twice about it to Harvey and he never knew what happened to her. I don't think he wanted to know."

Murtz put the cool barrel of the pistol to Nancy's head. "How do you know all of this? How do you know more than I do?"

There was no fear. She stared at him with her cold eyes, never blinking. "Are you sure you want to know?"

"I want to know."

"I slept with him. I slept with the miserable prick. We were lovers. You learn a lot from someone when you share a bed."

"You slept with him?" *Where the hell did that come from?* "And he told you about —"

"About Shelley O'Dell, about Libby Hellman? He did."

"The fucker. I knew I shouldn't trust him. And he told you about Randi?"

"That must be a new one, Danny. Harvey and I had barely talked to each other in the last year."

It didn't surprise him. He had enough on his plate without worrying about who his attorney and secretary were shagging. But if it was going on behind his back, so be it.

"So what broke you two up?" *Shouldn't have trusted him. The son of a bitch had no business telling Nancy his business during pillow talk.*

"It's not important, Danny."

"Oh, humor me. I could use a little humor. The dying girl on the floor, your dalliances with my attorney, the deaths of my attorney and my bodyguard."

He left out the wounded girl in the guest cottage.

"I could use some goddamned humor."

He could hear his voice, ringing in his own ears. He was practically yelling, his eyes stinging with tears.

"So tell me, tell me you conniving whore, tell me why you two quit communicating."

"Damn it, Danny. Let me stand up."

"All right." He motioned to her with the gun. "Get up."

"We quit communicating last year when you hired Raymond."

"Raymond?"

"We started . . ." she hesitated, "Raymond and I started an affair."

"What?"

Did his entire staff find this woman hot? First of all Murtz had sampled the wares, then Harvey, then Raymond. In the last twenty-five years there may have been others. He didn't really want to know.

"When Harvey found out, he threatened me. He told me that Jason's job was in jeopardy. And after knowing what he was capable of . . ." she hesitated, "what *you* were capable of —"

And then it hit him like a bolt of lightning. He knew what had happened. "You killed Harvey, didn't you?"

"You're guessing, Danny?"

"No. I saw you, didn't I?"

"And if I said yes? If I told you that I did end his life, if I told you that I did it to save both of us, would you hold it against me? He was holding you hostage, and threatening Jason!"

"Fuck Jason." Murtz slashed at her face, the pistol hitting her high on the cheekbone and drawing blood.

"My God, you killed Harvey."

Nancy raised her hand to her face, covering the wound.

"Of all the hypocritical things to say."

"I didn't kill him. And you almost had me believing I did. You bitch. You killed Harvey, then tried to make me feel guilty."

"You are a murderer, Danny. You killed women because of your insatiable appetite for drugs, alcohol, and sex. So don't judge me, you sanctimonious prick. Don't you ever judge me."

More blood, dripping from her face and mixing with the blood already coagulating on the floor. Jennifer Koenig moaned and for a fleeting moment Murtz thought about blowing both of them away on the spot. But then good neighbor Bill would be back sticking his nose into everything. Murtz pushed the gun into Nancy's stomach and shoved her backwards. "Turn around and walk out that door."

She kept her hand over the cut as she followed his instructions.

"Where are we going?"

Murtz flipped off the light switch.

"We're going to the guest cottage. There's someone there I'd like to introduce you to."

CHAPTER FIFTY-NINE

Sever walked toward the house. It was late, the gunshots had spooked him, and he wanted some time to elapse. There had to be a plausible explanation for those shots. But wait a minute — this was Danny Murtz. There didn't have to be a plausible explanation at all. There was a good chance that Murtz had given up and either gone to bed or gone on one of his late-night adventures. Sever entered the pool gate and gazed at the water for a moment. Last night he'd sat next to the pool with Murtz's attorney. Sometime during the night Harvey Schwartz had drowned. Dead girls, dead attorney, and attempts on Sever's own life. You took your chances.

The rear door was open, just like Murtz said it would be, but the hall was dark. He stood inside the entrance, hesitating, wondering if he should just walk in.

"Danny?"

No answer.

"Danny?"

It was much too quiet. Then he heard the soft moaning. Like a kitten with a mournful meow. His instinct was to step back, turn around, and leave. The interview could happen another day. Instead, he took a step forward, straining to pick up the sound again.

"Help me."

He stopped, his eyes adjusting to the dim light. He looked down and froze. He'd almost stepped on her. The girl lay sprawled in the hallway. Sever ran his hand over the wall, looking for a light switch. Finally finding it, he flipped it on. The soft overhead light illuminated the girl's body, her T-shirt covered in blood.

"Help me." Her eyes fluttered open and she squinted in the light.

Sever knelt down, instinctively touching her cheek. The girl he'd tackled from last night. Things just kept getting weirder.

"We need to call a doctor."

He couldn't move her. The injury looked too serious to risk a move.

"No." She forced the words.

"Take me away. They'll kill me."

Her breathing was labored and she coughed.

"They?"

"Danny and Nancy."

He had to call a doctor. There were rooms off the hallway. There had to be phones. He wondered if there was such a thing as 911 on the island. "Nobody's going to kill you."

"Take me with you. Please."

She coughed again and spit up blood. Internal bleeding? He wasn't a doctor, but the situation seemed pretty desperate. Murtz hadn't finished the job this time, but he'd come damn close. Sever checked out the first room, an office to the right, with a phone on the desk. He picked up the receiver. Punching the zero, he waited. Somebody had to provide some medical attention or it didn't appear this girl was going to make it out alive.

CHAPTER SIXTY

Murtz's foggy brain retraced the steps from last night. The pool, a bad hangover, and someone raising a heavy bar high in the air. Harvey and Nancy had argued, maybe about *the boy*, maybe about her romp with Raymond, or maybe about Murtz, but it was clear that she'd caved in his head and pushed him in the pool. He vaguely remembered the images.

"He was going to take you down, Danny. He was constantly holding you up for more money."

"Keep moving."

He shoved her along the flagstone sidewalk with his free hand. They approached the door and he fumbled in his pocket for the key, keeping the pistol trained on her the entire time. She was a murderer with more strength than he would have imagined. Busting Harvey's head open. He wasn't about to give her a fighting chance. Unlocking the door, he kicked it open and pushed her inside.

"What are you going to do?"

She turned, a defiant look in her eyes. The cut on her cheek had turned a deep purple and she touched it gingerly, the wound still wet with fresh blood.

"Are you going to kill me, Danny? Because whether you know it or not, you need me. Right now you need me more than you have ever needed anyone. Harvey's not around to clean up after you anymore. You'd better have someone in your corner."

He heard her, the murdering, psycho bitch, but he didn't trust anyone.

"In that room. Move it."

"Danny, you're making a big mistake. I'm on your side. Let's keep it that way."

Now there was a tremor in her voice, an uncertain quality. The domineering lady wasn't so sure of herself anymore.

"I said get in the room." He pointed ahead to the closed door.

"Danny, please." Begging. She was actually pleading with him.

"Nancy, I'm going to do what I need to do. Get the hell into that room."

She took baby steps, trying to stop the inevitable entrance into what could be her death chamber.

"Open the door."

She turned the handle slowly, stretching the seconds as long as she could. Was she going to lash out, try to pick him off like she did Harvey? He was ready for her, standing just out of reach.

"Inside."

She turned, blocking the entranceway and walked into the room.

"What the hell is this?" She spun around, a puzzled look on her face.

"Do you recognize her?"

She shook her head.

"Do I recognize who?"

Nancy stepped aside, turning back toward the bed. The window on the far wall was shattered, large shards of glass littering the floor as if someone had broken in, and the bed was empty except for scraps of used packing tape. There was no one in the room.

CHAPTER SIXTY-ONE

Her shoulder throbbed, piercing bolts of pain shot through her head, and she wanted to throw up. Jennifer Koenig desperately needed to eliminate all of that pain. She wanted to die, but her strongest instinct was to survive. There was no way to explain the conflict, even to herself, but it all converged at once and she closed her eyes to block it out.

The reporter had left, telling her to trust him. Hell, she had no choice. She'd trust anyone over Danny Murtz or Nancy Steiner. Jennifer had heard the lady admit to killing Harvey, proving that Murtz and Nancy were cut out of the same cloth. Both of them were cold-blooded killers.

She could hear him talking in the office down the hall. Harvey's office. "Hello." She tried to shout down the hall to him. Pathetic. For a woman who'd made a living projecting her voice, she could barely raise a sound. "Hello." Now there was only silence. She tried once more, the metallic taste of blood in her mouth. "Hello."

Then he was there. In the hall, standing beside her.

"There's an ambulance on its way."

"No. Just take me out of here."

He bent down, touching her cheek. She tried to shake him off, the offending hand stroking the scar where Danny Murtz had pistol whipped her. "No. You —" She didn't know his name.

"Mick."

"You were in Harvey's office."

"The ambulance is coming."

She coughed, the strong taste of fresh blood covering her tongue.

"Please, shut up!"

She saw the surprise in his eyes. Good. Maybe she could get through this without coughing her lungs out.

"Harvey's office. There's a computer."

He continued to stroke her, trying to calm her, and if she'd had any strength left at all, she would have coldcocked him. She had no strength, so he was safe.

"Okay, there was a computer on the desk. A laptop." This guy seemed to understand.

Praise Jesus. "Get it."

"What?"

Jennifer coughed again.

"Harvey kept," she couldn't keep up the conversation. She felt weak, sick, and nauseous, and she knew she was going to pass out at any time, "records."

"Records? Danny's records? The gold records?"

Jesus. Not records as in recorded music. The reporter was an idiot. If she had to trust her survival to someone, this wasn't the person she would have chosen.

"Accounts. Accounts of Danny's activities."

"What kind of activities."

She closed her eyes. Why didn't he get it? She was dying and if she died, there had to be a reason. She had to take Danny Murtz down with her or the entire exercise, the entire trip, would have been useless.

"Tell me."

He had clear, strong eyes. Maybe he could be her savior.

"Get the computer. Danny Murtz killed a friend of mine. The information is on that computer." She couldn't say it any clearer.

CHAPTER SIXTY-TWO

Murtz froze, staring at the bed and waiting for the other shoe to drop. And even in his drug-crazed mind, he understood that Michelle hadn't broken out. Someone had broken in. That meant that Sever or someone else knew about his clandestine activities. Someone had broken in and helped the blond bitch escape. Who?

Nancy stared at him, no comprehension on her disfigured face. Fuck her. The useless cunt was as good as dead. It was just that Murtz didn't want Bill, the next-door neighbor, banging at his door again, asking why he was shooting off his pistols.

"Who was in here?"

Life was so much easier when Harvey would say, "Lock yourself in your room. Give us two hours and it will all be handled."

"Danny." She was dangerously close.

"Stand back." The gun wavered in his hand.

"What do you want from me? Are you going to kill me?"

She didn't have a clue.

"Danny, give me the gun."

No, it had worked before, but now he was in charge. Was Sever still going to show up? Where was the blond, Michelle? Who the hell broke her out?

"Danny!" She screamed at him. "Listen to me."

Murtz stared blankly at her, hearing her and understanding her frustration, but not really caring.

"Danny, I don't want to die. You don't have to do this. We can solve whatever problems you've got and get out of this. Okay?"

It wasn't okay. She was responsible for some of these problems.

"Danny, I killed Harvey because he was going to destroy Jason's life."

"Anything for your kid. And what the hell do you think is going to happen to *the boy* now? Now that all of this shit is coming down?"

That seemed to calm her down. She buried her head in her hands and quietly sat down on the rumpled bed. Finally, she looked up. "Who was here?"

"Michelle. I found her going through papers in Harvey's office. She's part of it too. I'm sure she knows." Murtz gave her a grim smile. "Maybe Harvey told her what happened. Maybe she slept with him too."

"You were going to kill her?"

"I was."

"And me."

"Yeah."

"And?"

"Sever."

"A very ambitious evening, Mr. Murtz."

"Well, somebody had to do it."

She stood up and walked to the broken window, crunching broken glass beneath her high-heeled shoes.

"Let me give you a really good reason why you shouldn't kill me, Danny."

"I'm not sure it's negotiable."

"Let me try, okay."

Murtz nodded.

"When I started working for you, you and I had a couple of flings."

"Flings?" A little old-school.

"You know what I mean. I don't think that's come up in quite a while."

"And that's what you're using to negotiate with? That fact that we fucked?"

Nancy turned from the window, a frown on her face. He could see the lines in her face, the creases in her forehead. The thin, porcelain-like skin on her hands showed the outlines of her bones as she folded them in front of her. God, when had she aged like this? Truly aged. And when had he?

"Danny, as you so delicately put it, we fucked. And Jason is your son."

Oh, she was good. It set him back for a second. But she *had* walked out on him for a while. Enough time to have a kid? "How many people have you slept with in your life, Nancy? How many?"

"How about you, Mr. Murtz?"

"Hundreds."

"When you and I met, I'd never slept with anyone."

"Bullshit!"

"It's true. You were my first. Do you understand? I got lucky on the first try. Jason is your son, Danny, like it or not."

CHAPTER SIXTY-THREE

"They cautioned me against moving you at all. Only if it was necessary."

Her breathing seemed easier now, but she struggled between waves of nausea and pain.

"Did they caution you against Danny Murtz? He'll be back."

"Mick!"

Sever's head jerked up, and he grabbed for the Walther.

"Hold it, pal. It's me. I needed to check up on you, man."

Jordan stepped into the hallway, his hands above his head. "Hey, I always wanted to see how the really rich lived. I —" he paused, seeing the girl for the first time. "Whoa. Is she all right? Did you —?"

"Murtz did this. And she thinks he's on his way back to finish the job."

"Hey, there's two of us."

Sever took a deep breath. "We're not supposed to move her."

"But we're going to, right?"

Sever looked down at the blood-soaked, wounded girl.

"Yeah. She's definitely not safe here. Let's take her to the car. I don't know when the ambulance is coming, and I'm inclined to agree with the lady. If Murtz comes back, he'll want to finish the job."

Jordan cringed.

"St. Barts is not the greatest place to find yourself in a medical emergency, Mick. There are only seven resident doctors on the island, and Hôpital de Bruyn is not necessarily the best place for any medical care."

"We don't have a choice, Jordan. She needs help."

"Hopefully we can get her to St. Martin or Miami."

St. Martin. Home of the infamous honeymoon of a marriage that went nowhere.

Gently they picked her up, supporting her as best they could, Sever holding her head and shoulders, Jordan Clark supporting her lower body. She groaned, but seemed to deal with the pain. When they got to the pool deck Sever glanced over at the guest cottage sitting two hundred feet away. He saw the lights inside. Funny, he'd never really paid attention to the outbuilding, but now he was looking at everything in a whole new light. Maybe Murtz was back there. Why had he abandoned the young girl? What was going on in his warped world? Sever felt the Walther pressing against the flesh of his back, and the feeling both calmed and frightened him at the same time. He must be as crazy as Danny Murtz to constantly put himself in danger like this.

Sever supported her with one hand, opening the car door with the other. Gently they eased her in. One car blown up, deep scrapes on this car's body, and blood on the back seat. The rental company wasn't going to be happy with him. And this was going to cost the *Tribune* a lot more than they'd planned. The hell with it. They could take it out of his bonus.

"Can you hear me?"

She moaned.

"Jordan, can you stay with her?"

"You're going back there? Why, in God's name? You aren't getting an interview at this stage of the game."

"No. But I'm getting a story. And I've got an issue with that bastard. He and his attorney almost killed me."

"You are crazy."

"Yeah. I know. Stay with her, okay?"

"Mick, be careful. God be with you."

Sever nodded and walked back to the villa. There was a madman on the property. And what had the girl said about Murtz and Nancy? Was Nancy a part of this as well? It was tough to figure out a game plan when you didn't even know all the players.

CHAPTER SIXTY-FOUR

There was a time when he was in control. There was a time when he would make decisions on the spur of the moment and they'd all be good. Decisions on an arrangement.

I want the horns to swell at measure 82. A fat horn section. And bring the strings up under them. More reverb on the voice.

The song would soar to number one. There were times when he would make uncanny business decisions. He'd stopped productions of major recording stars at major recording companies until they'd paid him his asking price. And he'd made wonderful decisions on the material he stole from other writers. Danny Murtz stole from the best.

And he'd worked on his reputation of being the bad boy of the music business. Again, a great decision. In the entertainment industry, they respected you for being an asshole. Where else could you pull that off and get major respect, money, and your choice of women? Obviously, he'd made a big mistake in his choice in women. That was coming back to bite him in the ass, but he got the women nevertheless. Well, it was time to take control again. Enough of this self-pity crap. He didn't need Harvey, he didn't need Nancy. He was fucking Danny Murtz. Danny Murtz, by God.

He walked along the stone walk back to the house. God only knew where Sever had gone. He had to dispose of the girl in the hallway and take Nancy with her. Oh, Nancy had put up a good fight but a couple of whacks with the handle of his Colt had put her down.

Now he needed blankets from the house to wrap the bodies, then after midnight he'd drive them to the salt marsh. It didn't take much to dispose of them. He'd figured that out with the guy who currently resided below the slimy bog. The guy who was messing around with one of Murtz's poor choices in women. The guy who was stuck in the muck.

The back door was open. Well, of course. He'd hustled Nancy out of there and he forgot to close the door. He walked in and reached for the switch. Murtz clutched his chest, his heart banging inside the cavity. Where the hell was she? Blood everywhere, even a bullet hole in the wall that he hadn't noticed before, but no Jennifer Koenig. Where the hell?

He needed a drink. A line of coke. No question, he was an addict. The pleasure receptor in his brain required more and more foreign substances to feed it. Murtz opened the closet door, hoping with every fiber of his being that he'd dragged her back into the closet and just forgotten. More blood stained the white tile in the large hall closet, but blood was the only visible part of Jennifer Koenig that remained.

Murtz staggered down the hallway, heading for his office. The one sanctuary that could give him everything he needed.

CHAPTER SIXTY-FIVE

Sever stood outside the back door, wondering where to go with the situation. He and Jordan should have driven the girl to the hospital. Instead, he'd stayed to take on Murtz.

He was crazy, and Jordan Clark, who had no stake at all in this venture, was even crazier. The business mogul had put his life on the line to take down the music producer. Sever was still trying to figure that one out.

Was Murtz in the cottage or had he taken off for the evening? Sever had heard enough to believe that no matter what happened tonight, no major crime would be admitted. Major crimes had been *committed*, but none would ever be *admitted*. By the authorities or by the players.

He entered the hallway, pulling out the flat, black Walther PPK. Walther. A German company that manufactured weapons during World War II to fight the Americans. Strange how things turned around. The villa was quiet, eerily so. No noise, no sound whatsoever. Then he picked up the quiet hum of an air conditioner. And that was all. He was tempted to call out the owner's name, but he didn't want to telegraph his presence. Not now. Not after he'd removed the injured girl. Surely, if Murtz had returned, he'd be freaking out by now. He'd be having a heart attack, wondering where the girl had gone. Had she walked out on her own? Had someone rescued her? He could picture the crazy man wandering the house, looking for his intended victim. He'd be freaking out more than usual, and usual was bad enough.

Sever took soft steps, easing his way down the hallway. The first office on the right, the one with the phone, had the computer. The girl had been adamant that he take the computer. Information on Danny Murtz. Could he steal someone's computer? Even if that person was dead? What if the information was incriminating? What if the gendarmes would destroy the computer and all evidence that proved Murtz was a murderer? There'd be no record of the atrocities Murtz had committed. What if? What about copying the information to a disk? Then, if someone destroyed the computer, he'd have the information. It was stealing, but not quite as bad.

Sever stepped into the office, studying the black Dell computer. He had no idea how to find the file. Obviously Harvey was too bright to have a common password. This wasn't going to happen. Too bad. He'd made the moral decision but couldn't get past his lack of technical knowledge.

He turned to go, noticing the small pile of crumpled dollar bills, change, a credit card, and a driver's license on the corner of the desk. It appeared that someone had emptied the pockets of the attorney after his body had been pulled from the pool. Sever reached out and touched the bills. Still damp. The humidity in the atmosphere kept them from drying out. The license from Illinois framed the frowning face of Harvey Schwartz. And then he saw it. A small, black keychain. No keys. Sever examined it, then picked it up. He dropped the key chain in his pocket and walked out of the room.

CHAPTER SIXTY-SIX

He saw the office door ahead and breathed a sigh of relief. Just a minute to refresh. Just a moment to breathe, get a little substance, then he could figure out how to handle the situation. The office door? The door was closed. There was a door. He couldn't remember a door to his office. The opening was always, well, open. He had an open door policy. It was easier to throw someone out of the office when the door was open. But the door was closed. Oh, yeah. He'd closed it when he had heard the noise in the hallway, when Jennifer Koenig had come down the hall. He remembered pulling a door shut when he left the office, thinking that he didn't want anyone going in there. A big, solid mahogany door. He'd closed it. He felt like such an idiot. And where was that girl? Jennifer? He was a wreck, and needed some relief . . . now.

Murtz turned the handle and the door opened, the bright lamplight blinding him for a moment. The lamp was in front of him, right behind his big leather chair.

He shielded his eyes, trying to adjust to the brilliance. He'd used that bright light to intimidate people. Now, he felt intimidated. Adjusting to the light, he turned to the bar.

"Danny."

A soft voice but very determined. Where had it come from?

"Danny. Over here."

He turned, lifting the pistol.

"Right here, Danny."

She sat in his leather chair. His chair. Her blond hair hung around her face, almost silhouetted with the bright light behind her.

"Danny, put down the gun."

Fuck that. Nancy had told him the same thing and she was going to the muck tonight. Tomorrow she'd be buried in the salt marshes.

"I'm a cop, Danny. With the missing persons bureau in Chicago."

"Who's missing?" He kept his gun trained on her.

"Several young ladies. Jennifer Koenig for one."

Murtz wanted that drink. He wanted to walk to his desk and pour out some of the fine white powder in the right-hand drawer. But this bitch was trying to bust his balls.

"You're right. She is missing. She was here earlier this evening and now she's disappeared."

"Very funny."

"Oh, no. It's very true."

"Danny, you tried to kill me. And —"

"Listen you fucking bitch, if I'd wanted to kill you, I would have." Not entirely true. He just couldn't risk shooting her in the villa. Later, he'd take her out in a heartbeat.

"Do you see what's in my hand?"

Murtz stayed his distance, straining to see what she had.

"It's a pistol, Danny. I took it from your gun case. Very nice. A Smith & Wesson .45-caliber pistol. I've been trained on this gun. I could put out the eye of a cat at one hundred feet. And I could put yours out right here."

Damn, she knew her guns.

"Let me fix a drink before we start deciding who's going to kill whom. Okay?"

Murtz walked to the bar, his back to Michelle.

"I want you to put down the gun. And I want to take you back to the United States as my prisoner. When we're in Chicago, you'll be under arrest, and I'll come up with enough evidence to hang you."

Murtz belted down a glass of rum with a splash of Coke. He laughed, a hearty, loud laugh.

"Oh. Well, then let me get my jacket because it's probably cool in Chicago this time of year."

She sighed, keeping the pistol trained on him.

"I didn't really think you'd go along with my plan."

"You came over here with this idea?"

Michelle smiled. "No, no. I wanted to get as much evidence on you as possible. But when I found those papers, and then realized you wanted to kill me, I decided only one of us can leave this island alive. And I decided it's going to be me. So, I'm just explaining to you the only way two of us could walk out of here, and I didn't think you'd go for it."

Another belt of rum and Coke.

"You've got balls, lady."

He took another deep swallow and kept his gun trained on the Chicago cop.

"A battle of the .45s."

"It is."

"Michelle, is that your real name?"

She shook her head. "It is."

"Well, you're not exactly as you presented yourself, so I had to ask. Michelle, do you know where the name St. Barts came from?"

"No."

"In the late 1400s, Columbus discovered the island. He named it after his brother, Bartolomeo. It's as simple as that. Now you take Columbus. There was a risk taker, wouldn't you agree? Took a lot of chances and came up a winner."

"What's your point, Danny?"

"Today, people are putting him down. Seems he and his crew spread venereal disease to the Indians, caused all kinds of problems in the Western world."

"Are you buying time here, Danny? Because I'm not a patient person. Are you going back with me or am I going to kill you right here?"

"Hear me out. Columbus was a hero back then, because he made things happen. He found new worlds, explored new continents, and made a lasting impression. So he and his crew screwed around a little bit. So they were responsible for a couple of deaths here and there. Let's look at the big picture. For Christ's sake, Columbus discovered America!"

"Oh, my God. You're comparing yourself to Columbus?"

He smiled. "I knew you wouldn't get it. They never do. In the grand scheme of things, a few deaths don't really mean that much. Do you realize how much I've accomplished?"

"Do you realize you're delusional?"

"Tell me, what makes you think you can kill me and get away with it?"

"You told me, the bartender told me, there are no murders on St. Barts. None. If I kill you, I would either be the first murderer in the modern history of the island, or they would excuse the death and give it a spin. I think they'd excuse the killing. I think they'd turn their heads, and maybe be happy that you were gone. What do you think, Danny? Please, tell me quickly because I'm ready to blow a hole through your brain."

He'd kicked the shit out of her and busted some of her ribs. Murtz knew she had to be in pain. Her nose looked out of joint, so he'd done some damage there as well. He didn't think she'd have the guts to shoot him, and if he could just get close enough to put a foot into her rib cage she'd fold. He knew it.

"How did you get out of the cottage? Sever?"

Get her talking, distracted, take one step closer. She was hurting, he could see it in her face.

"No. Not Sever."

Murtz took another step.

"Pretty good trick."

"You killed Jennifer Koenig, didn't you?"

One hand with his drink, one hand with the gun. No more gunshots tonight. He took a long swallow of his rum and Coke. Another step.

"No. Not yet. But I fully intend to."

"Who did you kill?"

"Years ago there was a hot-shot record producer, and there were Shelley O'Dell and Libby Hellman. There's a guy rotting away in the salt marshes near Saline Beach. Oh, and a girl named Randi Parks. A wannabe singer. She really wasn't that good. Why the hell does this matter to you?"

"My God, you are so matter of fact about all of this. I don't think it bothers you at all."

"Why do you care?"

"Because," she raised her voice and he saw pain in her eyes, "it's my job to find out what happened to these people. And to make sure that scum like you are off the street."

Murtz laughed again.

"Off the street? Sweetheart, I'm as far away from the street as you can get. Have you looked around? This isn't the ghetto."

"Why?"

"Why what?"

"Why did you kill them?"

"Because it didn't matter. Because they were insignificant in the big picture. I didn't plan on killing most of them, but they became inconveniences."

Now he had her. He saw the dazed, confused look on her face. She kept her free hand on her chest and the gun hand dropped, just a little. She was getting tired.

"Do you think you're some kind of god? Is that it?"

Yeah. That was it. A rock god.

"I'm surrounded by people who protect me. I've got almost everything I want. And right now what I want is for you to go away and leave me alone."

She struggled to stand and he fired the drink glass at her head. As she raised her hands in self-defense, the glass hit her head full force and shattered on impact. Murtz kicked out, planting a foot firmly on her chest. Michelle let out a lungful of air, dropped the gun, and collapsed.

He picked her up and, with a grunt, threw her over his shoulder and walked out of the room. This time no one was going to break her out of the cottage. He'd see to that. *Down the hall to Harvey's office, get his laptop, and out the door. Don't fuck around with the rock god. You might get hurt.*

CHAPTER SIXTY-SEVEN

Sever stopped cold. Danny Murtz must be in the house, and the noise was coming from his office. Grabbing the Walther tightly in his hand, he walked slowly down the hall. All he had to do was walk out the door, get the girl into the ambulance, and fly back to Chicago.

Except for one small detail. Someone wanted him dead and he needed to clear that up. He silently approached the doorway, holding the pistol in front of him. A bright light shown behind a leather chair and he struggled to make out the rest of the room. A massive oak desk to his right, bookshelves, a wet bar, and an empty leather chair. Sever stepped into the room looked around. He heard a slight rustle to his right and started to turn. Something came down hard on the back of his head and he saw the bright-colored lights just before he lost consciousness.

The next thing he knew there were voices, mumbling, and he struggled to sit up. Then he realized he *was* sitting up. In the leather chair. He squinted, trying to make sense of the situation, and finally he was able to open his eyes all the way. His bruised scalp throbbed and the inside of his head felt like it would explode. Someone had really let him have it.

"I'm sorry for the pain."

Sever looked up, expecting to see Danny Murtz. "You?"

"Me."

"So when you're not bartending, you double as a hit man for Murtz?" The pain pounding in his head.

"Mick!" Jordan Clark stepped into the room. "We've got a serious problem."

"No 'How are you? Hope we didn't hurt you too bad.' "

"The girl, she's with Murtz. We've called the gendarmes, but —"

Sever gingerly touched the back of his head.

"Look, Mr. B. didn't know it was you. He came in to check on Michelle, saw the empty chair and you from the back. He thought you'd done something to her."

"The gendarmes?"

"They should be on their way, Mr. Sever." Mr. B. shrugged his shoulders.

"But they won't make it in time, will they?"

Clark stepped forward. "This Michelle, she wanted to handle Murtz by herself, and it apparently didn't work out."

"Where are they? We've got to do something."

"Mr. B. thinks they're in the guest cottage. Seems she found some papers, letters from a Chicago newspaper, and Murtz caught her reading them. They were incriminating, naming some of the girls he'd killed."

"Jesus." The papers. He had to do something, anything. "He could kill her at any minute, take off with the body, and we'd never prove anything."

Clark cleared his throat. "We bought ourselves a little time. Danny's next-door neighbor has been very helpful. First of all, he shot out all four tires on the Jeep.

"Bill?"

"Yeah. He and Susan are watching the cottage to make certain Murtz doesn't leave. This Bill — he has a gun collection that makes Murtz's look like toys — weapons I've never even heard of. But, if we try to break in and get Michelle out of there, he'll kill her for sure."

He had to come up with a plan. The papers, the newspaper

articles. It was his fault they'd been stolen. "She was in the guest cottage —"

"Was," said Clark. "Michelle told Mr. B. to come looking for her if he hadn't heard from her in twenty-four hours. He took her at her word."

Mr. B. nodded. "I came to Danny Murtz's villa to see if she was all right. When I saw drops of blood on the sidewalk I followed them to the cottage out back." Bertrand motioned with his hand to the back door. "It seems Murtz broke Michelle's nose and it was bleeding when he carried her to the cottage."

Sever glanced at his watch. Time was running out.

"The shades were not tightly closed and I could see her through the window, lying on the bed. I broke the window. He had wrapped her in tape so I cut it off and took her out and brought her into the house. Even though she was badly bruised, she insisted on confronting the son of a bitch with one of his own guns. He apparently disarmed her, beat her again, and took her to the cottage. That's when I came in to see if she was all right, and found you."

"Bill and Susan are watching the cottage?"

"Just waiting for the asshole to show himself," Clark said. "I think the big guy would probably shoot Murtz on sight."

"We've got to get her out of there. I'm not going to wait for the gendarmes."

"Mr. Sever, that may not be a good idea."

Sever ignored the Frenchman. "Listen, there's a laptop computer down the hall, in Harvey's office. Supposedly that computer has details that could put Murtz away for life."

Bertrand threw up his hands. "But how does that help Michelle?"

Sever was already walking down the hall to Schwartz's office. The two men followed. Sever flipped on the light. Everything on the desk was gone.

CHAPTER SIXTY-EIGHT

Murtz heard the four shots, thinking someone was shooting at him. He screamed out the window telling them he'd kill the girl if they tried to get him. When he went to the Jeep, he figured out what the gunshots were for. No escape there now. Since then it had been quiet. Back in the guesthouse, Murtz wished he'd taken more than just the Colt. He didn't know who was out there or how many there were. Michelle was totally out of it and deadweight if he had to carry her anywhere. Nancy, with the rip on her cheek, was belligerent as hell, but what was new? She threatened to just get up and walk out, but she knew damned well he'd kill her on the spot. He'd taped her arms and legs together and finally taped her mouth shut. Enough about *their* son and Murtz's responsibilities. Enough. Just shut up.

And there was no reason to hold off firing his gun any longer. Somebody had fired four shots outside, blowing out his tires. By now Murtz was sure that Bill, the nosy neighbor, was already investigating. A prisoner in his own house. This was bullshit.

He heard the back door shake. Someone pulling on the handle. He got up from the wicker chair at the bar and walked to the door. Leveling the .45 at the center he pulled the trigger. The explosion echoed through the cottage as the pistol bucked in his hand, the ringing in his ears was like a good buzz. Whoever was trying to get in would either be dead or be having second thoughts about entering.

Now he heard noise at the front door of the cottage. Murtz glanced at Nancy, just making sure she hadn't made any headway in her attempt to free herself. She remained sprawled on the wicker couch, glaring at him and mumbling through the packing tape that covered her mouth. Tough old broad. He took aim at the front door and fired again. He had ammunition, a fully stocked bar, and enough cocaine to buy Miami, so they could keep it up all night. Trying to drive him crazy, get him to crack, but they were trespassing. They were the ones breaking the law. All he was doing was protecting his property. The more he thought about it, the madder he got.

This Michelle, Jennifer Koenig, Sever, even Nancy. They wanted to hang him for killing the girls. And there was absolutely no evidence. None. They could get him in court, hire the best lawyers, but there was nothing. Harvey had seen to it. Even the people Harvey hired, they didn't know who they were working for and they'd been paid well. So what was he worried about? Where did all this paranoia come from? The coke?

Murtz picked up Schwartz's black Dell laptop and set it on end on the marble-topped bar. He stepped back, four, five, six steps. He aimed at the Dell logo and pulled the trigger. Again, and again. The explosion was deafening. While the sound still reverberated through the building, he picked up the shattered case and threw it to the tile floor and the damaged screen snapped off the hinges. He reached down, picked up what was left of the computer, and heaved it at the mirror behind his bar. The case exploded in flying pieces of plastic as the mirror crashed to the floor.

He had a good idea what was on that computer. It's why he'd gone back to get it. He'd always been suspicious. Dates, times, places, even pictures of the deceased. He always thought it was probably Harvey's insurance policy. Well, now there really wasn't any evidence. None at all. Nada. Now let them try to pin a murder on him!

CHAPTER SIXTY-NINE

It was their intent to rattle him, to see if he would fire at them. They found out immediately.

"Well, we know he's definitely going to protect himself."

Sever, Bertrand, and Clark knelt down behind the rental car. The rental car with the scraped sides and the blood-soaked seats. Thank God Jennifer Koenig had been taken away in the ambulance and was no longer in the car.

Bill and Susan were behind the Jeep. A lot of people were at risk, especially the girl inside the cottage.

"There's one more thing we can try."

"Mick, the man is a lunatic. We can't assume he won't kill the girl." Jordan stood up and stretched. "I say we wait for the gendarmes."

Sever massaged his knee. Kneeling, standing up, getting his head bashed in, he was in a lot of pain. *Where the hell were the gendarmes? Ignoring the call? Busy doing something else?*

"Let me talk to him."

"And say what?" Bertrand asked.

Sever took twenty steps toward the cottage, ready to drop to the ground at the first sound of gunfire. They'd antagonized Murtz already, and Sever didn't want any more gunfire.

Cautiously, he took ten more steps. The first shot startled him and he hit the dirt, grabbing ground with his fingers. The second shot followed immediately as well as the third. There was no question in his mind. Murtz had killed Michelle. The son of a bitch had done it again.

Then the banging started, a loud crash and, finally, a sheet of glass shattering. The entire episode probably lasted thirty seconds, but seemed like thirty minutes. Sever stayed on the ground, praying that he was wrong. He didn't pray very often. Didn't even know if he believed in prayer, but he wanted that girl to come out of there alive, and a prayer right now couldn't hurt.

CHAPTER SEVENTY

"Danny Murtz."

Murtz heard the screaming voice. His ears were still ringing from the gunshots but he could hear the irritating voice.

"Danny. Is Michelle all right?"

Murz stepped to the window where the voice had come from. He kicked out the glass, then stepped behind the wall.

"She's fine, Sever. Do you two have a hot date tonight? Casa Niki?"

"Why not bring her out, Danny?"

"Why not come in and get her, Sever?"

The reporter didn't have the nerve.

"Danny, if I come in and get her, just tell me there will be no shooting."

What gall. The son of a bitch was trespassing on Murtz's property and still he was trying to make the rules. If he'd shown up when we was supposed to, he'd be dead by now. Murtz would have shot him for breaking and entering.

"Sever!"

"What, Danny?"

"You're trespassing. Get off my fucking property."

"Danny, the gendarmes are coming. Why not just come on out and we'll wait for them together."

The gendarmes. One quick phone call and he'd stop that.

"Sever, get off my property or I may take steps to get you off."

The guy was trespassing. Murtz leaned around to the window and thrust the Colt through the opening. He pulled the trigger and the explosion kicked him back a step. If he hit the intruder, so be it, but if nothing else it should scare him.

"Danny?"

"Sever."

"Do you want to be responsible for another murder?"

"Another murder? I wasn't aware I was responsible for any murders." He needed to put a bullet in the brain of the persistent reporter.

"Come on, Danny, there's no question you killed several women."

"No proof, Sever. None." *Prove it, asshole.*

"Let Michelle out."

"What about Nancy? She's here too. Want to come in and save her too?"

"Let them out."

"Yeah, Danny, let them out. Now." The voice came from the opposite direction.

Who the hell was that? Then it hit him, Raymond. The dumb-ass bodyguard who had the hots for Nancy. He must have come in late from the restaurant and caught some of the conversation. Now he had Raymond to contend with, and Raymond had a gun.

"Raymond, whose side are you on?"

There was silence. Of course Raymond would have to think about it, and thinking wasn't one of his strong points.

"Hey, Raymond, I'm talking to you."

"Let Nancy go, Danny. Don't kill her. Please."

Raymond could be dealt with. Nobody seemed to get it. There was no proof that he'd killed anyone.

"Danny?" Sever again. "Danny, Harvey had a computer. A laptop. Supposedly there's some pretty strong evidence on that computer that you killed several young women."

"Is that it, Sever? That's what you've got? Let me set your mind at ease, my friend. That computer doesn't exist. It's gone. Blown into a thousand pieces." He heaved a sigh of relief. Harvey was gone, the computer was gone. He had a clean slate.

The front door burst open, hitting the wall, and bouncing off the plaster. Murtz spun around and there was Raymond standing in the entranceway, gripping his gun with both hands.

"Let Nancy go. Now. You can treat people like shit, Danny, but when you threaten to kill them —"

Murtz pulled the trigger, and the gun erupted. The bullet hit Raymond midchest and the big guy slid down the wall, his eyes never closing.

"Danny, what was that?"

"Go away, Sever."

"What was the shot?"

"Raymond came in to save Nancy. He broke my door open, Sever. What was I supposed to do?" He shouted out of the opening.

No response. He stood by the window, waiting.

"Danny. The evidence on that computer —"

"I told you, Sever, the computer doesn't exist anymore."

"Yeah. I know. But the evidence does."

Bullshit.

"Harvey had a key chain, with no keys on it. He kept it in his pocket. When they pulled the body out of the water, you put it on his desk. It's a flash stick, Danny. Harvey loaded all the information from his computer on the stick, and it's in my pocket right now."

Murtz slumped against the wall by the window. Knowing how meticulous Harvey was, he probably did have a backup. The producer studied his Colt .45, and considered the damage he'd done with it today. He'd blown a hole in Jennifer Koenig's shoulder, bludgeoned Nancy's face, destroyed Harvey's computer, and killed his bodyguard. How much more damage could one gun do? He put the barrel of the gun in his mouth, running his tongue over the smooth metal. Kissing the barrel of the gun, the tangy, metallic sensation whetting his taste buds. The best thing to do was not to think about it, because he'd thought about it for years. The best thing to do was just do it. Danny Murtz pulled the trigger.

CHAPTER SEVENTY-ONE

Chicago caught a mild spring day for late April. A gentle breeze for the Windy City and highs in the upper sixties. Sever dropped by the *Trib* even before going to his townhouse. Bloomfield got up from his seat, walked around the desk, and actually hugged him. Sever stiffened imperceptibly at the display of male affection.

"Man, I am so glad you're safe. We were all worried, Mick. I would never have asked you to go if I'd known just how bad it would get."

Sever plopped down on the leather couch and gazed at the piles of paperwork on Bloomfield's desk.

"I'm in one piece. Some people didn't make it out at all."

"God, it must have been gruesome. His attorney and both of his bodyguards?"

"As far as I could tell he planned on at least three more. Jennifer Koenig, Nancy Steiner, and yours truly."

"Jennifer Koenig was sending us the letters, trying to get someone to focus attention on Murtz?"

"She was. And, she was dropping off letters to Murtz and making threatening phone calls, hoping he'd get a little crazy and careless. That was her way of getting revenge. It started when she dated Danny. He beat her up one night and carved her face with a pistol. When she threatened him, Harvey Schwartz threatened her entire family and sent some goons to scare the hell out of her. When she disappeared, Harvey thought she might have been killed."

"This guy was not only Murtz's attorney and handler, but cleaned up all of his messes. How much would you have to pay someone for that service?"

Bloomfield drummed his fingers on the desk. He didn't seem to expect an answer.

"Mick, the authorities in St. Barts are telling us that there were a number of accidents. A car accident in which, and I quote, 'A Samuel Jean, traveling at a high rate of speed, unfortunately left the well-marked road and his vehicle was destroyed in an explosion. Mr. Jean did not survive the explosion.' "

"Oh, it was an accident. No question. And I was the intended victim."

"We brought that up, and they claimed there was no proof that you were involved."

"Let me guess what the second accident was. Harvey Schwartz drowning in the pool."

"Right on the money, Mr. Sever." Bloomfield read from a sheaf of papers. "Attorney Harvey Schwartz suffered severe cranium damage due to a fall, and as a result of his fall, fell into the swimming pool and drowned."

"I can't prove it, Jeff, but I keep thinking Danny killed him."

"Why Danny?"

"Harvey knew about all the murders. He was basically blackmailing Murtz, raising the stakes every time Danny needed help. I think Murtz decided to eliminate the problem."

"Then there was Raymond. Here's the take on that. The official reaction to the bodyguard's death is he walked in while Murtz was cleaning his gun and it accidentally went off, killing Raymond."

"And what possible reason can they give for Murtz's death?"

"Suicide."

"You're kidding. Suicide? They got that one right."

"He was depressed over the fact that he'd accidentally killed his bodyguard."

Sever slowly stood up, stretching his leg and massaging the knee. It had been a long, cramped plane ride. "So no murders. Everything was explained away."

"They got Jennifer and Michelle on a plane to the States, and they'll claim more accidents happened to them. This Nancy Steiner, she stands to inherit a boatload of money once the courts get through with his estate, so she's not going to say anything. I hear she's got a useless kid who is following in Murtz's footsteps. Maybe we'll have a story on him in five or ten years."

Sever walked to the window and marveled at the view. The river, the lake, totally different from his fabulous view at the Manapany. Totally different from the view from Murtz's multimillion-dollar villa. God it was good to be home again.

"Jeff, I get the impression you're a little hesitant to run the true story on Murtz, when there's no evidence."

"I'm not sure we have a story."

"You may be surprised." Sever fumbled in his pants pocket and pulled out the key-chain. "I took this memory stick from Schwartz's office. Jennifer Koenig claims all the evidence you'd ever need was on Schwartz's computer. It makes sense that he would back up that important information, and this was his key-chain. You'll notice, no keys, so it had another purpose."

"You were waiting to spring this on me? Give me the damned thing. Let's get it into a computer and see what it's about."

Sever handed him the small plastic stick, and Bloomfield pushed it into a port. Within fifteen seconds a window appeared on the screen. The newspaperman tapped a couple of keys, highlighting certain sections of the memory. He studied the screen intently and Sever studied him. His expression was both serious and confused.

"This was the attorney's memory stick?"

"No question." Sever nodded.

"There's nothing on it." Bloomfield didn't look happy.

"Are you sure you're reading it right?"

"Mick, I make my living in communications. I know how to download a memory stick."

"Nothing?"

"Nothing. Sorry, buddy. We'll talk about the story later, okay? Hell, you haven't even been home yet. Relax, take it easy. We'll deal with this tomorrow."

Sever picked up his leather carry-on and said good-bye. On ground level he flagged down a taxi, remembering the last time he'd tried to get a taxi in Chicago. This time the experience was much safer.

You couldn't write a factual piece when the facts weren't there. Harvey Schwartz had done too good a job in covering up Danny Murtz's screwups.

The mail was stacked neatly on the kitchen table in his townhouse. Mrs. Olds, his housekeeper, kept everything neat and tidy. Bills, checks, a week-old *New Yorker.* Sever picked up his phone and checked his answering machine. He hadn't been able to access it in St. Barts, so he hadn't checked it in over a week.

"You have thirty-six new messages. Message one."

"Hey, Mick, it's Art. We need to go over your royalty statements for the estimated taxes. Call me when you get this."

"Message two"

"Mr. Sever, this is Carolyn at Dr. Miller's office. You're due in for your annual checkup and cleaning and I just wanted to set an appointment. Please call me back."

"Message three."

"Mick, it's Randi Parks. Again, I don't want to bother you, but —just a minute. I'm on the frigging phone. No, you can't. I'm sorry Mick. I was wondering when we could do the interview. Oh, you'll never guess who I'm hanging with tonight. Danny Murtz. You probably know him, but this is so cool. He's talking about maybe producing a CD for me. God, Mick. Isn't life just great?"